Birdie's BIKER

ROYAL BASTARDS MC

MISTY WALKER

Birdie's Biker
Copyright © 2020 Misty Walker

Cover Design: Simply Defined Art
Photo: Adobe Stock
Editor: Lawrence Editing
Formatting: Champagne Book Design

ALL RIGHTS RESERVED. This book contains material protected under International and Federal Copyright Laws and Treaties. Any unauthorized reprint or use of this material is prohibited. No part of this book may be reproduced or transmitted in any form or by any means, electronic or mechanical, including photocopying, recording, or by an information and retrieval system without express written permission from the Author/Publisher.

This is a work of fiction. Names, characters, places, and incidents either are the product of the author's imagination or are used fictitiously, and any resemblance to actual persons, living or dead, business establishments, events, or locales is entirely coincidental.

To the Ty-bot who, despite hating any book that isn't nonfiction, listened to me ramble on and on about my lawless bikers.

ROYAL BASTARDS CODE

PROTECT: The club and your brothers come before anything else, and must be protected at all costs. **CLUB** is **FAMILY**.

RESPECT: Earn it & Give it. Respect club law. Respect the patch. Respect your brothers. Disrespect a member and there will be hell to pay.

HONOR: Being patched in is an honor, not a right. Your colors are sacred, not to be left alone, and **NEVER** let them touch the ground.

OL' LADIES: Never disrespect a member's or brother's Ol'Lady. **PERIOD.**

CHURCH is MANDATORY.

LOYALTY: Takes precedence over all, including well-being.

HONESTY: Never **LIE, CHEAT,** or **STEAL** from another member or the club.

TERRITORY: You are to respect your brother's property and follow their Chapter's club rules.

TRUST: Years to earn it…seconds to lose it.

NEVER RIDE OFF: Brothers do not abandon their family.

PLAYLIST

"Walk with the Devil" by Karliene
"F**k Love" (feat. Trippie Redd) by XXXTENTACION
"Die Tonight" (feat. Upchurch) by Adam Calhoun
"Paint it Black" by The Rolling Stones
"Even Though Our Love Is Doomed" by Garbage
"Enjoy the Silence" by Denmark + Winter
"Afraid" by The Neighborhood
"Supermassive Black Hole" by Muse
"Mind is a Prison" by Alec Benjamin
"Little Monster" by Royal Bond
"Whole Lotta Trouble" by Cracker
"Girl, You'll Be A Woman Soon" by Urge Overkill
"Ain't No Sunshine" by Black Label Society
"Beast of Burden" by The Rolling Stones
"Mary Jane's Last Dance" by Tom Petty & The Heartbreakers
"The Whistler" by The White Buffalo
"Toxicity" by System Of A Down
"Devil's Keep" by Tyler Bryant & The Shakedown
"More Than A Feeling" by Boston
"Careless Whisper" by Seether
"You Spin Me Round" by Dope
"Alone I Break" by Korn
"Through Glass" by Stone Sour
"Sitting on Top of the World" by Chris Goss & The Forest Rangers
"River of Deceit" by Mad Season

Birdie's Biker

Chapter ONE

Bridgette

"Daddy, I need your credit card," I say, bouncing into the home office.

"You always need my credit card. You should learn the value of money, not spending my hard-earned paychecks on a new pair of shoes," he grumbles.

I bend down and kiss his cheek. "Like you even notice when I spend money on shoes. Besides, I know the value of money. I know I need it. I know you have it. And I know you'll give it to me. There's value in that knowledge."

Daddy pushes away from the desk and stands up enough to dig his wallet out of his back pocket. He can't say no to me, he's never been able to. It's why we own a mansion he didn't want to live in, why I drive a Rover he didn't want to buy, and why he's handing me his credit card right now.

"Spoiled," he mutters and returns his attention to his computer screen.

"Thank you, Daddy."

"Take Angelo with you," he says as an afterthought.

"Okay. I love you. I'll be back for dinner."

"Fine."

I watch him from the doorway, wondering why he's more distracted than usual lately. The last few weeks, he's been absent and increasingly frazzled. I grew up with him devoting most of his time to his business. Then Mom died, and it got so much worse.

Now, I rarely even see him.

I assumed it had to do with work, but he's stepped up security, too. I'm no longer allowed to leave without a guard, and there's someone standing outside his office at all times. I've asked him why the change, but he tells me it's only a precaution. That can't be it, though. He's aged ten years in three weeks, it seems. He's always on edge and he doesn't go into his office anymore.

I've taken two steps out of the doorway when his phone rings. Curiosity gets the best of me and I creep back to his office door, staying out of sight.

"I don't care how valuable it is, destroy it. Right now. We've held onto it long enough," Daddy bites out, angrier than I've ever heard him.

He pauses to listen to whoever's on the other end. His chair creaks the way it does when he stands up and the leather soles of his Italian shoes echo against the marble floor as he paces. I picture him running a hand through his short cropped inky hair that's graying at the temples.

"Goddamn it, Byron. If the government finds out about that vial, we'll both go to prison. Not to mention what would happen if the wrong person learns of its existence!" His voice quavers in fear, causing goose bumps to prickle up and down my arms.

Dad quiets again, listening.

I'm confused about what they're saying. What have they developed that's so dangerous? Daddy's company discovers lifesaving cures, not whatever this is.

"Fuck you, Byron. Bring it to me. I don't trust you to do the right thing. I'll destroy it myself."

"Can I help you, Miss Bridgette?" A voice sounds from behind me, causing me to jump.

"Angelo, I was coming to find you," I rush out.

I turn to see my tall, dark protector. Angelo has been working for Daddy for as long as I can remember. His slate eyes turn sharp and assessing, obviously not believing my story.

"Shopping." I hold up the credit card and flash him a wide-open smile.

Suddenly, a crack sounds against the wall. I rush around the corner and see Daddy's cell phone shattered into a million pieces on the ground. I stare at him expectantly, but he doesn't notice I'm back in the room. He stands in the middle of the space, staring at the wall, his arms down by his sides, his shoulders slumped, and his mouth gaping.

He looks… defeated.

"Let's go, Miss Bridgette. Let's leave your father be." He reaches past me and pulls the door closed, but not before Daddy's eyes meet mine. His are emotionless and hollow. Like he sees me but doesn't *see* me.

I turn on my heels and walk outside to the Rover, my mind reeling, wondering what's going on. Angelo holds my door open and I slide into the back seat. I take in our palatial estate through the window. The giant fountain sculpture, the neatly manicured lawn, the four other luxury cars lined up in the driveway. The only reason they aren't in the garage is because it's full of Daddy's project cars. The ones he works on every Sunday afternoon to relax.

Come to think of it, he hasn't been in there in weeks.

This can't be good.

"Angelo, is Daddy okay? Is there something going on at work, or—"

"He's fine. It's a stressful time for the company, but you know him, he always comes out on top." Angelo watches me from the rearview mirror as he drives away from the house.

"You're right."

His words calm me a bit because he has a point. Daddy succeeds in all he does. That's proven by the massive building that sits on the outskirts of downtown Reno. The one that finds lifesaving cures and vaccines to everything from the flu strains to cancer. The scientists develop them, and Daddy sells them off to giant pharmaceutical companies for more money than we could spend in ten lifetimes.

He's successful, to say the least.

Ten minutes later, Angelo parks in front of the large outdoor mall. I'm meeting my friends Lindsay and Ruby for a day of shopping. Summer has arrived and we all need to update our wardrobes for the warmer months. There are pool parties and barbecues to look forward to, and last year's clothes won't do.

I spot my friends in line for coffee and rush over to them. We hug and squeal like we haven't seen each other in a year, but really, we hung out last week.

Our friendship is superficial. We run in the same circle, so it only makes sense for us to be friends. But I know one or both of them would stab me in the back in a heartbeat. And honestly, I'd do the same. We walk a tightrope with no net, waiting for the wind to blow and knock one of us off. It's happened to other girls we've hung out with, and it'll happen again. To me, if I'm not careful.

"Are you feeling okay? You seem puffy." Ruby's green eyes scrutinize me.

"I'm fine. I see your hairdresser got a little overzealous with the scissors this week," I return.

"I knew she took off more than a quarter inch. That bitch." Ruby tugs on the ends of her auburn hair, like she can make it grow back faster.

"I told you to wait for Emil. He's worth scheduling two months out." I step up to the counter and order a nonfat iced latte, no flavor.

My friends order their drinks and we're off to shop, Angelo trailing closely behind. We walk into a boutique swimsuit shop and gather a dozen suits each. We separate into lavish changing rooms with chaise lounges and flutes of champagne waiting for us. When you're this rich, people don't question your age.

I strip down to my thong and choose a red, strappy suit first. It's technically a one-piece, but it's nothing more than a bandage wrap. Only covering the essentials. My ass not being one of those essentials. The cherry color pops next to my creamy complexion and white blond hair. I brush a fleck of mascara away from my brown eyes and take in my appearance.

I'm not puffy.

"Ready?" Lindsay calls out.

I step out and we spend a few seconds judging each other, getting ready to spew whatever snub we can think up.

"Don't you think we should reserve red for someone more… *experienced*," Ruby says with a finger tapping against her pink lip. "Like maybe Lindsay?"

"Bitch!" Lindsay huffs out. "At least I don't look like a gorilla in that poop brown suit you're wearing." She points between Ruby's legs. "Also, your pubes are showing."

I cover my laugh. Lindsay always cracks first. Ruby and I could banter like this forever and not break a sweat, but Lindsay is easily triggered.

"Liar. I got waxed yesterday," Ruby says, but she bends in half to get a better view.

"Skanky or not, I'm getting it. I'm in charge of bringing the cake this summer." I return to the changing room and close the door.

At eighteen years old, we should be packing for college or at least traveling the world. But instead, we're spoiled princesses slinging insults and fighting over pubes. It's as if we didn't even graduate high school last month. The only thing that's changed is we don't go to class. But it's not expected for us to do more.

Our lives are set, we don't have to work. We don't have to get married if we don't want to. We don't even have to move out of our parents' houses.

I can predict our futures with certainty. One of us will develop a pill habit, followed by a lifetime of going away to the "spa" for three months every year. One of us will be a serial ex-wife, marrying and promptly divorcing when we find someone with more money or power. And one of us will come out as a lesbian and take a job as an art dealer.

Hint, the last one will be Ruby. She's a clit licker if I've ever met one.

We try on the rest of our bathing suits, arguments forgotten, and walk out spending three thousand dollars each on scraps of fabric we'll wear once and then have our maids clear out of our closets come fall.

There has to be more to life than this.

Chapter TWO

Loki

"W-What are you doing here?" the fat fuck sputters from behind his messy desk.

"I think you know why we're here." I pull my leather gloves on slowly, drawing this out.

This is my favorite part. Watching them squirm. Witnessing their eyes turn from shock to terror and the moment they realize they're there to meet their maker. It's a heady notion to have people fear you. Having them cower with just one glance. Not one fucking thing in the world can make you feel more powerful than taking a life. It turns mere men into gods.

Normally, I don't give a fuck why we're hired to take out the proverbial trash. I don't care. As long as there's a fat paycheck on the other side of the kill, it's none of my business. But this time, I know who this asshat is. Zach Wesley is a slimy bastard who owns a string of strip clubs from here to Vegas.

That alone doesn't mean shit. I love strip clubs. What's not to like? Naked, morally corrupt women who use their bodies to earn cash. That's the best kind of chick. One who won't get clingy after you wet your dick. One who'll let you do all the filthy things your mind can conjure just as long as you can pay.

They're not that different from me and my brothers. Except while they're spreading their legs, we're ending lives. They don't ask where your dick has been, and we don't ask why you need someone gone. We're all just trying to pad our pockets.

But Zach Wesley is a sick fuck, and he deserves everything he's about to get. The strip clubs he owns are where the girls go when they're too old for his other business. The underground side where the child molesters feed their sick and twisted addictions. Kids as young as nine are ripped from their tiny villages around the world and brought here. They're drugged to make them agreeable and then used and abused until they age out of Zach's fucked-up system. Then they're tossed on stage to continue servicing perverted schmucks until they're no longer valuable. That's when they're killed off like cattle and tossed in incinerators.

I don't have much of a moral compass, I've proven that time and time again. But I never fuck with kids, and I try not to fuck with women. The only two rules I follow that don't involve the club.

"I-I have m-money." Zach spins in his executive chair to where his safe is.

I glance over my shoulder at my brothers, both of them grinning. Now we know we can get a double payday out of this kill. I love it when that happens.

We move in like a pack of hungry wolves.

"This one's mine," I growl out and stalk over to where the fuckwad is spinning the dial on the safe.

I wait until the door springs open before grabbing him by his oily mullet and yanking him back until his head is lulling over the back of the chair. With my other hand, I pull my knife out. Typically, we're given detailed instructions on how the client wants the death to occur. They're too big of a pussy to do it themselves, but that doesn't mean they haven't dreamed up the way they would do it. With Zach, they gave us free rein. Our contact just wants him gone.

I flip the blade out and admire the weapon. It's deeply curved like a claw. One side sharp enough to filet a fish, the other is serrated, strong enough to saw through concrete. The second Zach sees the sinister knife, his eyes go saucer wide and bug out.

Good. That'll make my job easier.

"Hold him," I demand of Kahn, my VP, and Goblin, my Enforcer.

They lock his legs down by holding them between each of theirs, then they pin his arms down to the sides of his chair.

I use the hook tip to pierce through his eyeball. The scream he lets out is loud and pierces my eardrums painfully, but not enough to be heard over the blaring music coming from the club right outside this door. I give it a tug and pop it out of its socket. It hangs from an optic nerve, reminding me of old Looney Tunes episodes when that gray cat would see something shocking.

"Don't do this. My men. They'll be here any second. They'll kill you for this!" he howls.

"Oh, you mean the guys who're guarding the door? The ones we bought for a C-note?" Khan taunts.

I shake my knife free and move to his other eye. The fucker has his eyelid squeezed tight, like that'll stop me. I stab right through the lid and tear it open as I pull his other eye free.

There. Now the fucker won't be able to see when he meets Hades. That'll make it even more terrifying.

Zach howls, snot running down his face, mixing with the saliva dripping from the corners of his mouth. He's pathetic as fuck. Hardly worth all this effort, but my need to make him suffer the way he's made hundreds of kids suffer is strong.

"What should we do now?" I muse and shake his other eye free from my pig sticker. "Maybe cut off your shriveled-up balls?"

I drag the blade down his face. Even the lightest touch slices his skin open as I go. I continue down his neck, stopping at his jugular. I'm sure he's hoping I'll dig in and end this right here, but he's not that lucky. I gouge his shoulder, leaving my blade embedded to free up both my hands so I can rip his shirt open. Buttons fly and ping off the walls.

He screams out again, muttering incoherently. A mix of empty threats and begging. None of which will help his situation.

With the lard-ass's hairy belly and chest exposed, I yank my knife from his flesh and continue my descent. I slice off his pudgy man tits, doing my best to humiliate and cause the most amount of pain.

I grow annoyed with all his blubbering, so I stab into his fat gut, once again needing both hands to silence him. I tear off a strip of duct tape we brought along and stick it to his forehead for safe keeping. Then I pull my blade free and slice through both optical nerves.

With his eyeballs in one hand, I use the other to plug his nose. He holds his breath for a long minute. My brothers and I share impatient looks, waiting for his mouth to open. When it finally does, I quickly shove his eyeballs inside and then seal his lips shut with the tape.

He sputters and wretches, his stomach revolting. Liquid bile and vomit leaks from the duct tape, but not much. He chokes and I know my time is running out. He'll inhale the puke into his lungs and die if I leave him like this. It's tempting. No doubt it wouldn't be a pleasant death, but I have something else in mind.

"Mind if I take a page from your book?" I ask Goblin.

"Go for it, brother." He shrugs.

I step back while Goblin and Khan each grab a side of Zach's head. With one quick and forceful thrust, I stab right into the top of his head. Easily piercing through his skull and cutting into his brain. Zach goes silent and his head flops forward when my brothers release him.

Done.

I walk into the attached bathroom and wash off my gloves and blade. I root around through the medicine cabinet until I find an unopened first aid kit. I pop the top of the small bottle of alcohol and dump it all over my knife. I flip it closed and dry off. When I come back into the office, Khan and Goblin have already emptied the safe, shoving the cash into a rucksack.

We walk out, slapping some cash into the hands of Zach's men. The shitheads make me sick. They have no loyalty. A man should believe in what he does and die by his convictions. Right or wrong, if you're doing it, you should be willing to meet Hades if someone threatens your livelihood. I have zero respect for men who can be bought.

But a deal's a deal, so they'll get paid and then like fucking snakes, they'll slither around until they find the next hole to crawl into.

We straddle our bikes, strap on our domes, and peel out down the road. The fresh air is cool on my overheated skin after being in that stuffy office. The scents of earth, motor oil, and freedom fill my nostrils. My Goblin Bell jingles underneath the bike, trapping evil road spirits and protecting me.

The stars are out in force, not a cloud in the sky, and the moon illuminates the road ahead, guiding us home. Today was a scorcher, but living in the high desert means at night, we're given a reprieve and the temperatures drop dramatically.

Reno has a confusing climate. We're surrounded by snow-capped mountains and evergreens, but we're resting on a bed of sand and sagebrush desert.

I grew up here, watching as things changed on the exterior, but underneath the flashing lights, clean streets, and manicured landscapes, it's still the same. Owned by crime lords and dirty politicians doing back alley handshakes with suitcases full of cash.

We pull into the warehouse district where our clubhouse is, and the tall iron gates open at our arrival. One of the prospects, Clint, waves us through. We park and by the time I'm pulling off my helmet, Trucker is at my side.

"How'd it go?" He puts a cigarette to his lips and offers one to me. I take it and we both light up.

I try not to be annoyed at having my dad hassle me every time we get back from a job. He may have given the prez patch to me, but in his head, it's still sewn onto his cut. In his head, I'm not ready. But he lost his ability to lead the day Ma died, and he was forced to pass the torch to me, even though he hates me. Whether her death was my fault or not, I was there. Therefore, I'm responsible.

"Fine. It's done." I take a long drag, letting the thick smoke burn my lungs and even out the sharp edges of my mind.

"Are you sure?" he asks.

"Yes. Jesus Christ. I don't need my daddy checking in on me to make sure I did a suitable job. I've got the prez patch now. Best remember that."

I walk away, not wanting to rehash the same fucking fight he picks with me every goddamn time I see him. I wish the old man would walk away and pick up a hobby. I laugh to myself thinking about his ass out on a golf course. His grease stained jeans and leather cut scandalizing all the polo wearing motherfuckers.

I make my way to the bar and knock on the old oak bar top. It's seen better days, but it wears the history of our chapter on it like a textbook. Every time we've been raided, every brawl that's broken out, every shot that spilled and soaked into the grain. It's as much a part of our club as the hand-carved table we sit around in the Chapel. It's as much a part of our club as the old man outside stewing.

"What can I get you, Prez?" another prospect, Jake, asks.

"Gimme a bottle of mezcal."

"Sure thing." He pushes around a few bottles until he finds the tequila I asked for.

"Thanks, bro." I take the bottle and head to my room, careful not to make eye contact with any of the brothers. Trucker soured my mood and I don't want to shoot the shit. Maybe after I work my way through the bottle, I'll feel better.

I shut and lock my door behind me. I take in the room. Trucker gave it up when he stepped down. He said it was only right, but I don't perceive it as my space yet. I only see him. His bed, his TV, his fucking bathroom. The place he locked himself away to grieve the loss of his wife.

I've changed the bed, I bought a new TV, and I painted the fucking walls. Didn't do shit to erase the memories.

I sit down in my chair and open the bottle. I don't need a shot glass, or a lime, or any of that pussy shit. I guzzle it down in between puffs of my cig. Tequila and cigarettes. The only thing I love more is pussy, but until I get rid of this nasty mood, I won't be leaving to find a snatch to bury myself in.

When I've had just enough, I set the bottle down and get out my tattoo gun. I'm not an artist. Not even a little. A guy downtown who's a friend of the club did all my ink. But my tally marks are for me, so I need to be the one to put them onto my flesh.

I wipe down the skin of my pec with disinfectant and set the little bottle of black ink out. I take in the four marks I've already etched. They're crude lines that could pass as kindergarten scratch, but each one represents a life I've sent to Hades. It doesn't matter if they're perfect.

I take the tattoo gun to my chest and carve out the fifth line. Even though I've been behind the scenes on a shit ton more kills, these are the ones done by my own hand.

Usually, I let my brothers do the honor, not because I don't have the stomach for it, but because I'm the one who plans each of these visits. I'm the one who vets clients and makes the game plan. It's their job to execute. We all have our strengths and mine is in the planning.

But now and then, the rage that burns deep in my belly gets too hot, like a pressure cooker ready to burst. I wait for something to come across my table I feel a certain way about, and I take all my frustrations, all my anger, all my hurt, and I expel it on my victim.

Each time, I think it will calm the fire inside me and atone for my mistakes. But it doesn't. No matter what I do, I'll always be the one who Trucker blames for Ma's death. And instead of fixing me, each kill takes a little piece of my soul. Soon there won't be any left. Not that it fucking matters. I don't need a soul. That's not how you make it through this life.

I look down at my handiwork, wipe away the excess ink, and put away my tools.

Another mark. Another death. Another reason I deserve this prez patch.

Chapter THREE

Bridgette

I wake up to the sound of a loud *pop*. At first, I lie there and listen. But when another *pop* fills the air, I jump out of bed, throw on my robe, and run down the staircase. With my eyes trained on the foyer below, I trip on something lying across the bottom step and fall face first into the marble tile below.

I sit up shakily and look at what I stumbled over. My mouth opens to scream, but nothing comes out. Angelo lies hunched over, blood trickling down his face from a circular wound in his temple.

A gunshot wound. Someone shot Angelo!

I crawl over to him and place my shaky fingers over his pulse point. When I don't sense a heartbeat, I jerk my hand away.

He's dead.

My lip trembles and my eyes well with tears. I slap a hand over my mouth. If whoever did this is still here, I can't let them find me. But even my heavy breaths sound like wind whipping through the large, open room.

Another gunshot echoes through the foyer. It's close, like it's coming from Daddy's office. I crawl on hands and knees, not trusting my wobbly legs, to the closed door, careful to keep my movements silent.

I pull myself to standing and put my ear to the door. The sound of my racing heart and heavy breaths are so loud, the voices arguing angrily on the other side are muffled. I close my eyes and take a deep inhale and exhale to calm myself down and try again. The only voice I recognize is Daddy's.

"Where is it? Don't make me find your pretty daughter as an incentive to get it from you," the unknown man threatens.

A chill runs down my spine, and the hair on my arms and the nape of my neck stands on end. I'm scared. Daddy needs to give him whatever it is he wants, so he'll leave. He *needs* to leave.

"I don't have it! I told you, I destroyed it already," Daddy says, his voice unsteady.

He's lying. Why would he lie?

There's a scuffle and a *crack*, like the sound of someone being hit.

"Don't play games, old man. You're not taking me seriously. Your partner, Byron, didn't take us seriously, either. I'd tell you to call and ask him what happens when I get the brush-off, but he's indisposed right now. Actually, he's indisposed indefinitely. But maybe you'd be more apt to comply if you had something to lose standing in front of you. Marco, go find Mr. Davis' daughter, please. What's her name? Bridgette?"

Footsteps grow louder and my eyes widen. If he's coming for me, I need to run and hide.

"Okay!" Daddy yells out. "I was going to destroy it tonight, but I haven't yet. It's in my safe."

The footsteps move away from the door, and I breathe a sigh of relief. There's more shuffling and then the *beep* of Daddy's safe opening.

"Look at that. Thank you for your cooperation. Now you have two weeks to get me the cash. If you do, I'll return this to you and you can do whatever you want with it. But if you don't? Well, let's just say jail time won't be the worst of your punishment. While you're safe behind bars, your daughter will be all alone, unprotected. She might need a man like me to keep her safe. I'm not a gentle lover, but I'm sure she'd get used to my particular tastes."

The walls close in on me, and black spots fill my vision. Despite how cold this house is, no matter the time of year, beads of sweat dampen my brow.

"You have it, now go. You'll get your money." Daddy's voice is stern, but I recognize the false confidence. He's being held at gunpoint in his office and Angelo is dead. He must be every bit as terrified as I am.

"Sure. Okay. We'll go. Marco, bring the car around."

I run, but I don't go back upstairs to my room. If they end up searching for me, that's the first place they'll search. Instead, I go through the formal sitting room, through the kitchen, and out the back door. The motion light clicks on, startling me. I hope they don't notice it from the front of the house.

Sophie, our Rottweiler, runs up to me. Her ears are forward and she's huffing in distress. She must've been going nuts not being able to get inside but sensing the danger.

"Come on, girl." I snap my fingers and she jogs at my side.

The chilly night air chafes my skin, and the freezing,

damp grass numbs my toes. But I don't stop. I've made it halfway across the football-field-sized lawn when another gunshot sounds. I freeze in place.

No. No. No. They didn't shoot Daddy. He's my only family. But he's the only one left in the house, the only one left to shoot.

The tears I've fought spill free. My nose runs and I don't even have it in me to wipe it away. The mixture mingles and drips down my chin.

Sophie bolts toward the house, but I stop her with another snap of my fingers. She's all I have left now. She reluctantly turns around and marches back to me. Her eyes are worried, and she's visibly stressed. She's trained to protect us, but Daddy must not have brought her inside for the night before those men showed up.

With Sophie back at my side, I take off again. This time I don't stop until I get to the pool house. I quickly type the code into the door to unlock it and slam it shut behind me. I flip the deadbolt and slide down the glass door until my ass hits the tiled floor.

Sophie crawls into my lap, nuzzling me. I wrap my arms around her large, muscular body and sob into her fur. She doesn't move. She stands guard over me, her eyes scanning the grassy lawn behind us. I lean into her, letting her ground me. If I let go, I fear I'll break apart into a million pieces.

Every inch of me aches with loss.

I don't know how much time passes before I get my wits about me enough to stop crying and try to form a plan. I lift my robe to my face and wipe away the snot and tears. Sophie tries to help by licking my cheeks. Despite my devastation, I let out a sad laugh.

What do I do now?

My mind races with my next move. I don't have my cell phone and Daddy had all our landlines disconnected years ago. The pool house is a large studio, so I glance over at the microwave and see it's one in the morning.

How long do I wait?

I squint over my shoulder into the dark and decide enough's enough. If Angelo and Daddy have been murdered, what does it matter if they kill me, too? It won't. I'd welcome death over this feeling of utter helplessness and heartbreak.

"Come on, Soph. We need to go back." On trembling legs, I stand up and leave the pool house.

The motion lights turn on again, temporarily blinding me. Sophie prances a few steps ahead on high alert. When I get to the back door, I listen carefully. I hear nothing, so I turn the knob silently.

I walk on tiptoes back the way I came. Sophie runs ahead, growling low and menacing with her nose to the ground. I stop in the foyer, noticing Daddy's office door is wide-open now. The silence is eerie as I pad to the threshold and peek inside. The only light in the room is the gas fireplace burning in the corner, but it's enough to see him. He's slumped over his desk, face first. I rush over to him.

"Daddy?" I whisper out. I shake him gently, but he doesn't move. "Daddy?" I cry louder this time.

He still doesn't move. I push his shoulders to force him to sit. His head lulls lifelessly and white-hot fear courses through my body. It's one thing to think he might be dead and a whole other to see it with my own eyes.

Then I spot the bloody stain that's seeped through his white button-down shirt near his shoulder, and my world falls apart.

"No. No. No."

I push his executive chair away from his desk and climb into his lap like I did when I was a little girl. He'd spin in circles until I was so dizzy, I turned green. But it's been a long while since the last time I've done that. Lately, I've been a selfish brat, only coming to him when I needed something.

Suddenly money means nothing, and the only thing I need is for him to wake up.

I pound on his chest, shouting, "You can't die! I need you!"

I wrap my arms around him and his head flops onto my shoulder. I clutch him tight, willing my beating heart to leave me and enter him. Frantic tears fall and I gasp for breath, unable to calm myself. Sophie rests her gigantic head on my thigh and whimpers.

It just doesn't make sense. They need him for his money. Unless he said he wouldn't give it to him. That's the only thing that makes sense right now. But even that doesn't seem right, because Daddy would do anything to protect me. Anything.

It's been that way since Mom died ten years ago from cancer. That's what made him start this company in the first place. He didn't want any other kids to suffer the way I did. He's an honorable person. He doesn't deserve to die, and I don't deserve to lose yet another parent.

A soft gurgle fills my ears. I push him off of me. Although his head still hangs, it's not quite so limp. I cup his cheeks and lift his face to mine. His eyes barely open, just tiny slits, but I see it. I press two fingers to his neck and pick up a slight thrum.

"Oh my God."

I jump out of his lap and search around for his cell phone. I can't find it, so I sprint up the stairs, trying hard to see Angelo's lifeless body. I find my phone on my nightstand and dial nine-one-one.

Daddy's alive. I just pray he can stay that way.

Chapter
FOUR

Loki

A knock sounds on my door, followed by a muffled, "Church is in five, right?"

"Right," I yell out and then roll over to the no-name, naked bitch and say, "Time to go."

She doesn't move, so I slap her ass. She squeals but still makes no effort to get up.

"Just let me stay, then I'll be here when you're done," she whines, and her hand blindly reaches over to cup my junk.

"Not gonna happen, darlin'. Don't leave no one in here when I'm not around." I push her hand away and stand up.

As I dress, I watch as she makes a production out of getting out of bed. She lifts to all fours and spreads her knees wide, giving me a full view of her bare pussy and puckered asshole. She looks over her shoulder and licks her plump bottom lip.

I walk into the bathroom and slam the door shut. She was a fun afternoon fuck, but that's all it was. A fuck. It's all bitches are good for and the ones who believe their magic pussy will get me to lock her down are delusional. There ain't no pussy good enough for me to give the old lady title to.

I wash my face. I look older than my thirty-five years. Smoking, alcohol, and a hard life have made sure of that. You don't grow up in a motorcycle club looking like a freshly picked peach. I grab my beanie off the hook and pull it over my messy hair. I put on my black leather cut and I'm ready.

When I return to the room, the bitch is gone, and thank fuck for that. I'm not above physically removing a girl from my room, but I'd rather things be more civil than that.

I lock my bedroom door after me and walk down the hall to the great room. A bar runs the length of the far wall. To my right is a large open area with a few leather couches, a pool table, a dartboard, and an old-school jukebox that only plays hard rock.

A few of my brothers are lounging with the hang-arounds and club whores, most with a beer in hand. It's three in the afternoon, but there's never a wrong time to drink and get your dick wet in our clubhouse.

"Church," is all I say as I open the door to the large, soundproof room.

It's dark in here, no windows, and the only decor being framed pictures of our fallen brothers, an enormous wood table with the Royal Bastard logo carved in the center, and high-back chairs. Enough for all the members of the board.

My brothers file in one by one, leaving their cell phones in a basket with Clint to guard. Trucker and the old-timers are absent. Not surprising. Trucker rarely shows up for anything unless he has a reason to chew my ass out, and the rest only show for the party. They leave the business to us these days.

Not that they don't deserve it. They built this club with their bare hands and grew our business from nothing.

I slam the gavel around and all the chatter between brothers stops.

"I've called Church because we have a new client," I say.

Khan hands me a file folder and I open it. I hand a stack of papers to Goblin.

"Take one and pass it around." I give him a chin lift.

When everyone has a copy, I give them a few minutes to read over the information.

"Since when do we recover stolen items? We're hitmen, not hide-and-go-seekers." Goblin's deep voice rumbles through the room.

"Since the payday has two extra zeros on the end," I say.

"What do we even know about this guy? Who stole whatever it is he wants back?" Goblin tosses the paper onto the table. "I vote no."

"We're not voting yet. Not until I say my piece." I stand up, gaining the attention of the room. "This guy, Martin Davis, needs his shit back in a hurry. He didn't want to tell me too much on the phone because he was in the hospital with a gunshot to his shoulder.

"Whoever broke in killed his business partner before breaking into Davis' property and killing one of his men before they shot him. They meant it to be a warning shot, but these guys aren't fuckin' around. He wouldn't tell me who they are, but it sounds bad and he can't go to the cops because it's illegal for him to even have whatever was in that vial." I search every face at the table, hoping they see things my way.

"I don't know, man. We go after low level crime lords, business deals gone wrong, and cheating husbands with vindictive wives. This seems out of our scope of abilities," Sly argues.

"We can't do it on our own, but we have contacts everywhere and we've done enough favors around this city. It's time for some repayment."

"This is crazy shit, man." Moto pinches the bridge of his nose. "It sounds straight up out of an episode of that crime show Khan's always blasting Monday nights. It doesn't even sound real."

"I was suspicious, too. But I did a bunch of research on this guy. Everything he told me lines up with what I could dig up." I hold up the spec sheet with all the information I've collected so far and point to contract total. "Pay close attention to that payout amount. You're not seeing things. That's six zeros."

Moto whistles. "Sure could use a cut of that."

"We all could. This clubhouse could." I stand up, pressing my fists on the table. "Now you know everything I do, so let's vote. All in favor, raise your hand."

I scan the room while each brother considers his options. I just need a majority, not all of 'em. And I'll be glad to take the cut of any motherfucker who doesn't want to join in.

Khan raises his hand right away. My VP has my back, regardless. Goblin glances around before lifting his. And now I have my Enforcer. Roch, my Sergeant at Arms, nods and barely lifts a finger, but a yes is still a yes. Moto and Sly have a silent conversation before giving me a thumbs-up. I knew if I have one, I'd have both. Which is good because I need my Road Captain and Treasurer.

"There're my boys." I slam the gavel down. "Now let's get fucked up. Tomorrow we all go to Davis' house so we get more information and start planning."

We leave the Chapel and head right to the bar. Jake lines up shot glasses, already knowing how things go after a meeting. Tequila is poured and passed around.

"To six zeros." I hold up my glass.

"Six zeros!" A chorus of cheers come back at me.

We slam our glasses down and Jake divvies out bottles of beer with the caps popped. He's a good kid. Give him a little more time and he'll be patched in, no doubt.

We turn to the great room where the hang-arounds are playing pool and darts while the club whores busy themselves trying to look appealing so one of us will choose them. The movie on the big screen shows a thick chick with huge fake ass boobs bobbing up and down on a dude's dick. Porn's all well and good, but real live pussy is where it's at, so I grab my beer and make my way over to the sofa where a few of the club whores are pretending to chat. They fucking hate each other. To them, this is a competition to see who can bag a biker first. They only pretend to be team players so we don't kick their drama filled asses out on the street.

I plop down in between a blond chick with creamy skin and a brunette with a bronzed glow. I'm sure they have names; I just don't give a fuck enough to ask. I span my arms wide and they snuggle in. Being the prez means a lot of tough decisions fall on my shoulders and my guys look to me to make sure everyone stays paid and whole. It's a lot of responsibility and pressure. But being the prez also means I get first dibs on pussy and tonight, I'm taking two.

"Ladies. How are we feeling?"

"Better now that you're here." The blonde rubs up and down my chest.

"Much better." The brunette grips onto my thigh.

Goddamn. It's good to be me.

While Thing One and Thing Two do their best to tease me, I scan the room to see how my brothers are faring.

Khan's huge ass is chatting up a chick who probably weighs less than his thigh. I cock my head, wondering how he'll get it in. He might break this one, but he's got a type. Tiny things he can throw around.

Moto and Sly, the fuckers, have a redhead pinned between them. She's got her ass resting on the edge of the bar and my brothers are each latched onto a tit. They get off on banging the same chick. Whatever clears their pipes, I'm not about to judge them.

Goblin's hunched over the other end of the bar. No doubt overthinking this job. He's serious as shit. If you're itching for a good time, don't make eye contact with him because he'll lock you into a conversation about something he saw on the news or some other fucking thing. The guy hardly goes after the chicks, and if he does, it's only when he finds a smart one. He's good to have around for jobs, but not so much to party with.

Roch is missing, no doubt out back with his pack of pit bulls he's rescued from dog fighting rings. The only exception is his chihuahua. She's the pack leader. No idea why those huge-ass dogs listen to her when the bitch weighs three ounces soaking wet. Roch's road name comes from the patron saint of dog lovers. Those dogs are his babies, and nobody better even look sideways at them.

"Let's go do some shots," the brunette whines.

"Yeah, sure." I bring my gaze back to the bitches at my side.

And that's how the rest of the night goes. Lots of drinking, chain smoking, and a ton of sex. There's not one man alive who wouldn't want to be in our shoes.

We ride our bikes out to the middle of the desert. There ain't nothing around here to see for miles. That is, until we come across a massive house. Mansion is probably a better word. We get buzzed in through the gate and park next to a giant fountain sculpture of a man with water squirting from its pecker.

Rich people are so fucking weird.

"At least he's good for the money." Moto removes his sunglasses and scans the property.

We're greeted at the door by two strapped motherfuckers the size of Khan. Davis must've stepped up security since being shot.

They lead us into an office with tall, book-lined shelves and a sitting area next to a picture window that overlooks the pool. Davis sits behind a substantial desk. He's squirming around and his face is pale. Either from having his house overrun by bikers, or the pain from being shot a couple days ago.

I move to shake his hand before realizing his arm is in a sling.

"Sorry," he says.

"No worries."

There isn't anywhere for us all to sit, so we stand, towering over the small man.

"Does your being here mean you've taken on my… issue?"

"Yeah, but we need more information on who these fuckers are." I fold my arms over my chest.

"My men have done some research after combing through the surveillance footage. We believe they're part of the National Crime Syndicate. A smaller, local branch of the Italian Mafia."

"Fuck." I look over at my brothers. The same darkness that flashes behind my eyes does the same to them.

Two years ago, the Corsetti crime family were the ones responsible for the death of Ma. Trucker had us running guns at the time and the Corsettis decided they wanted to take over the market. They made this known by breaking into the clubhouse late at night. Trucker and Ma didn't stay the night often, preferring to be in their home, but we'd had a barbecue that night and they both had too much to drink. Trucker was passed out in his room, but Mom and I were up late talking the way we used to do.

It happened so fast. One second we were laughing, the next I was watching her die. The brothers charged out of their rooms firing. We killed a few of their men, but neither of the Corsetti brothers.

It started a war. Trucker wanted to punish everyone responsible. At some point, all of us younger guys had to sit down with the old man. He didn't listen. We were losing too many people. It was a bloodbath.

Behind Trucker's back, I negotiated an end to the violence. We gave up the gun market in exchange for a truce. It was that, or we'd be wiped away. It was the only way we'd survive. Trucker lost his mind and eventually was forced to hand over the prez patch to me.

It's the smartest and dumbest thing I've ever done. I earned the respect of my brothers and lost the respect of my dad.

If that's really who's behind this, it could mean another war. More bloodshed. But now we're more prepared. We've built our numbers back up. And we aren't the ones being surprised this time. We'll be the ones on the offense, killing every fucking one of them if we have to.

Davis continues, "They're looking for a big payday, coming after me since my company grossed over two billion last year."

I whistle at that.

What kind of business can gross that much cash?

"I know." He holds his good hand up in a pacifying manner. "My team of scientists and medical professionals developed a cure for a certain type of cancer and the profit potential is astronomical. We sold it to a pharmaceutical company for a sizeable sum. That was in addition to a few other less lucrative deals. I'm being honest with you because that's the only way you'll be able to catch them. I'm trusting this information won't leave this room because confidentiality was part of the sale." He leans back in his chair, wincing with the movement.

"So they want your money?" Moto asks.

"Yes, and they're holding the vial ransom until I give them a hundred and fifty million in cash. They gave me two weeks, and that was four days ago."

"Why not just give it to him? It sounds like you can afford it." I shrug.

"Because that money has the potential to do a lot of good. The more we can reinvest into other cures, the more lives we can save." He sighs. "I'll pay it if I have to. But if I can recover it before the ten days and pay you guys a smaller amount of money, it's a risk I'm willing to take."

"And what if you go to the cops? Wouldn't they have a better chance of getting this shit back?" Goblin asks.

"Even though we didn't mean to engineer this virus, we did. If the full vial is used in the right conditions, it could wipe out half the country, and possibly even spreading around the world. More likely, they'd use it in smaller doses to kill off the enemies of whoever owns it. And by not destroying it right away, we committed a crime. I might go to jail for the rest of my life. That also isn't an option for me."

"How did the Corsettis even find out?" I ask.

"I'm uncertain, but the only thing that makes sense is my business partner's responsible for the leak. I found it weird that he fought me on destroying it. I assume he was shopping it around, finding anyone who would have the need for a weapon of mass destruction. Possibly, he thought the Corsettis might be interested. All I can guess is they didn't want the virus, but instead wanted to use it as ransom." Davis hands me a folder. "The man who shot me said Byron was his first stop and he… he killed him. I can't confirm that because there hasn't been a body found, but I also can't get ahold of him. If I were you, his house would be my first stop."

"You know what we do, right? We're not the guys who knock on doors and take no for an answer. If we do this, we're doing it our way. No questions asked." I flip through the file, making a note of the name, Byron Billings, the business partner.

"I've had a bit of time to contemplate this while I was in the hospital. Whatever you guys have to do, I won't get involved. I also don't want to know about it. I just want the vial back."

"Okay. We require half the cash up-front, the other when we deliver," Sly demands. His mind is always on the money.

"Of course." He carefully stands and walks over to a

duffel bag sitting on the table by the window. "Here's the first half."

Sly takes the duffel, opens it, and flips through a few of the stacks. He gives me a nod.

"Okay. We'll start today." I lead my men toward the door.

"There's one more thing," Davis calls out.

We stop and turn around. The man looks sheepish, staring at his oriental rug like it's got titties drawn on it or something.

"Yeah?" I ask.

"It's my daughter. I'm terrified for her life. These men"—he chokes out—"they threatened to do things to her. Terrible things. I'm worried she'll be their next target, especially as we get closer and closer to the deadline. I only have a few men I can trust right now, and it's not enough to keep both her and me safe."

"I don't understand what that has to do with us," Khan grumbles.

"I need you to protect her. I need her safe. I can't think of a better place than with you all."

"No. We don't babysit bitches." I shake my head.

"Please. She's a pleasant kid. She's a bit defiant and headstrong, and she won't like this at all. She might fight and throw a tantrum. Ignore her but keep an eye on her. And you have my permission to do whatever you need to do to keep her safe."

I look at my brothers for guidance on this one, but none of them will meet my gaze, worried they'll be put on nanny duty. We don't need a kid hanging around, especially not some spoiled brat. But if this is a deal breaker, we can just lock her in the basement until this is over.

"Throw in another twenty Gs."

"Done."

I blow out a breath. "Fine. If you're convinced your daughter is safer with a gang of bikers, you must be desperate. We'll take her."

"I need you to promise me she won't be harmed."

"We're not the kind to tuck her in at night and make sure she eats square meals, but we won't hurt her, if that's what you mean. We probably won't be her best friends, but she'll be safe," I say.

"Okay. That's all I'm asking. Thank you. This means a lot to me." He picks up his cell phone, types a message, and not two minutes later, the girl walks in.

Only, she's not a girl, she's a hot as fuck woman. Probably not much older than eighteen, but she's no kid. Whatever she was going to say dies on her lips when she sees us and she just stands there, mouth gaping. My eyes lock on her, taking in every womanly curve, her long blond hair, her pouty lips. Her whole goddamn package. My cock twitches and threatens to harden.

She's going to be a bigger problem than finding the vial.

Chapter FIVE

Bridgette

Daddy texts me to come see him immediately. Scared something is wrong, I fly down the stairs and into his office. I expected to find him alone. But that's not the case. Instead, there are six gargantuan men in leather vests. The room is large and open, but with them in here, it's cramped. Both their demeanors and their size fill the space to capacity.

"Who are they?" I ask Daddy but keep my eyes on them.

Anxiety claws at my insides, threatening to shut me down. After what happened with Daddy, I haven't been able to relax. I can't sleep, I can't sit still, even though I'm exhausted. Every day that ticks by is a day closer to Daddy's deadline. He won't talk about it with me, he won't tell me his plan. He said it's for my own good, but he's wrong. The not knowing is what's killing me. I can't leave the house, I keep Sophie next to me at all times, and I stole a handgun from the safe.

Late at night, I pace my room, listening for any sound of forced entry. The guard Daddy assigns to my door doesn't ease my mind either. I saw what they did to Angelo. Bodyguards are mortal. They can die. They can make mistakes.

"I've hired these men to handle my situation. I've also asked them to take you somewhere secure and watch over you."

"No," I say vehemently.

"Sweetheart. Be reasonable. Please. You aren't safe here. You know it. It's why you haven't been eating or sleeping. You need to be out of harm's way." He stands in front of me. His good hand grips my arm. His eyes pleading.

"No, Daddy. I don't even know who they are." I take a step back out of his grasp.

A scary man with a beanie on his head takes a step toward me. His gaze roams my body, making me uncomfortable. Like I'm a steak and he's ravenous. He thrusts his hand forward for me to shake. "I'm Loki."

I cross my arms, ignoring his pleasantries. His hand drops and those eyes darken in a terrifying way. An evil way. These men aren't here to protect me. They're not nice.

"I'm Kahn, darlin'," the largest of the bunch says. "And this is Goblin, Roch, Moto, and Sly."

"This is Bridgette," Daddy says.

I huff a breath and stamp my foot. Why is he trusting them? It doesn't make any sense. Using one evil to fight another. I've begged him to call the cops, but he's worried about getting in trouble. While I understand, this whole situation is beyond worrying about your own skin.

What Daddy's company did was reckless and dangerous. All that should matter is getting the vial back and saving the lives of innocent people who might be affected by the virus.

"I'm not taking the bitch biting and clawing. If she wants

to stay here and risk her life, that's on her," the first man, Loki, says.

"Can you give me a moment with my daughter, please?" Daddy asks.

"We'll be outside," Khan says, and they file out.

I watch them leave and notice the patch sewn onto the back of all their vests. The Royal Bastards MC? Daddy hired a motorcycle gang to take care of me? He's lost his mind.

The door closes, leaving us alone. Now that they're gone, the air isn't as thick, making it easier to breathe.

"I'm not going anywhere without you. I won't do it," I say.

"You have to. I can't keep things together while also worrying about you. I'm doing everything in my power to make sure I can walk away from this, but I can't do that and keep you safe. Please, sweetheart. It's only for a few days. Then you can come and get back to your regular life. I'll even give you your own credit card."

His words prove how shallow he thinks I am. And maybe he was right before all this happened. But now? Now, the last thing I want to do is go shopping or see my stupid friends. The only thing important to me is making sure I don't lose my last remaining family member.

"But who will watch over you? If I'm not safe, that means you aren't either." I loop my arms around Daddy's neck and hug him tight.

I inhale the cool, clean scent of his aftershave. The same one he's used since before I can even remember. It's comforting knowing some things haven't changed.

"I have my own men. They'll protect me. And if I don't have to divide them between me and you, they'll be able to focus on me and the house. It'll be okay. I promise. Go with them. Please." He pulls back and kisses me on the temple.

"They're scary. I don't think I'm any safer with them."

"I looked into them. They're not nice men, but they don't hurt kids. You'll be fine. Keep your head down. It's only a few days."

Silly man still sees me as an eight-year-old girl who lost her mom. Not as a woman who might not be safe with a group of bikers.

"I'll go, but you have to promise I can come home if I don't like it there."

"Of course. If anyone does anything that makes you nervous, call me. I'll have them bring you back."

"Fine. I need to pack a few personal items."

"Thank you, sweetheart."

I leave his office, wondering what I'm getting myself into. I've seen *Sons of Anarchy*. Jax Teller was sexy, making me fantasize about all the things a man like him could do to me. But this isn't a TV show. This is real life, and hot or not, these bikers are scary.

I gather my things, mostly comfortable clothes since I don't plan on going anywhere until this is over. Then I move to my bathroom where I collect my toiletries. By the time I'm done, my Louis Vuitton crocodilian backpack and my overnight bag are full. I put my phone and charger in my purse and grab my pillow.

I maneuver down the stairs and outside where Daddy is talking quietly with Loki. It gives me a minute to study the dangerously attractive man. He's in worn jeans and underneath his vest is a simple wife beater. His skin is tanned dark from the sun and he has slight wrinkles around his eyes and lips. His arms are muscular and tattooed. I wonder what his hair looks like under his beanie. He's handsome in a way that makes your heart skip a beat, both in fear and attraction.

I clear my throat and all the men turn to look at me.

"I'm ready," I say.

Loki approaches me with a helmet. He crowds my space, smelling of cigarettes and motor oil. Two scents that on a normal man would make me recoil, but on him they smell manly and strong. He puts the black, matte dome helmet on my head and adjusts the straps to fit. Even tightened all the way, it's loose and flops to the side.

"It's too big, but it'll have to do." He looks down at my feet where my luggage is sitting. "You can't bring all that."

"I have to, it's all my stuff," I argue.

"Darlin', you're riding on the back of a bike, not a minivan. I don't have a trailer for you to cart your entire bedroom with you."

"It's not my entire room. It's only my toiletries and some clothes."

"It's too much. You can take this." He picks up my backpack.

"That only has my clothes. I need my shampoo, my conditioner"—I glare at him—"my makeup."

"You don't need any of that shit." He tosses my backpack to the giant man, who puts it on. "Let's go."

"I'm not going anywhere without my makeup." I place my hands on my hips.

Loki picks up my overnight bag and my pillow. He hands it to Daddy, who accepts it while his eyes plead with me to not fight this. But I need my toothbrush, my nighttime face mask, my eye cream.

"Daddy can drive me," I suggest.

"Darlin', get on the bike," Loki demands.

"No," I say with all the confidence of a twig in a tornado.

"Darlin'," he warns, his features darkening.

"My name is Bridgette."

"Get on the bike, Bridgette."

"Not without my toothbrush."

He grabs the overnight bag from Daddy and I'm proud I stood up to him and won. Except I didn't. My jaw drops as he releases it to the ground, crouches and unzips it. He digs around, tossing my things all over the driveway. Daddy watches helplessly, his eyes wide.

"Stop it. What are you doing?" I march over and try to take my bag from him, but he looks up at me and what I see sends my pulse racing. His eyes are ruthless and cold, and there's a snarl on his lips.

He throws all my expensive products out one by one until he finds my Sonicare. He holds it out to me. I take it and tuck it into my purse.

"I need the charger. What if it goes dead before I come home?"

"Get on the fuckin' bike," he says through clenched teeth.

Not wanting to piss him off anymore, I give Daddy one last hug and walk over to his motorcycle.

"Not mine," Loki whispers close to my ear, his warm body suddenly right behind me. "The only bitches I allow on my bike are the ones I plan on fuckin.'"

My eyes widen at his crassness. Was he raised in a trailer park? It's the only reason I can see for him to have such terrible manners.

I look around, wondering whose bike I'm supposed to ride. One of the men I haven't even heard speak waves me over. The name tag on his vest says he's Roch. I wonder what sort of name that is. Despite being part of this gang, he has kind eyes, and he looks softer than the others.

Roch takes my purse and shoves it into a saddlebag. He

places his hands under my arms, and I squeal. He lifts me up and plops me down on the bike. He does all of this without saying one word to me, let alone making eye contact. These men are all Neanderthals. I'm not some *thing* they can pass around.

But I stay silent. I need to get through a few days and then life can go back to normal like Daddy said.

I don't want it to go back to normal.

The thought gives me pause. But the more I think about it, I don't want to keep living the life of an heiress. I'm not qualified for anything else, but I'll figure it out. I can use this time with the bikers to think about it and make plans.

Roch lifts a leg over his bike and sits down, making my chest flatten against his back and our thighs touch. I scoot away but run out of space on the seat. He reaches behind him and grabs my hands. He yanks roughly, forcing me forward so I'm flush with his body. He wraps my arms around his middle and pats them, like he wants me to stay like this. I jerk them off of him. I'm not snuggling into this biker.

He sighs loudly, reaches behind, and grips my hands almost painfully in his. He brings them around and holds them there tightly in his hold.

He starts the bike, sending vibrations through my core. It's loud and obtrusive. As he takes off, he lets go of my hands. But now that we're moving, I wouldn't let go if he asked me to. This isn't safe. It's terrifying and I feel like I'm seconds from flying off. I grip onto his T-shirt tightly.

We pull off onto the highway and I press my forehead into his back. I hate this. The wind and the engine are so loud, I can't hear anything else. The cars we pass are so close, all it would take is one drifting from its lane and I'd splatter all over the asphalt.

What the heck did Daddy get me into?

Chapter SIX

Loki

I lead my men down the highway, heading back to the clubhouse. Things didn't go exactly as I planned, but we got twenty Gs more out of Davis.

And his daughter.

I smirk, remembering the look on her face when I told her she wasn't riding on the back of my bike. This bitch is so innocent. I'm almost looking forward to showing her the clubhouse. To making her join us for a party. The deer in the headlights expression she gave me earlier would be nothing compared to how she'd react to seeing orgies play out on the sofa.

I fall back a little so I can see how she's liking the ride. Roch pulls up alongside me. He pushes his cut out of the way so I can see the death grip she has on his shirt. Looking behind him, I see her smashed to his back. Her eyes are squeezed so tight, she could probably turn coal to a diamond between her lashes, and her forehead is pressed against his cut.

I shake my head and move out in front again. Is this bitch

for real? I've never met anyone so wholesome. It should make me want to go easy on her, to coddle her, and handle her with kid gloves.

It doesn't.

Instead, I want to defile her. Expose her to all the dirty things I've seen in my life. Watch the innocent light in her eyes dim. I'd be doing her a favor. Life isn't all shopping and lunch dates with friends. Not real life.

Real life is fucked up and messy, and I want to dirty the fuck out of her. Especially after witnessing her bratty behavior back at her house. If her dad hadn't been there watching, I would've bent her over my knee and spanked the shit out of her. That thought turns me right the fuck on. I want to see her pale, creamy skin pink up underneath my palm.

I push that away. I don't need any distractions right now. We're about to walk into the biggest fight we've ever been in. I need focus and a clear head.

We park our bikes side by side in the clubhouse parking lot. I could tell any of my brothers to give her a tour, but instead I find myself grabbing her backpack from Khan and waving her over after she's off Roch's bike. She stumbles a bit, and Roch steadies her before giving her ass a pat to get her moving.

She startles and shoots a glare over her shoulder. Her hair is windblown, and her yoga pants and tank top are askew. She straightens herself as she walks over to me, a scowl firmly fixed on her beautiful face. It's the same resting bitch face she's had since I met her. I don't imagine I'll get anything but that until we turn her back over to her daddy.

"Let's go. I'll give you a tour." I open the door and allow her to step in first. She looks surprised, but my mama taught me manners. I just don't always use them. "This door leads to the Chapel. No one's allowed in there except patched in members."

"Patched in?" she asks.

"Only brothers with this patch"—I show her the back of my cut—"can enter. That means you're one of us. This is the bar. There's a kitchen through those doors. This room is where we hang out."

She turns in a circle, taking in the large space. I wonder what she's thinking, but not enough to ask. I have a feeling whatever comes out of her smart mouth will just piss me off.

"There are bedrooms down here." I motion to the hallway. "But you'll stay down here."

I open the door that leads to the basement stairs. I thought about sticking her in a spare room, but I want to test her, see how weak she really is. So, the basement will do.

"Down there?" She gulps, looking down the unlit corridor.

"Yeah, darlin'. Down there. Let's go." I grab her hand and give it a tug, but she digs her heels into the ground.

"Isn't there anything up here?"

"No. There's not. The bedrooms up here are for the brothers. Not a spoiled brat we have to babysit."

I yank harder, sending her stumbling forward. Everything with this bitch has to be a fight.

When I finally get her down the stairs, I pull on the string to turn on the hanging lightbulb. The only room we ever use in here is the kill room. If our clients have someone they need information from before taking them out, we bring them down here. That room is hidden away behind a wall of shelves that are piled high with boxes. But it's on a hinge, so it's easy to swing the shelves out and get to the secret room. You just would never know it.

The flooring down here is concrete and there's no sectioned off rooms. It's just framed roughly with two by fours. We have dreams to put in a few more bedrooms and have another lounging space since upstairs gets crowded, but our finances haven't allowed us to do it yet. It's what we'll use part of our payday for.

I pull a canvas tarp off the couch, sending dust balls flying through the air. Bridgette coughs and sneezes, like even dust is too much for her delicate system.

"It's a little rough, but it'll be okay for a few days."

"Are you joking right now? I can't tell if you're trying to scare me or you're serious."

"Dead serious, darlin'. This is the only space we have open. I mean, if you want to share my room, you can. Just be warned, I like to bring *dates* back with me. I'm sure they wouldn't mind if you watched, though. Maybe you could even join—"

"This is fine." She closes her eyes, takes a breath, and then reopens them. "I'll be fine."

"There's a cot over there." I point to the corner where a military style cot is set up. "There's probably some clean bedding upstairs. Ask one of the club whores. They do the laundry around here."

"Club what?"

"Whores. Patch pussy. Whatever you want to call them. There's Tabitha, who's been around for a long time or Sissy. She's usually around. Ask one of them."

Her eyes go wide and I laugh. This bitch is something else. I've never met anyone this obnoxiously innocent. I'll bet she's a virgin. She has to be. Unless some country club, sweater vest wearing dick hole has gotten to her, and even then, I'd still consider her a virgin because until you've been fucked properly, you don't know what sex is. My cock jerks in my pants, liking that idea of me being the one to show her.

Jesus Christ, I'm gonna have to find Tabitha to take care of my problem. I need to be sucked off if I have any hope of keeping away from this bitch.

I've made it up four steps before she calls out to me.

"What am I supposed to do now?" she asks, her voice trembling.

"Whatever the fuck you want. Just stay on the property and stay out of our meeting room. Other than that, I don't give a fuck."

"Where are you going?" Her eyes meet mine. She looked innocent before, but now she looks pathetic. Like a baby bird who's just hatched and is terrified of everything and can't do anything on their own.

"I've got shit to do."

I take the steps two a time to get away. I don't need her looking to me for guidance. I can't help her. I just need her to stay out of my way and we'll be fine.

I walk upstairs and find Goblin at the bar. He's hunched over all the information we collected from Davis. I take the stool next to him.

"Watch this." He presses play on his phone, pulling up the footage from Davis's security feed.

There's no doubt it's the Corsettis. I'd recognize that rat bastard, Dom, anywhere. The other guy appears to be one of his goons. I blow out a breath, watching as the camera angles switch as they walk right in, kill the bodyguard, and then storm into the office. Goblin fast-forwards through them talking and stops the moment Dom shoots Davis in the shoulder.

"I can't believe we're going against them so soon after—"

"What do you think your old man'll say about this? Think he'll go all nuts again?" Goblin interrupts, not wanting to talk about the past.

I study my Enforcer while thinking it through. I've known Goblin since we were in Pampers. His old man was Trucker's Enforcer back in the day and was one of the men killed by the Corsettis. I'm sure it's painful for him to think about starting a war back up.

"Yeah, he'll probably fly off the handle. I'll wait to tell him. He's looking less homicidal these days. I'd like to keep it that way."

"So, what's our plan?"

"I had Sly pull some aerial maps of their compound. I put some feelers out there to find out which building Dom lives in. I think he'd keep the vial where he can get to it quickly." I scratch my chin, going through possibilities. "But I also don't think he'd be risking carrying it around with him. If we can get in when we know he and his dad are out, I think that's our best bet."

"Sounds good. We need to make sure they don't know we were hired. If he thinks Davis is trying to gather the cash, he won't be expecting an ambush." Goblin pulls at his beard.

"I'm also trying to find out Dom's cell phone number. Sly said he could pull text messages and show calls in and out. I know a guy who's friends with Dom's cousin. I helped him out of a sticky situation with a hooker last year. He owes me." I cringe thinking about dragging the slut out of the hotel room, her face blue from some breath play gone wrong.

The sound of sex distracts me, and I turn around to see what's playing today. A chick is getting anally plowed by a huge black dildo and then held open, gaping. I roll my eyes. Her butthole is one double penetration away from prolapsing. Not sexy at all.

"Hey, Prez." Moto drags his attention away from the giant asshole on the screen and comes over to the bar. "How's it going?"

"Just going over our game plan. Don't have much yet. Waiting to hear back about a few things." I pull a cig out and light up, holding the smoke in my lungs for long seconds before blowing out. That first drag is always the best.

"And the girl?" Moto pulls his long, black hair into a ponytail, securing it with a rubber band.

Looking at him, you wouldn't think he'd be in an MC. Most Japanese bikers ride crotch rockets and choose to street race, not ride a Harley and earn their money by killing. But he's earned his spot here. While we all can work on our bikes, Moto is our gearhead. He can build a bike from scraps, or fix a bike using only a wrench and a prayer.

"What about her?" I ask.

"Is she going to be trouble?"

"I set her up in the basement. She'll be fine."

"Seriously?" Moto asks incredulously. "Why didn't you put her in one of the many empty rooms we have?"

"All that perfection needs to be muddied up a bit." I chuckle.

"You're such a prick," he says, but now he's laughing too.

The front door opens and Khan walks in. The fucker barely fits through the doorway. He had to have his bike specially made for his huge ass. His personality is just as outrageous. He's the guy who'll do anything on a dare. He's also loyal as fuck. He stood by my side when I went behind Trucker's back to end the war with the Corsetti family.

"Hey, man. I went over to that Byron guy's house. It's been tossed and he ain't there. Don't look like he's coming back, neither. Found some blood spray on the wall." Khan grabs a chair from one of the tables that are scattered around next to the bar. He flips it around and sits on it backward. The wood creaks under his weight.

"That's what I expected. Thanks for checking it out," I say.

"No problem." He scans the room. "Where's the bitch?"

Moto, Goblin, and I bust up.

"My guess is throwing a tantrum downstairs."

Bridgette

He left me here. I can't believe he left me in this disgustingly dirty cesspool. There's no way I can live down here. I just can't. My nose is itchy and my eyes water from the dust and the cot he expects me to sleep on has a mattress so thin and stained, it gives me hives just thinking about trying to lie down on it. There are spiders in the corners, and it's bone-chilling cold.

Humans aren't meant to live like this. I feel the tears coming, but I swallow them down. That's what he wants and I refuse to give him anything he wants.

I know what he thinks when he sees me. Weak, frail, pitiful. Which is exactly how I feel right now, but I can't show him that. I need to put on a brave face for Daddy. He needs to focus his energy on helping these guys find that vial, not on his daughter who is so blind to the world, she didn't even know people like the ones upstairs existed.

I decide to find bedding and maybe a vacuum to suck the

spiders up. I ascend the creaky stairs, holding my head high. I can do this. I refuse to find club whores, as he put them. But maybe Roch will help me. After being plastered to his back for the ride here, I feel closer to him than that idiot, Loki.

I open the door at the top of the stairs and the sound of someone moaning fills my ears. Not moaning in pain, this sounds almost pleasurable. I walk into the large room with the sofas and what I see shocks me. Many of the men I met earlier are playing pool or sitting at the bar. That's not what has my attention, though. It's the pornography on their enormous TV that has me frozen in place.

Heat overtakes my body and I know I've turned an embarrassed shade of red.

"Bridgette, where you goin'?" someone asks.

My feet carry me out the front door. I don't even think before I take off running. Thankfully, I'm wearing workout clothes, because I put my tennis shoes to use. My feet pound into the loose gravel as I make my way to the gate.

I jostle the iron bars, trying to figure out how to open them.

"Darlin'! You can't leave," someone else yells and I hear footsteps nearing where I'm standing.

I know I have only seconds before they catch up to me. I climb the gate and have one leg over the top when someone yanks on my hand, sending me flying back the way I came. I hit the ground face first with a thud, tiny rocks embedding themselves into my skin. I look up to see Loki standing over me, a pleased smirk on his stupid face.

The tears fall then. Dripping down my dusty cheeks and soaking the gravel underneath me.

"What the fuck do you think you're doing?" he shouts.

"I can't do it. I thought I could be brave, but I can't. I can't stay where there're spiders and the reason I was sneezing is because I'm allergic to dust, you asshole. And then they were watching pornography, like it was cartoons. I just can't." I rest my forehead on my arms, still on the ground.

"Did you say 'asshole'?" He chuckles.

"That's what you got out of that? That I swore? Well, guess what, fucker? I swear." It sounds wrong even to my ears. It may be the first time I ever said the F word. It's not appropriate in the circles I frequent.

"Fucker, huh?" He bends down and lifts me up.

A stinging pain shoots up my knee. I sit up a little in his arms and see my leggings torn open and my knee is bloody with rocks embedded in the wound. It has me crying all over again.

"Why didn't you at least try to catch me?"

"You run away and make me come get you, you'll pay a price. This time that price was falling on your face," he says with no emotion, like a robot. Like he didn't just force me to take a six-foot fall. "Next time, I might spank your bare ass. You keep pushing, your punishments will get more and more severe. Just test me, darlin'. I guarantee you won't like it."

"Put me down," I say.

"You sure?" He quirks a brow.

"Yes! Put. Me. Down. Now. I don't need your help."

His arms open up and once again I'm falling. This time I land on my butt and a sharp pain shoots up my tailbone. I go to yell at Loki, but he's walking away. Not a care in the world.

I scan the area and the other men are standing in a line, entertained by what just happened. I try to stand up, to get away, but everything hurts, so I stay put.

Guess I'm going to live here now. On the dirty ground. Still would be better than the basement.

"Got ya." Roch helps me up and then wraps an arm around middle to hold me up. "Clean up."

I think he'll take me back into the clubhouse, but he leads me over to the side and through a gate. A pack of pit bulls come running toward us and I squirm to get free from Roch's hold. This day has been bad enough, I don't need to be mauled by rabid dogs.

"Shh." His grip tightens. "Won't hurt. Might lick."

I watch as the dogs, tails wagging and tongues hanging out, swarm around us. They jump up, trying to get attention, but Roch has them all sitting with just a movement of his hand.

We continue to make our way around the back of the house where there's a roughly built casita. He helps me through the door and into a cozy, tiny home. The living space has two couches covered with blankets. There's a kitchen with just a hot plate, a sink, and a mini fridge. He guides me into a separate room that has a bed in it, but there's also a toilet and sink in the corner. This must be where he lives. He sets me down and opens the medicine cabinet above the sink.

While he's busy digging around, the dogs fill the room. I can't count how many because they're always in motion. A gray dog with a splash of white on his head comes over and rests its big, square head in my lap. I notice her ears are cropped short to her head, leaving almost nothing at all. She also has scars all up and down her body.

I look over at the man still rooting in the cabinet. Like most of these bikers, he's tall and muscled. But he's the only blond. From the hair on his head, to his closely trimmed beard. Not the white blond I am, but more of a golden blond. He's handsome, gentle, and has a peace about him I didn't get from the others. I can't believe he's the one responsible for this dog's injuries. Despite being in a motorcycle gang, he doesn't seem to have a mean bone in him. There's no way he could hurt these animals.

He pulls out a red box and then kneels is front of me. He smiles at the dog snuggled into me.

"Bella." He nods to the dog, whose eyes are closed now.

"She's sweet. What happened to her?" Bella licks at my wound and Roch brushes her away. She reminds me of my Sophie. Always wanting to take care of me. God, I miss her. I'll bet she would have so much fun in a yard full of other dogs to play with.

"Fighters. 'Cept Karen."

"Karen?"

He pulls open the hood of his sweatshirt, opening the pouch where a tiny chihuahua is sleeping. I reach over to pet the dog, but he jerks the hood out of reach.

"No."

"Okay." I pull my hand back. Obviously, he's more protective of her than the others.

He pulls out a pocketknife and flips the blade up. He reaches for my leg and I block him, which is stupid because he could just as easily stab my arm, but it's enough that he looks up and sees my shocked expression.

"W-what are you doing with that?" I ask.

"Knee's fucked."

I consider him, studying his navy-blue eyes. They're intense and hard, but there's not a hint of malice, so I move my arm.

He cuts a slit into my leggings, right above my bloody knee. Then he rips the fabric off and drags it down my leg. I watch as he carefully picks rocks out with fine-tipped tweezers. When he's satisfied, he dabs it with alcohol. The sting has me hissing. He puckers his lips and blows on it, soothing the hurt. It's so sweet, I want to cry again.

Instead, I clear my throat. "So, you rescued all these dogs?"

He nods.

"And you live out here with them?"

Another nod.

Not much of a conversationalist, but I don't care. I like him. He applies antibacterial cream and a bandage, then flips each hand over to inspect my scratched-up palms.

"No bandage," he says.

"I don't think so either. Thank you, Roch."

"S'okay. Go," he mumbles, and I realize a full sentence is not in his list of abilities.

"Go where?"

He points outside.

"I really don't want to go back in there. Can I just hang out here with you and the dogs?" I ask hopefully.

I like it out here. It's peaceful despite the constant clicking of the dogs' nails on the tile floors and a few who are wrestling and nipping at each other.

"No." One word is all he says, but it crushes my hopes of this being a place I can hide.

"Oh. Okay." I stand up on rubber legs, still sore from both my falls.

I hobble out the door, but I turn to steal one more look at Roch. He's on the bed now, surrounding by tail-wagging dogs. He gives each one scratches and kisses on their noses.

It's sweet, but something about it is almost sad. Like this is his happy place. Not in the clubhouse, not with his brothers, but out here with his rescued dogs.

I cut through the yard, avoiding the many piles of poo. I see a back door, and even though I don't know where it leads, I walk through it.

I step into an industrial-sized kitchen. Long, stainless steel countertops with an eight-burner stove and a double oven line one wall. Two wide refrigerators sit side by side with a deep freezer next to them. This kitchen could prepare enough meals for a restaurant.

Or a house full of bikers.

It's then I notice the woman peeling potatoes over a garbage can. She's pretty in an overly done way. Her blond hair is in a high ponytail, secured by a neon pink scrunchie. Her eyes are lined black and her eyeshadow is sparkly gray. Her lashes are fake, and her lips are painted a neon pink, matching her hair accessory. She's in a crop top and although the garbage can is blocking her bottom half, if I were to guess, she probably has a miniskirt on.

She's studying me with a frown, probably wondering why I only have one pant leg and I'm limping.

"Hi." I wave and smile.

She rolls her eyes and goes back to the potatoes.

Wow. Okay.

"I'm Bridgette." I try again.

She huffs and looks up again. "Do you need something? 'Cause I'm busy here."

"No. I just…" I trail off and walk through the swinging doors to my right.

I end up behind the bar with a man I haven't met yet. He's

younger than the rest, clean-shaven with gelled back brown hair. He puts more effort into his appearance than anyone else I've met. His vest has a prospect patch plastered on the back.

"Oh, hey." He reaches around me, pulling a bottle of liquor from the shelf. "Can I get you something?"

"No. I'm okay."

I look out into the sizeable room. The TV isn't showing sex anymore, and there are a lot more people here than there were before. Mostly men, but quite a few women wearing not much more than lingerie. I blush thinking about walking around a room full of men wearing an outfit like what they have on.

The one person absent is Loki. Which is good, I guess, but I still wonder where he is.

"Hey, darlin'," Goblin says from where he's sitting at the bar with Sly. They both have a bottle of beer and a shot glass in front of them. "Come sit a minute."

I walk around, trying my best not to show how much my knee and bum are aching. I attempt to hoist myself onto the stool in between them, but it hurts too badly. Goblin hops down and lifts me up like I weigh nothing. These men have a habit of just picking me up and placing me where they want me.

"Thank you."

"I see Roch got you fixed up." Goblin reaches over the bar, grabbing a bottle and a second shot glass. He pours the liquor and sets it in front of me.

"I'm eighteen." I push it away.

"So? You afraid the cops'll come bust ya? Newsflash. They don't come around here." He pushes it back.

"I've never had alcohol. I don't think it's a smart choice."

Daddy has a glass of wine at night, and I've had a sip or two of champagne. The bubbles stung my nose, and I sneezed for five solid minutes. But I keep that to myself. I don't think it counts.

"Come on. You can't live in a clubhouse and not drink. It's practically a rule." Sly holds his shot up in a toast.

I eye mine for a moment, praying it's not an awful idea, and then clink it against his and take a sip. I cough and sputter as the liquor burns its way down my esophagus.

"Jakey? Can we get some water?" Goblin asks while banging on my back. "Here you go, darlin'."

I gulp the water down, disappointed there wasn't a wedge of lemon in it to help remove the taste of the vile alcohol from my mouth.

"I'm fine," I gasp.

"You aren't meant to sip it. You're supposed to just shoot it down the hatch. Gives your body less time to react," Sly says.

"Sorry."

Goblin laughs. A full-on belly roar that's contagious. It must be, because soon I'm laughing along with him. I don't know why, but I am.

"Don't apologize." He shakes his head. "Damn it, you're cute."

"I think I'll go now. I need to find bedding for the cot."

"Sissy," Sly calls out.

A blond woman saunters over. She's wearing a lace dress that's completely see-through. Her breasts must be silicone because they're perfectly round. I avert my eyes, uncomfortable with seeing so much of her.

"You need somethin', baby?" She wraps an arm around Sly affectionately. He lowers his face to between her boobs. I hear him inhale as I look anywhere besides at them.

"Jesus. These tits. Worth every fucking penny the club spent on 'em." He hums into her skin. "Take Bridgette here to find some sheets and a blanket, will ya?"

"Sure." She turns to me. "Come on, honey. I'll show you where they're at."

She takes my hand and walks me down the hallway Loki said all the bedrooms were located.

"Thank you," I say.

"No worries. Us girls have to stick together around here." She winks and opens up a closet where neatly folding linens are.

"I'm not… I mean, I'm just here—" I stumble over my words, trying not to be rude by telling her I'm not a club whore.

"Why are you here?" She hands me a set of black sheets, a gray comforter, and a pillow.

"I don't want to be. I tried to leave, but then this happened." I motion to my leg. I want her to feel bad for me and help me to get out of here. I'd sooner sleep on the streets than in this place.

"Yeah, well. If I were you, I'd just do what they say. It's not in your best interest to make enemies of them."

She seems nice enough; so I try to enlist her help.

"Do you think you could help me?" I ask.

And just the way Loki's eyes darkened earlier, her green eyes deepen in color and her lips purse tight while she stares me down.

"Fuck no. Are you crazy? Go on and get out of here." She points back down the hallway and then mumbles to herself, "Bitch thinks I'm gonna go against the club. Ha! I don't have a death wish."

I limp back to the basement door. I take another look around. Everyone seems so happy. Loudly telling animated stories to each other. Throwing darts at a board. Drinking and laughing.

And here I am. All alone.

Back downstairs, I make up the bed and curl into the fetal position on my side. I spot my purse next to the cot. I reach in and find my wallet, my lipstick, and my toothbrush, but I don't find my cell phone or my mini bottle of pepper spray. I upturn the bag, dumping it on the ground. I know I put my phone in here, and I never leave the house without my mace.

Yet, they're missing. I scramble off the bed and over to my backpack. I dig through it, emptying its contents. No cell phone.

What the heck?

Chapter
EIGHT

Loki

"Fuck. Just like that," I moan.

I grip the back of her head and push my cock deeper down her throat. I release her and she licks up and down my shaft, rolling my balls in her palms. She latches onto my head and sucks so hard, she pulls the beginning of an orgasm from me.

I open my eyes and see Tabitha's black hair. Not my blond captive, like what I was picturing in my mind. Suddenly, this blowjob doesn't feel quite so good.

I grip the base of my cock and shove it down her throat. I'm angry now. Both because it's not Bridgette on her knees and because I'm picturing the prude bitch in the first place. After she tried to run today and then ran her mouth off, I had to walk away. The next week and a half will feel more like an eternity.

A banging on my door has Tabs popping off me. The door flies open, and Bridgette comes storming in. One pant leg is cut above her knee and she has a bloody bandage covering her injury from earlier.

"I want my cell phone ba—"

Her words die on her lips as she takes in the scene. Tabitha on her knees, tits hanging out, and a fist wrapped around my hard cock. I smack her hand away and tuck myself painfully back into my pants. This'll be uncomfortable for a while.

"After you knock on a door, you're supposed to fuckin' wait until someone tells you to come in. Otherwise, what's the point of knocking?" I spew.

"I'm just going to go." Tabitha stands up, pulls her dress up, and shuffles past Bridgette.

"Obviously, if I'd known what you were doing, I would've."

"Never come barging into my room again."

"Trust me, I won't. Now give me back my cell phone." She holds her hand out, palm up.

"No."

She blinks rapidly, like it's not the answer she thought she'd get. Probably not an answer she ever gets.

"Yes," she says. "It's mine."

"It'll be hard to give it to you since it's crushed into a thousand pieces out in the parking lot and the SIM card is flushed down the toilet. But you're welcome to go try and put it back together and go fishing for the card." I push past her and out the door. I'm tired of this bitch.

"Why would you do that?" she yells after me.

"Because I don't know if someone was tracking it. If you're trying to hide from the bad guys, you can't go around with a phone that anyone has had access to." I turn the corner and take a stool at the bar. I give Jake a chin lift and he brings me a beer. "Thanks, man."

I have the bottle to my lips when someone smacks the back of my head, sending beer spraying down the front of my shirt. I turn my head to see Bridgette, arms folded across her chest.

"I need a phone. Since you broke mine, get me a new one," she demands.

The music turns off, and the room goes quiet around us. Only a few muffled whispers come from the game room. There's not a person here who'd dare speak to me like this, let alone lay a hand on me. And Bridgette is about to find out why.

I hop off the stool and stalk toward her. With every step I take, she takes one backward. I don't stop until she's pressed against the wall behind her.

"I don't know who *you* think you are. *You* don't demand things of me. *You* don't shove me. *You* are a guest here. Or that's what I thought our agreement was. But as it turns out, you don't know how to act right. Get your ass downstairs and go the fuck to bed. You'll need the sleep because tomorrow I'll be teaching you some manners."

I'm so fucking pissed she disrespected me in my fucking house, but if I punished her right now, I'd likely kill her. I'm proud of myself for having enough wits to know I can't be near her in this moment.

"I *hate* you."

"Feeling's mutual, princess. Now go."

She slides sideways until she's beyond my reach. Then she throws open the basement door with so much force, it cracks against the wall and the doorknob puts a hole in the sheetrock. I fist my hands at my sides and go after her. Fuck waiting until I've calmed down. She's gone too fucking far.

Khan steps in front of me, resting a hand on my shoulder.

"Not right now, bro. Not when you're this pissed," he mumbles so no one else can hear him.

It would normally be a sign of disrespect for him to stop me from doing anything I want to do, but in this case, he's right. We don't need to explain to her dad why she won't be coming back.

I seethe, trying to calm down. Roch is leaning against the doorway to the stairs, arms folded and eyes down. If I didn't know any better, I'd think he was guarding her. But that can't be right. I'm his President. He wouldn't dare go against me.

"Yeah, okay." I walk over to the door and shut it. Not that it would stop me from getting to her, but the more closed doors between us, the better.

The music starts back up and my brothers gather around me. Cheering me on to take shot after shot. This is why I joined the club. Not because Trucker wanted me to take over his legacy. Not because I love the lifestyle, even though that's a strong contender. No, it's this. Blood makes you related, but loyalty makes you family.

By three in the morning, we're all stumbling to bed. I fall face first into my mattress and let the alcohol lull me to sleep and pull me into tormenting dreams about Ma.

I see her at one of the club barbecues, setting out a vat of potato salad she made and watching proudly as the family she and Trucker created laugh and enjoy a relaxing Sunday. Then the dream turns into a nightmare as the night they shot Ma floods my mind. Images of her body jerking as bullet after bullet hits her and then the way Trucker collapsed when he found out have me begging to wake up.

But I don't. I just relive it over and over. Each time with

more detail. It's no wonder my own father hates me. I didn't protect her. I should've seen it coming.

I'm such a fucking failure.

I bolt upright to a banging on my door. I'm drenched in sweat, despite not having a stitch of clothing on or any covers, and the A/C pumping chilly air through my vent.

"Just a sec," I yell. I get up and pull on a pair of sweatpants.

I open the door to Khan, head hanging and looking worse for wear.

"What time is it?" I ask, dragging a hand through my damp hair.

"It's a little after six. Jake was making rounds this morning and the basement door was open. She's gone, man. Don't know when or where she went, but she bolted." He winces in preparation of my wrath.

"FUCK!" I roar. "She couldn't have gotten far. We have to find her."

"Jake is out looking. He feels like shit, man."

"He should. He was on night watch and he let a little girl sneak past him." I tug on a T-shirt and my cut. "Let's ride."

My VP and best friend follows me outside and to our bikes.

"We checked the footage. She was small enough to climb between the spot where the gate meets the fence. Looked like she went left toward the highway," he says.

"I swear to Christ, I'm gonna kill her if she isn't already dead." I straddle my bike, not bothering with a helmet.

We ride a couple miles down the highway and then pull

off to the side. We live in the fucking desert. She can't hide behind trees, but she can walk between the hills that line the roadway.

We hike our way through the sagebrush and behind a hill. A rattlesnake pops out, its jaw unhinged, showing threatening looking fangs.

"Don't fuck with me," I mutter and walk right past. It scurries off because even a deadly snake knows better than to cross my path, yet I can't keep a five-foot nothing brat in check.

I look up and down the shallow river that flows between hills. I don't see her, but I do see fresh footprints in the soft sand. Small, girly footprints.

"This way." I point to the right and we pick up our pace.

"What're you gonna do with her when we find her?" Khan asks carefully.

I think as my boots cut through tumbleweeds and rocky sand. An idea crosses my mind, a damn good idea. I pull out my phone and shoot a text to Roch. He won't like it, but he'll do it. He seems to have a soft spot for the girl. That better change real quick.

"You'll see," I say.

Ten more minutes of walking, and we finally see her. She's resting on a boulder, hunched over and heaving. She doesn't notice as we close in on her. Khan and I glance at each other. He stretches his arms out, preparing for the inevitable fight.

"Look who we ran into," I call out.

Her head jerks to the side and her eyes go wide as saucers. She stands up and quickly scans the area, probably trying to figure out how she'll get away.

"Don't run, darlin'. Didn't work out so well the first time. I'm sure you remember," Khan says.

The bitch doesn't listen, of course not.

"I haven't even had coffee yet," I grumble before breaking out into a sprint.

Khan catches her before I get there. His long-ass legs can go twice as fast as I can. He throws her over his shoulder. She kicks, screams, and flails about like a two-year-old who didn't get a cookie after dinner. I roll my eyes. Khan grips her by the hip and his other arm goes around her calves to prevent her from kicking him in the nuts. She pounds on his back, but I doubt he feels it.

"You're more trouble than you're worth, bitch," I say. "Should've asked your daddy for a lot more money."

"Put me down right now!"

I shrug my shoulders at Khan. He turns toward the river and with a push to her hips, he throws her into it. It's not even waist deep, but it's enough to immerse her entirely when she lands on her ass. She jumps up, sputtering and gasping. The water's snow runoff and icy cold year-round.

"You'll pay for this!" She brushes her hair from her bright red face.

"You done throwin' a tantrum?" Khan asks, holding out a hand to help her back up onto the bank.

She ignores it, falling back into the river before she manages to make it out. Her thin tank top does nothing to hide her naturally perky tits and puckered up nipples. I've never wanted to fuck someone I hate this badly. I wonder if all that piss and vinegar would come out in the bedroom.

"I'm not going anywhere with you. I don't care if I get killed. It would be better than being around you," she replies to Khan, but her brown eyes are on me.

"Not an option. We only get the twenty Gs if you stay

alive. Now be a good little girl and let's walk back to where we parked our bikes." I point back the way she came.

Her arms fold over her chest and she pops her hip out. Her lips flatten into a line and she scrunches her forehead. I'm sure she thinks this will stop us, that we'll consider her feelings and give in. It's probably what's happened her whole life. But she just looks like an angry otter. No matter how much they show their teeth, they still look cute as fuck.

I walk over and grip her by the messy bun on top of her head. I yank, hard, and pull her by her hair toward the bikes. She howls in protest, but I don't let up. She trips and stumbles over rocks, trying to keep up with our fast pace. At one point she falls, but I tug her up by her hair and keep going.

I thought for sure the tears would flow freely by now, but she doesn't cry. She smacks at my arm and hurls insults, but her eyes stay dry. Stubborn bitch. That's something I can respect. The outbursts and threats piss me off but being strong-willed and determined are two things I admire.

When we get back up to the highway, I pull her so we're face-to-face.

"Listen up. If I let you go, you'll lose your attitude and walk to my bike. I'm not above dragging you, but it'll save me from having to kick some dude with a hero complex's ass who will no doubt pull over to save you."

Her eyes light up and I know she likes this idea.

"I don't lose fights. That innocent guy will end up at the hospital with a broken nose and a crushed windpipe. You sure you want to be responsible for that?"

She sighs. I let her hair go and she rolls her head, stretching and rubbing at her neck.

Like a little duckling, she follows me to where we left the

bikes. She doesn't wait for me to tell her where she'll be riding, she just goes right to Khan's Harley. He lifts her up and over his custom chopper before climbing on himself. Already knowing the drill, she wraps her arms around his middle. Or at least as far as they'll go, which is only to his sides. Then she rests her cheek against his back.

It irritates me she snuggles into him so quickly. Maybe she thinks she'll fuck him and he'll feel bad for her. Fat fucking chance. She's not fucking any of the brothers and when we get back, I'll be making that crystal fucking clear.

She thinks she's so clever. Just wait until she sees her new accommodations.

Chapter NINE

Bridgette

I've almost fallen asleep by the time we pull into the clubhouse. I snuck out around four in the morning after spending half the night pacing around the basement. Too scared of all the creepy crawlies to fall asleep. I was losing my mind and had to get out of there.

I tried to stay hidden, thinking if I could just make it to the city, I could find someone to let me use their phone. I didn't think they'd find me so quickly.

Khan parks and helps me off the bike. I don't even care if I'm eaten alive by the spiders anymore. I need sleep and to lick my wounds. Both physically and emotionally. It's time to rethink my plan of leaving and come up with a new one that includes just surviving this nightmare.

I walk through the door and veer to the left to go downstairs when Loki's deep voice stops me.

"Where you goin', darlin'?"

"Downstairs."

"You're not staying down there anymore. You've lost your right to privacy. You're in my room now." He points down the hallway.

"But I—"

"'But you' nothing. Come on."

He grips my upper arm and yanks me roughly to his room. It's infuriating how every man in this place thinks he can put his hands on me. It's demeaning and rude.

He opens the door and suddenly, being manhandled isn't as insulting as it was five seconds ago. My stomach drops at what I see. A tall kennel sits in the corner of his spacious room, like what you put your dog in, but maybe two welded together to be taller.

"What's that for?" I whisper, but I already know. He's putting me in there.

"Welcome to your new home." He holds his arms wide, an irritating smile on his face.

"You can't expect me to stay in there." I wrap my arms around myself protectively. This situation just went from bad to worse.

"Expectations have nothing to do with it. I know you will." He unlatches the door and holds it open.

"I won't. I'm not a dog. You can't do this!" I sound whiny even to my own ears, but he can't be serious. "When Daddy finds out about this, he'll kill you himself."

"Your daddy doesn't exist in your world anymore, little birdie. I'm your daddy now and this is your home." He shoves me inside and latches the door behind him. "I'm going to get a cup of fuckin' coffee. I had to skip mine this morning so I could deal with your annoying ass. Get comfy and if you behave, someone'll bring you some breakfast later."

Then he's gone, slamming the door behind him. The tears I'd been fighting as he pushed and pulled me through the desert earlier can't be fought back now. I didn't want to show him how badly he was hurting me, tormenting me. But he's gone, so I let them flow.

I scan my surroundings. There's a foam pad covered by a blanket and pillow for a bed. My backpack full of clothes is in here, and that's it. A sudden rush of anger fills me, and I yank on the door of my cage. There's a hefty-looking padlock holding it shut, but the bars are thin metal. There has to be a way out. My cheeks heat and my jaw clenches.

I hate Daddy for sending me with them. He knew they were terrible men. He knew they were callous and cruel. He trusted his money to be enough to make them take care of me. He's always relied on his money to be enough.

Even after Mom died, all he did was throw money at the problem. Hiring me therapists and sending me to private schools. Giving me his wallet to go shopping instead of giving me love and attention. He thrust himself into his job, almost obsessed with finding cures to cancer. He's a noble man, but when you're a little girl who just lost her mom, all you want is your only living family member to be with you.

Thoughts and feelings I never identified before flood my mind. I'd gotten used to my life. I'd replaced human affection for physical items. Even my friends are shallow and insincere. But now that everything has been stripped away from me, I'm seeing my life for what it really is. And I hate it.

I wrench the bars apart, trying to stretch them before realizing they're so closely spaced, even if I pulled them as far as they'll go, I still won't be able to get out. I yell out in frustration, the exhaustion from earlier turning into anxiety and claustrophobia.

I can't get out. I can't escape.

My breaths come faster and my heart pounds. My vision narrows and my head feels light. I fall back onto the foam pad that does little to cushion the bars that run along the bottom of the cage. I curl into a ball, gently rocking myself.

I won't come back from this. I feel myself changing into someone unfamiliar. Good or bad, I can't be sure. But either way, the old me leaves with my tears, no hope of ever coming back. I've been so stupid. So oblivious to the realities hiding in dark alleys and riding motorcycles like they own the world.

If it's the last thing I do, I'll make them pay. I'll burn this club to the ground if I have to. I'll steal that vial and infect every person within these walls. They won't even see me coming. Why would they? I'm just a dumb girl they can treat however they want and do with as they like.

That's not me anymore.

When I wake up, I have no idea what time it is. Sunlight is still streaming through the window, but it's low in the sky, making me think it's evening.

I blink my eyes to clear my vision, noticing a tray of food just inside my cage. A crudely made sandwich and a bottle of water. My tummy rumbles, though, so I pull the tray to me and devour the processed turkey and cheese between two slices of cheap, white bread. There isn't a vegetable to be seen, but I'm so hungry, I don't even care.

I open the bottle of water and drink it until only drops remain. I realize I've had nothing to eat or drink since I left my house yesterday. No wonder I was so famished.

It's then I remember I also haven't used a bathroom and drinking all of that water has reminded my bladder it needs to be emptied. I stand up and look around to see if there's something I might've missed. I was right when I thought it was two crates stacked together and welded. I see the joints, but whoever did this knew what they were doing. It's solid and unyielding.

"I have to pee!" I shout at the top of my lungs.

Muffled music rattles the walls, so I doubt anyone can hear, but I try shouting again and again until my voice goes hoarse. The urgency to relieve myself grows. I jangle the cage and try yelling one more time.

"Jesus fuck. I hear ya. Hold the fuck on." Loki opens the door, looking fresh as a daisy. He's changed out of the sweatpants and T-shirt he had on earlier, into a worn pair of jeans and a clean black tee that stretches over his chest and arms. His tattoos are on full display and he has the same black beanie on I've never seen him without. Short black curls peek out around the cap and I wonder how long it is.

No, I don't. I don't care what his hair looks like. He's a disgusting human being who has me caged like I'm not a living, breathing human being.

"I have to use the bathroom," I say, although I'm embarrassed to admit it.

"That sounds like a problem. There are two solutions I can come up with and I want you to think long and hard about which option you want." He sits on the edge of his bed, studying me. "You can either act like the lady you were raised to be, and I can let you use my bathroom, or you can act like a rabid dog and I can bring you a bucket. Choice is yours."

Despite the irritation I feel toward him, he's degraded me enough today. I need a proper toilet.

"Can I use your bathroom, please?"

"You'll behave?" One eyebrow lifts in question.

"Yes. May I shower too?" I know I'm pushing it, but I'm itchy from my bath in the river earlier.

He blows a breath out and rubs at the back of his neck. Then a sly smile breaks across his lips. The bigger it gets, the more scared I am.

"Sure, Birdie. Grab your stuff. I'll let you shower."

I scrutinize him, wondering what he has up his sleeve. But whatever it is, it has to be better than going the rest of the day without getting clean. I pull out another pair of leggings and a tank. Every shirt I own is cropped because that's the current trend, and in my former life, I kept up with whatever was in style. Not anymore. When I get home, I'm burning every single shirt that bares my midriff. I'll start wearing whatever I want to wear, not what my friends expect me to.

I discreetly tuck a bralette and a pair of panties between my pants and shirt and then stand, ready to leave this prison.

"If you make me chase you again, your cage will get smaller and smaller until there's hardly room for you to stand. Don't test me." He puts a key in the lock, and it pops open.

He yanks on the roughly made door until it swings out. I don't move. I know if I appear too eager, it'll feed his sadistic need to control me. He motions for me to walk out and I take slight steps until I'm free. It's the same air as what's in there, yet it seems thinner, cleaner, freeing.

I walk around the cage and into the bathroom. I push the door closed, but before it latches, he stops it with his foot and forces his way in. I stare at him, wondering what his game is now.

"You haven't earned the privilege of being in here alone."

He rests his butt on the sink, his hands clasped in front of himself.

"But I have to use the bathroom."

"I heard you the first time. Go right ahead, I'm not stopping you."

"Please, Loki. Don't do this." My fits have gotten me nowhere, so I resort to begging.

"My little birdie finally realizes who's in charge now. Adorable, but no. If you need to take a piss, go right ahead." He reaches over and lifts the lid.

My head falls forward, but the urgency in my bladder is almost painful. A urinary tract infection is not what I need right now, so I set my clothes down and drag down my pants and panties. I sit sideways on the toilet, gaining as much privacy as I can. My ears burn in shame and I try hard to urinate, but it won't come out.

"I don't have all day. In case you forgot, I have a vial to steal."

"I can't, okay? It's too humiliating."

He must flip on the faucet, because the sound of running water fills the room. I void my bladder and wonderful relief flows out of me. I quickly wipe and flush. I pull my pants back up, only to realize he won't be leaving me alone to shower either.

I've never been naked for a man. I've kissed a few boys while I was in high school, but I didn't feel comfortable enough with anyone to share my body. The boys at my school were just as fake as the girls, and while Ruby and Lindsay didn't seem to mind, I wanted my first time to be special.

I turn the water on in the walk-in, glass-enclosed shower and let it warm. I steal a glance at Loki, but he has his phone out and his thumbs are moving fast and furious, typing out a message.

I quickly undress, keeping an arm over my breasts and a

hand covering my privates, I back into the shower, staying as modest as I can. Deciding if he has to see anything, I'd rather it be my butt, I keep my back to him.

The warm water feels amazing after how difficult the last twenty-four hours have been. I wet my hair and scan the products he has in here. An all-in-one shampoo and conditioner mix that I know will tangle and ruin my hair, a bar of soap, and two small travel sized bottles of shampoo and conditioner. The same stuff I use back home. I peek over my shoulder to see Loki still focused on his phone.

Is it a coincidence? Maybe one of the women he's been with have left it in here. That's the only reasonable excuse. I take care of my hair first, then I wash my body with the bar soap. I wish there were a razor for me to shave my legs, but I'm not about to ask him for any favors.

Once I'm clean, I turn the water off. I look at the rack, but there is nothing hanging there. I open the steamed-up shower door to find Loki standing right there, holding two gray towels. He scans me from top to bottom, before his eyes land on my breasts. I quickly cover myself back up. He thrusts the towels at me and goes back to his perch on the sink, but not before his lips part and his eyes go half-lidded.

I wrap a towel around my hair and then dry my body off. I hang the towel over the glass wall of the shower and dress behind the cover it provides.

"You about finished? I've got shit to do," he gripes.

"I'm done. Thank you." I offer politeness he doesn't deserve. "Do you happen to have a brush?"

"Tabitha brought a bag of girly shit." He hands me a bag with a popular beauty store logo on it.

So the shampoo and conditioner were for me. Interesting.

I open the bag and find a brush, a comb, a hair tie, and a book. My nose stings at the kindness, which is stupid because I'm being caged like an animal. But when you've been stripped raw, the smallest comforts are special.

"Thank you." I pick my dirty laundry up and walk out of the bathroom.

"Give me your clothes. I'll have one of the girls wash them."

"I can do it. If you'll let me, I can be helpful," I offer.

"Yeah, right. I'll bet you don't even know how to do your own laundry and I don't know if you remember, but there isn't a washer and dryer in your new home." He rips the dirty clothes from my hands.

Without being asked, I take the bag and step back into the cage. He locks it up and tucks the key into his pants pocket.

"Can I use your cell phone to call my dad, please?" Surely, he'd send for me if he knew how I was being treated.

"I spoke with him earlier. I let him know you're doing well and will see him when this is over."

"I promise I won't tell him anything. I just want to hear his voice." *Lies.*

He ignores me. "Someone will be by with dinner soon."

Then he's gone and I'm alone again.

I sit on the foam pad and take my time brushing my hair. I braid the long strands over my shoulder since I don't have a hair dryer or a flat iron to keep them tame. Then I pull out the book Tabitha gave me. It's a trashy romance with a Fabio looking man and a woman in Victorian-era clothes on the cover. I've never read a book like this, but I'll do anything to keep my mind busy and away from the dark thoughts of my reality.

Chapter TEN

Loki

"So, where are we at?" I ask my brothers.

I've called Church so we can all get on the same page. Our plan is a living, breathing thing, changing and developing with every hour.

"I hacked into the cell phone provider of the cell phone number you gave me. It's not Dom's, but his brother, Anthony's. He has been texting Dom, though. Only superficial shit, nothing that's helpful," Sly reports.

"Have we heard which building Dom lives in?" Goblin asks.

"Yeah, it's the big one, like we thought. It's good because there are more points of entry, but bad because it's a big fuckin' house to search," I say, studying the aerial images.

The main house is in the center of smaller houses, most likely belonging to the many family members and their goons. It makes it even more challenging to get in, but not impossible.

"I did a little scouting, snuck on to check out their

security system. They have cameras that track movement throughout. But their security system is mostly brawn, with guards walking the grounds constantly. There're also motion detectors in the main house." Sly points to various points on the map.

"You snuck on?" Khan asks, surprised.

"Don't call me Sly for nothing."

Sly is our newest member. He did some freelance work for us on a job we had. He's a hacker, wanted by the FBI on all kinds of charges for breaking into different government agencies. But they only know an online username he was using at the time, not his actual identity. He likes to live on the edge, always seeking an adrenaline high. It makes him valuable and also risky to have in our club.

On one hand, he'll do whatever the fuck we ask, no matter the danger. On the other, he always pushes things just a little too far. Waiting for the last minute to jump, staying inside a system until they've almost tracked his location, whether or not he needs to.

"So, can you disable their security?" I ask.

"Yeah, that won't be a problem. What'll be a problem are all these meat heads they have circling around. We'll have to drop 'em. It's the only way I see us getting past." He sits back in his chair.

"I don't see that as a problem. I've got a new silencer just waiting to be used," Khan says.

"We'd have to get them all at nearly the exact same moment. Otherwise one will radio over and if there's no response, everyone will go on high alert and game over," I say.

"And there's this security station here." Sly points. "This is where all their cameras link to and where the guard is who checks in with all the others. It's locked and behind bulletproof glass. We can't get to this guy."

"Make 'em come out," Roch chimes in for the first time.

"How?" I ask.

"Karen."

I raise my brows. We've used his dogs before. They're vicious protectors and will rip anyone to pieces who dares come onto our property or threaten us. But never Karen. That bitch is his baby and he keeps her tucked away safe at all times.

"How can Karen help? They'd be able to squash her like a bug, no matter how snippy she gets," Sly says.

Roch pulls Karen out of his hood. "Draw 'em out."

"Maybe send someone in after her?" Goblin asks. He deciphers Roch-speak better than any of us.

"If we did that before we started firing, it could work. There'll probably be some guys inside we'll have to deal with. But we'll just send Khan in first." I smack my best friend's chest.

"Who are we sending to search for their missing dog? If any of us do it, we'll be made immediately," Goblin says.

"Girl." Roch jerks his head toward my room.

"No." I shake my head. "We're supposed to protect her, not send her into danger. Plus, they might already know what she looks like. They did their research."

"Whores," Roch says in explanation.

"That might actually work." Goblin scratches at his chin. "Tabitha and Sissy can make her over. A little sex appeal might even distract them. She can say her dog went through the fence and then work around to asking if they can locate her with their cameras."

Roch nods, his plan forming with just a few words out of him.

"No," I deadpan. I refuse to put her life in jeopardy.

"Think about it, Prez. A pretty, youthful girl who lost her tiny dog. They'd never suspect she'd be playing them. If she can get that door to the security booth open, we're golden. Take him and the others out, we'd have plenty of time to go through Dom's shit. Find the vial and get out." Sly bounces in his seat, either because the plan is coming together or because he's been sitting too long. He can never just be still.

"It's an excellent plan," Goblin says, and the others nod.

"Fine, but one of us will be assigned to her and be ready to pull her out if shit goes bad. I doubt Davis will care about the vial if it means his little girl ends up dead." I pin each of them with a meaningful stare.

"So, when do we do this?" Goblin asks.

"I think we should spend a couple days doing surveillance. Look for patterns in shift changes, when and where they guard. Get familiar with their operations. Hopefully Dom has some kind of schedule so we can know when it's safe to break in. If not, we'll figure that out later." Sly shrugs.

"That's smart. Let's do it. I want you all on a rotating schedule for surveillance. Sly, I want you to scope out a few different vantage points we can access. Let's plan for this to happen in three days," I say.

"Sounds good. Now let's drink." Khan gets up and moves to the door.

"Girl," Roch says, stopping everyone's departure.

"What about her?" I narrow my eyes on him. I knew the fucker was after her.

"Caged."

Most of the time I can deal with his cryptic communication, but I don't have the patience for it right now and especially not with her.

"And she'll stay caged. I'm tired of spending my time chasing after her." I step toward my brother, who's still seated, giving me the upper hand.

"Keep her safe." He pounds a fist to his chest.

"Like fuck you can. She'll stay where she's at. It's not up for discussion."

His nostrils flare and his breaths come out in puffs, like he's one of his dogs. The guy's been living out there with his canines for too long.

"You got a problem with that?"

"No, Prez," he bites out.

"Didn't think so." I turn my back on him and walk out.

I don't give a fuck what he wants. She's mine to keep safe, she's mine to torture, she's mine to do whatever the hell I want with. At least until I hand her back to her daddy.

I head straight to the bar while lighting a cig. I need to calm the fuck down before I attack a brother or take my frustrations out on my little pet.

Tomorrow the partying stops. Surveillance will start, all possible scenarios considered, and a plan made for each, then putting it all together and going through it over and over until it's burned into our skulls.

But as for tonight, we're going all out.

Khan stands in front of his smoker trailer, rotating huge slabs of meat. The smell is mouthwatering. A few of the club whores and the wives are spreading side items onto a picnic table, along with utensils and condiments. Kids run around the yard, the old-timers play horseshoes, and everyone's in a good mood. Everyone except Roch, who's in his shack sulking like a little bitch.

It's weird he cares for the girl. I've never seen him have any emotion for anything besides his dogs. When I texted him to weld two of his dog crates for Bridgette, he didn't even reply. I half expected my room to be empty when we got back, but like an obedient boy, he did what I asked.

I don't know a lot about Roch's life before he came to the club. Trucker brought him in after being dishonorably discharged from the army. For as timid as he comes across when you first meet him, he changes when we go out on a job. His instincts sharpen, and like his canine counterparts, he can smell danger. He knows when something is off and turns brutal if anything goes south. He completely checks out mentally and might be the most sadistic of us all.

I push away the urge to barge into his place and ask him what he wants with the girl. Instead, I gather a plate of food to take to my pet. If I didn't think she'd try to escape in the chaos of the barbecue, I'd let her come out and hang. But I don't trust her for nothing.

I open the door to my room to find her curled up on her side, reading some shit book Tabitha snuck into the bag of toiletries I had her put together. She sits up when she sees me. Despite her politeness and obedience during her shower, I saw the indignation she was trying to hide. Just like now, the corners of her lips turn up in what I think is supposed to be a smile, but it's a sneer. She can't hide her true emotions from me.

"I thought you might need to piss, and I brought you supper." I set the plate on my dresser and dig the key out of my pocket.

"I do." She stands up and moves closer to the door.

I unlock it and lead her to my bathroom. I pull my phone out of my pocket and pretend to be interested in whatever's on the screen, but I'm not. I wasn't earlier when she stripped down and showered either. I watched her from my periphery like a creeper. She has the smoothest, creamiest skin. Not a single blemish mars her perfection. One brief glance of her tits had my cock wanting to salute them. They're the perfect handful with bite-sized nipples. She kept her back to me while she washed, and my eyes didn't leave her heart-shaped ass the entire time. I wanted to strip down and spend an hour exploring every inch of her.

"Do you have to stand there while I pee?"

I shake the indecent images from my mind and look up from my screen. She's sitting on the toilet, pants around her ankles, and bent forward to hide her naked thighs.

"This is what happens when you're naughty. Need the faucet on?" I ask.

She rolls her eyes. "Yes."

I flip on the faucet and go back to my phone. I hear the tinkle of her peeing and then a rustle as she puts herself together again. I look up and our eyes lock. She steps slowly toward me, almost seductively.

What game is she playing?

She holds my gaze, her innocent brown eyes peering up at me. Her long, dark eyelashes flutter and she bites her bottom lip and drags her teeth over it until it pops free. It's fucking sexy as hell. I'm seconds from reaching out and pulling her against me, when she sidesteps me and throws a shoulder into my chest to push me out of the way. I flip around and study her in the mirror as she turns on the water to the sink and washes her hands.

Such a fucking tease.

After she's dried off, I grab her by the upper arm and take her back to her cage. I hand her the plate of food and lock her back up. She plops down on the pad and glares daggers into me, shoving a heaping fork of food in her mouth.

"What the fuck is your problem?" I ask.

"What's my problem? I went from living in a mansion with a pool and a workout room to living like this. I can't wait for this to be all over so I can leave this place and never see your face again." She grabs the ends of a rib and tears her teeth through the meat. Even that's sexy.

"It didn't have to be this way, Birdie. You could be outside, enjoying the cookout. You did this to yourself."

"Are you so weak, so pathetic that you get off on locking up a naive girl? God, you must have the tiniest dick," she snarks.

"I'm sure you remember from yesterday that's not the case at all. Do you want me to remind you? Maybe I'll give you a taste. You'd like that, wouldn't you?" I pretend to unbuckle my belt.

"Keep your disease infested penis away from me." She sets her food down. "I can't even eat. Just the thought of getting anywhere near that thing turns my stomach."

"Keep telling yourself that. Have a miserable night." I step out and slam the door behind me, rattling the walls.

How can someone so fucking beautiful on the outside be such a fucking bitch on the inside?

It's then I get a genius idea. Apparently, she hasn't hit rock bottom yet. But that's okay, because by the end of the night, I'll break her. I'll fix her attitude and put her in her place.

I snag a beer before stepping back outside. I eye the talent hanging around tonight. Tabitha and Sissy are always around, but I need someone new for what I have in mind. I spot a blonde sitting by the fire pit with a couple other chicks. *She'll do.* I walk up and throw my arm around her shoulders. When she looks up, it's blue eyes I see, not brown. I push the disappointment down.

"Hey, darlin'. You wanna go have a drink with me?" I ask.

She giggles and has an entire conversation with her friends with just her eyes. Then she nods up at me and I wrap my arm around her waist. We walk inside and to the bar. We have a couple shots, eat some food, and party with my brothers. Layla is a veterinary assistant. This is her first time at the clubhouse, but her dad is a Harley enthusiast, so she's used to being around bikers.

I don't care what this bitch says, she's not used to our brand of bikers. This is proven when Khan, Sly, and Moto drag out some shopping carts they found who the fuck knows where. They start small fires on the lower rack and climb in. Some of the hang-arounds poise themselves to push the carts, and Tabitha yells, "Go!"

Then they're off. Racing each other as their asses toast to a crisp. Layla covers her eyes and digs her face into my neck while everyone else cheers and places bets. I hold her close, letting my hands roam her body.

By the end of the first lap, my brothers are forcing the shopping carts onto their sides just so they can get out. I laugh my ass off as they scoot across the lawn trying to put out the burning embers on their asses.

The families leave soon after, and that's when the party really picks up. The club whores lose their clothes and it's a sex free-for-all. The girl at my side watches like she can't believe what's going on. She's innocent like my birdie. Even her friends lose their tops and get in on the action. I bring her to the bar to sit and watch.

I'm certain she's going to bolt until I notice her rubbing her thighs together and her fingertips trailing along her cleavage. I crash my lips to hers, devouring her like she's my next meal. She doesn't fight it and I know she's down to fuck.

"You wanna go back to my room?" I breathe out.

"Sure."

I grab her hand and pull her down the hall. I throw my door open, Layla straddling me and my hands cupping her ass. She doesn't pull away from me long enough to even breathe. I lay her down on my bed and climb on top of her. I pull her shirt up and over her head. Her fat tits spring free. Her nipples are big and round, not like the tiny little bites of Birdie's, but these are hot, too.

I suck one into my mouth and she cries out. She unbuttons her cut-off shorts and pushes them down her legs. It's hurried and rushed, but I've been hard since I took my captive and I'm desperate for a release. I also know I don't have much time before we're inter—

Birdie clears her throat, and Layla bolts upright, throwing her forehead into my nose.

"Fuck," I shout as blood trickles from my nostrils.

Chapter
ELEVEN

Bridgette

I wake up to heavy breathing and moaning. I rub at my eyes, trying to make sense of what's happening. That's when I see Loki has a half-naked girl pinned under him. A pang of hurt strikes me and I hate myself for it. This man has been nothing but cruel and mean yet seeing him with another girl bothers me in a way I couldn't predict.

I use the ache to fuel my anger. How dare he lock me up and then force me to witness him having sex with some slut? It's disgusting and a whole new level of degradation I can't allow.

I clear my throat. The girl cracks her forehead against Loki's nose, and he curses.

Good. That'll teach him.

"Who's she?" the blond bimbo asks.

"No one." He tugs his shirt off, wipes at his nose, and tosses it across the room. He pushes her back down, like I'm not even here.

"I'm the girl he's locked up in a cage. If I were you, I'd run. He might lock you up, too." I stand up and grab the bars, shaking them, making as much noise as I can.

"Loki?" Her voice pitches high.

"Her daddy asked us to babysit. She couldn't listen to basic instructions, so she's being put in a time-out. Pretend she isn't here, darlin.'"

He separates her thighs and latches onto her neck. She doesn't push him away. I can't even believe this. Is this what I've been missing while living in my ivory tower? If so, I want to go back. Things weren't perfect, but they were better than this fresh hell. I push down the sadness and replace it with resentment.

"Did the genital warts clear up, Loki?" I ask in a mock curious tone.

The girl sits up again, this time avoiding injuring him.

"She's lying. My genitals are clean. Why don't you pull my pants down and check?"

I hear his buckle clank, and then the teeth of his zipper going down. Is this chick seriously going to ignore a warning like that?

"I can't do this. I'm sorry." She slides out from under him, grabs her clothes, and darts out of the room without dressing first.

Loki drops his forehead to the pillow and breathes out a frustrated breath. Obviously, he saw this going very differently.

"Oh, darn. Your little friend left." I lie back down on the foam pad, pleased with myself.

Loki says nothing, but he reaches into his pocket and stalks over to me. Shadows fall over half his face, but the moonlight that's streaming in through the window illuminates the other side. It's what I see there that has me thinking I've pushed too far. His face scrunches in anger and he pants like a wild animal. The muscles on his arms and chest ripple with the movement of unlocking the cage. He throws the lock against the opposite wall with such force, I'd bet it's embedded in the sheetrock. Though I can't see to know for sure.

"Get the fuck over here," he grinds out.

"No. Thank you. I'm fine right here." I stretch out, taunting him against my instincts to back down.

"I don't give a fuck what you want. Get off your ass and get out. You don't want me to come in and get you."

"Aw, poor big, dangerous biker couldn't get it in with an easy lay. That must be embarrassing." The words fly out of my mouth with no thought or concern for my well-being.

"All right. The hard way." He has to duck to enter. The cage is plenty tall for me, but not for this enormous man.

He bends down, grips my arms, and yanks me to standing. He walks me backward out of my prison walls. His penetrative gaze almost hurts, it's so intense.

"Put your hands against the wall." He points to the far wall.

"Why?"

"Birdie, you don't want to fuck with me right now. Hands. Against. The. Wall." He punctuates each word.

I turn around slowly and do as he asks. I crane my neck around to see what he's doing. He yanks his belt from the loops and folds it in half. A crazed, sadistic smile crosses his beautiful lips.

He brushes my hair over my shoulder and leans in. "No matter how I punish you, take away your freedom and your dignity. It doesn't matter. You just push and push. You act like a child and children get spanked."

He crouches, pulling my pants and panties down as he goes. My ears burn with the humiliation of having him so close to such a private place. A place no man has seen. He's slow to make his way back up my body, pausing at my butt. He bites into it, hard. I yelp and my arms leave the wall to cover myself. He stands up and forces my hands back to the wall.

"Don't move. If you do, I'll give you more lashes than you've already signed up for," he whispers into my ear.

"Lashes? You're going to spank me? You really are a special kind of jerk."

"Yeah, Birdie. I'm going to beat your ass raw." He wraps an arm around my hips and tugs, propping my butt out.

"You think I care? I don't. Do whatever you want to me. The only thing this proves is you're a freaking maniac who feels threatened by a little girl," I taunt.

I'm sick of the way he's treating me. Nothing has worked with him. I've been rude, evasive, polite, I've tried it all. He's the same bastard, regardless. If he thinks demeaning me this way will make me obey him, he's got another think coming.

I hear leather cut through the air, and then the force of it as it strikes my backside. At first, I don't feel anything but pressure. But seconds later, a scorching hot sting spreads along my skin. I whimper. The pain is one thing, but it's the indignity that has a knot forming in my throat and tears stinging my eyes.

"Count," he demands.

I can't. If I open my mouth, the only thing that will come out is a cry and I don't want to give him that satisfaction.

"That's fine. We'll just repeat one over and over and over again. You know what I do for a living, right? I kill people.

Beating you bloody is nothing." He rubs the smarting skin, his fingers delving between my cheeks and against the lips of my vagina.

I look up at the ceiling, begging for my body not to respond. How could it? This is embarrassing. Maddening. Infuriating. The least sexy thing to ever happen. An invasion of the most sacred part of me. And yet, I feel the tingles of arousal.

He pulls away and I hear the whistle of the leather before it lands on my sit spot. It hurts worse than the first, but I know he's holding back. If he weren't, it would cut my skin open.

"You ready to count for me?" His strong body presses into me, and I can feel the hard length of him through his jeans. This is turning him on. It should disgust me, but my sex throbs. I should not be turned on by this. Maybe I have more daddy issues than I thought.

"One," I whisper, giving in.

"I can't quite hear you." He bites down on my earlobe.

"One," I say louder.

"Good girl. Six more and then this'll be over."

I nod rapidly. Not understanding why I'm suddenly compliant. He palms my sore flesh, dipping his fingers deeper. Pressing through my pussy lips until he meets the spot I already know is wet. I expect him to say something, to make me feel even worse because my traitorous body is reacting to him, but he just hums his pleasure.

In rapid fire succession, the belt jumps from cheek to cheek, never hitting the same place twice. He seems to have forgotten he wanted me to count. He was only after my compliance, and I'm grateful because I have no words. My skin heats in more ways than one, and my breathing picks up. I take each swat, only yelping when he reaches six. He tosses his belt and scoops me up. Tears I didn't even know were falling dampen my cheeks. I'm a mess of warring emotions. Confusion, fear, sadness, excitement, arousal. It's too much.

So, I cry.

He lays me down and tucks me into his chest. I want to be mad; I want to kick and scream, but it's felt like forever since I've had affection of any kind and it feels good to be held. Daddy tried his best to replace Mom, but he couldn't while also building his company. Attention, hugs, time, it all fell by the wayside.

This has been the longest day and a half of my life. I can go back to hating him later. For now, I just want his comfort. He strokes my back and whispers shhs into my ear.

"Such a good girl. I'm proud of you," he compliments, and it confuses me even more.

He was so angry with me. Why is he proud now? Why do I take his pride and allow it to seep into my heart? I don't understand any of this.

He presses a kiss into my temple, and the tenderness brings on a whole fresh wave of tears. I'm lying half naked with a cruel man who just whipped me, and I can't imagine anywhere else I want to be more.

I do something I've wanted to do since I met this man. I remove his beanie. And he doesn't stop me. I marvel at seeing him like this for the first time. His black hair is flattened from the hat, but the ends flip up in every direction, telling me he has a slight curl. He looks more human like this. Less like scary criminal.

"Close your eyes, my little bird," he murmurs.

I do. And I sleep better than I have since before this nightmare began.

Chapter
TWELVE

Loki

I wake up with Birdie still snuggled into me. Our legs entwined, her bare pussy straddling my thigh, her grapefruit shampoo invading my nostrils.

Last night did not go as planned. I thought Layla would go along with it. Girls will usually do whatever fucked-up thing I want. Screwing me with a girl watching seemed like child's play. But she bolted, and I was so fucking pissed. I anticipated spanking the shit out of Birdie and then shoving her back in her cage. But when I exposed her perfect ass, instead of backing down, she egged me on. She didn't whither under the weight of my belt; she was brave. Even more, when I pressed into her heat with my fingertips, she was wet. She got off on it. I was surprised and strangely pleased. I have no idea how such an innocent girl can have such a steely spine.

By all accounts, she should've retreated into herself by now. She should've rocked herself to sleep, staring off into space. I'd bet money on the worst thing to happen to her before me was a broken nail. She makes me curious. Makes me want to get to know her more. And that's dangerous. Way too fucking dangerous.

This is why I untangle myself and get out of bed instead of allowing myself to enjoy this quiet moment with a bitch I respect. I pull on a T-shirt and walk out to the bar. The club whores have a breakfast buffet set up with bacon, sausage, scrambled eggs, and pancakes.

I make a plate and take it back to the room with a cup of coffee. Something tells me she's a dieter, so naturally I drenched her pancakes in butter and syrup. Her coffee has a bunch of sugar and heavy cream, too. I tell myself it's to piss her off, but deep down I know it's because I think she's too skinny. She could stand to put on some weight while she's with me.

She's not in bed when I open my bedroom door and the bathroom door that was open when I left, is now closed. I'm assuming she's taking advantage of the privacy. I'll give it to her this time, but no more. I like not having boundaries between us. I'm sure she doesn't appreciate it like I do, but I don't give a fuck. She can have all the alone time she wants when she goes home.

I set her food in the cage. Something else I'm sure she won't like, but today shit gets real and I can't be worried about what she's doing.

"Hi." She steps out from the bathroom with wet hair and fresh clothes on.

"I don't remember saying you could shower," I say.

"I don't remember asking." Her eyebrows furrow. My birdie was expecting me to be a changed man.

"I've got shit to do. Your breakfast is in there." I point inside the cage.

"Don't make me go back in there. I won't run, I promise."

"Thing is, I don't trust you and I'm too busy to babysit. Don't fight me, you won't win."

"But I thought—"

"You thought what? That last night changed something? It didn't. Come on, you're wasting my time."

She studies me for a minute. I can see her mind spinning. She nods and does as I ask. I lock up after her, avoiding her eyes. One night of me softening changes nothing. Twenty-four hours ago, she was walking along the highway to escape. Neither of us can change in such a short amount of time.

I take a quick shower and then leave my room without a second glance or a goodbye.

"Gob, need you to watch over the girl." I take a seat on the sofa next to him.

"I can keep an eye on her out here if you don't want to leave her in there," he offers, setting the newspaper he'd been reading down.

"She stays," I growl. "She's too sneaky and the last thing we need is to be chasing her down while we're going against the Corsettis. Let her out to pee and bring her lunch. That's it."

"All right, Prez." He opens the newspaper back up and goes back to reading.

I get up and walk outside. Khan is already straddled on his bike. We're on the first surveillance shift for the day. Sly rented the house to the north of the Corsetti property that sits higher up so we should have a good vantage with a set of binoculars.

"Let's ride," Khan says, pulling his dome on.

Twenty minutes later, we pull into the driveway of the

rental. I use the key Sly gave me to unlock the house. We find Moto and Sly in the master bedroom upstairs. They had the overnight shift and they both look droopy-eyed and exhausted. Coffee cups and empty snack wrappers litter the ground.

"How'd it go?" I ask.

"As expected, considering we were still half-drunk from last night." Sly tilts the laptop screen to me. "We've logged shift change, the times they make rounds, and who goes where. These are the pictures of who was around last night. I tapped into the local copper computer system and ran facial recognition on them all. If you take pictures today, just load them on the laptop and I'll run the software on them later."

"Cool. Will do." Khan folds himself into the camp chair Moto and Sly had been using. I watch wide-eyed as the aluminum bends but doesn't break, surprisingly. The motherfucker's too big for cheap chairs.

"Dom pulled in around one in the morning. His car is the blacked-out Maybach, so you know what to look for." Sly hands me a pair of high-powered binoculars.

"Okay. We're good here. You guys go get some sleep." I take a seat in the other chair, fitting a lot more comfortably than Khan.

Moto and Sly take off, and then it's a whole lot of boring as fuck watching. The guards seem to operate on a half-hour rotation, each one moving to the next section of the property in a circle until they end up where they began, and that's when there's a shift change.

I'm surprised they don't vary things. Keeping a strict schedule leaves you too vulnerable to attacks like the one we'll be doing the day after tomorrow.

"How was your night last night?" Khan asks.

"Not that great. Turns out having a chick in a cage is a turn-off." I laugh at myself.

"You're such an asshole." Khan slaps me on the back. "Speaking of the girl, how's she handling her seclusion?"

"As good as can be expected." I don't say more because it's none of his goddamn business.

"Not gonna lie, brother, the whole locking a girl up is kind of hot. I wish I would've had the idea first."

"No shit. Might leave it in there for the future."

Khan's right. Having a girl at your mercy is a turn-on. If I wasn't keeping her in there for her own safety, it would be an even bigger turn-on. I'm a kinky bastard, always have been.

I ride hard.

I play hard.

I fuck hard.

Growing up with bikers as your role models, there really was no other way for me to end up.

"We have movement," I say, spotting two men in suits walking out to the Maybach.

"That's definitely Dom. The other guy must be his driver." Khan pulls out the camera and takes a couple pictures.

"You think our plan will work?" I ask.

"It either will or it won't. Seems easier to swallow when you know there are only two options."

"True, and honestly, I just want this over with. I'd rather go back to popping cocksuckers and making the easy money. This thing with the daughter and having to plan this entire takedown? It's nothing I ever want to take on again." I set the binoculars down and rub at my eyes.

"Agreed, brother. Although, I don't think you mind the

girl. It would've been easy to send her packing and tell Davis she's too much, but you fought hard to keep her," he says while pretending to be absorbed in watching the property when we both know there ain't shit going on right now.

"It's twenty grand. I didn't want to walk away from that," I shoot back.

"What's twenty Gs when we're getting a much bigger payday overall?"

"It's got nothing to do with her. I'll be glad to get rid of her. She's a fuckin' headache."

"Bullshit," he says through a fake cough.

I glare at my brother. Whatever he's thinking is wrong. I don't care about the bitch. Sure, she's sexy as fuck, but she's been nothing but trouble. I like my women easy in every way. Easy to get in their pants and easy to get rid of 'em. Birdie is nothing but difficult. As soon as this is over, I'll send her packing and never think of her again.

Liar.

Goblin and Roch relieved us after eight hours of watching. Dom's guards' routines are like clockwork. They're making this too easy. We leave the same instructions for them that Moto and Sly left and then head back to the clubhouse.

We walk in to the scent of Mexican food. Tabitha and Sissy are setting out dinner. It's a small spread since everyone's been told not to come around for a while to limit distractions.

"Smells good, ladies," I say, eyeing the dinner.

"Thanks, baby. We know how much you like tacos." Sissy winks at me.

"That I do, darlin'. I'll be back in a minute."

I walk down the hall to my room, wanting to check in with Birdie. I'm relieved when she's right where I left her. Her nose in a book, looking pathetic on a thin foam pad.

"You hungry?" I ask, removing my cut.

"I shouldn't be since I was locked up all day doing nothing." She closes the book and sits up.

"I'll bring you some dinner." I open the door to leave, but then decide maybe since she's been good, she deserves a little treat. "You wanna come out of there and have dinner with us?"

"No, thank you."

"Why?" I narrow my eyes on her.

"Everyone out there knows you've been keeping me locked up. It's embarrassing. Plus, I've seen what you guys do out there and it doesn't interest me. I'd rather stay right here and have dinner alone."

"Suit yourself." I leave her to sulk, but as I'm plating up food, I can't help a little niggle of guilt. It's easy to keep her locked up when she's being a brat and annoying the fuck out of me. It's harder when she's resigned.

I take both our plates to my room, still undecided if I'll sit and eat in there with her. I should just drop it off. Leave her be. Yet here I am.

I set the plates on my dresser and unlock the cage.

"Come on out. We can eat together."

"Why?" She eyes me speculatively.

"Why not? Fuck, woman. You don't want to go out there, so I thought I'd be nice and let you stretch your legs, but if you're gonna be a bitch about it, I'll throw your food on the ground and let you eat it like a dog."

"You'd like that, wouldn't you? Make me feel even worse about myself than I already do."

"Just stand up and come sit down. Why does everything have to be a fight? Jesus Christ."

She stands up, nose in the air like the rich cunt she is. Her hair is a messy pile on her head and I still haven't seen her in anything but workout clothes, but she's still the most beautiful woman I've ever laid eyes on. She'll have to rely on her looks to make it through life since her personality is lacking.

She sits gingerly on the bed next to me, and I wonder if it's because of the belt I took to her last night. I hand her a plate of food, watching as she studies it, poking at the rice and beans with her fork.

"What's wrong now? Never had Mexican food?"

"I have. It just hasn't ever looked this… beige."

"It's fuckin' tacos. The only colors are brown for the meat and yellow for the cheese and shell. Anything else is for decoration."

"Our chef, he makes tostadas with lettuce, tomato, guacamole, green onions, you know, vegetables. Things you need to stay healthy." She scoops up some beans and brings them to her mouth like she's about to ingest poison.

"I'm proof you don't need that shit to survive. I've had nothing green in years." I take a big bite of my taco, devouring half of it all at once. The taco sauce drips down my chin. I wipe it with a finger and lick it off.

"You eat like a pig." She takes a dainty bite of her own taco.

"Well, you eat like a damn bird."

"It's called manners. You could use a lesson."

"Not useful in my life." I crunch into another taco.

"At least chew with your mouth closed."

"Birdie, I ain't never eaten a taco with a closed mouth." I waggle my brows at her.

"Gross."

"You wouldn't think it was gross if it was your taco I was devouring. You'd be screaming my name like, 'Oh, Loki. Lick my sour cream. Munch my meat.'" I laugh because that was a damn good analogy.

"And there goes my appetite." She sets her plate down next to her.

"Mine's just getting started."

I watch as her eyes widen, and she scoots farther away. I reach for her and the second she tries to block me, I dart to her side where her plate sits and dig into her food.

"Oh, you thought I was going to"—I wave a fork around her center—"don't worry. Your V-card is safe. I don't fuck virgins."

"How do you know I'm a virgin?" she asks, offense clear in her tone.

"It's written all over you. From your legs that are always locked up tight, to the way you cock blocked me last night. You couldn't stand being a voyeur for your first sexual experience."

"That's not why I stopped you last night. You're a caveman, so you don't understand just how rude that was. You were visually raping me. Is that what you are? A rapist?"

"Visually raping? You really are a dumb bitch."

"Don't call me a bitch." She stands up, putting her hands on her hips.

"It don't mean nothing. It's just another word for female."

"No, it's not. It's derogatory and you've done enough to make me feel like crap to last a lifetime."

"Maybe it is where you're from, but it's not here. There's a lot of things you don't understand about my world. That don't make you right and me wrong." I stack our plates and set them on the nightstand.

"Yes, it does. It also makes you an asshole." She trails off at the end like she's still uncomfortable saying the word.

"You haven't seen just how big of an asshole I can be."

"I'm pretty sure I have. I have the bruises to prove it."

I guess she was sitting awkwardly because of last night. I wish I could say it taught her a lesson, but clearly it didn't. Her mouth is still too smart for her own good.

"You better watch your tone, or I'll do it again."

Her mouth closes and her eyes cast down.

"That's what I thought. Now it's time for my little birdie to go back in her cage. I've got some business to tend to."

"Fine." She walks in and sinks to the pad. So small, so dejected, so gorgeous.

I lock her up and pick up the trash from our dinner.

"You want the light on or off?"

"Doesn't matter. You're just going to do whatever you want to, anyway."

"I'm giving you a choice. Now stop being a cunt and tell me."

She scowls at me. "On. I'd like to keep reading."

"I'll be back later."

"Try not to have a slut with you this time."

"Jealous?"

She ignores me and opens her book. I shut the door behind me and feel almost disappointed to be leaving her. She tries my patience and infuriates me more than anyone else, but in a world where all the bitches around me do nothing but agree, it's a little refreshing.

Chapter
THIRTEEN

Bridgette

I read through the love scene in this romance book for the eighth time. I finally feel like I understand why everyone makes such a big deal out of sex. If this is what it's like, I don't know how anyone gets anything done besides lovemaking. It sounds so romantic, two bodies becoming one. My cheeks heat and I feel the same tingle in my core I felt last night with Loki.

I'm in the middle of reading about the Duke ravishing the peasant girl for the ninth time when Loki walks back in. If he weren't so attractive, it would make this whole thing so much easier. His chiseled jaw line covered by just enough scruff to be manly, his worn clothes that on anyone else would look unkempt, but on him they just add to his bad boy appeal. And of course, the beanie.

But last night, seeing him without a shirt, all muscled and tattooed. It was too much. He has these V-shaped muscles with a script tattoo along the curve traveling below his waistband. Despite how angry and scared I was, I'm not blind and I'm still a woman.

He says nothing, just strips down to his underwear and walks into the bathroom. I hear the shower turn on and then five minutes later he walks in with just a towel tied around his waist. He ignores me while I pretend to be engrossed in my book.

He opens his drawers and pulls out a pair of boxers. The towel drops to reveal his muscled behind. It's whiter than the rest of him, and that somehow makes it more forbidden. He pulls up his underwear and then turns to me.

"Mind if I turn out the light?"

"No, it's fine." I dog ear the page I'm on like I don't already have page one hundred and fifty-three burned into my memory.

Darkness shrouds the room, and I hear him climb into bed. It's silent for a long while, but both of our thoughts are so loud, it would be a miracle if either of us can sleep. I pull the thin blanket up to my chin and try to get comfortable, but it's impossible on such a small, thin pad. I toss and turn until deciding to flop onto my back.

"Can you stop moving, please?" he asks, irritation in his voice.

"Oh, I'm sorry. It's probably easy for you to settle into a king-sized memory foam mattress, but I'm over here on a dog bed. It's a little difficult to fall asleep when you can feel metal bars digging into your hip."

"If you want in my bed, you just have to ask. I'll warn you, though, the only chicks who sleep in my bed are the ones who ride my dick."

"What about last night? There was no riding. Actually, if

I remember correctly, you cuddled me all night." I don't know why I'm poking the bear. It never works out for me, and I can't take his belt again. I'm still sore.

What the heck.

Why am I having these thoughts, like it's the only reason I shouldn't want his belt? I don't want it because I'm not a naughty child being taught a lesson. I'm a grown woman who deserves respect and to be treated with kindness.

"That was a one-time deal. I'm not in the habit of making chicks comfortable enough to sleep over."

"God forbid you have a relationship with a woman and want them to stay over if there's not a chance of getting laid."

"I don't do relationships. I don't do sleepovers. Why would I want to when there's someone else to take her place the next night?" he argues.

"Because everyone needs love, security, and comfort. One day those good looks you rely on will be gone and you'll be all alone, miserable."

"Darlin', maybe that's what normal men have to look forward to, but not me. I'm the king of this castle and there will never be a shortage of bitches who think spreading their legs will make them the queen."

I'm quiet after that. What argument do I have? If he's happy living a shallow existence, that's none of my business. But for me, I want a Duke. I want someone to sweep me off my feet and fight to be the man in my life. I want someone who will work hard all day just so he can come home at night to be with me, make me feel like the most beautiful and special woman in the world. Not some biker who thinks there's always something better waiting to warm his bed.

I toss and turn some more, my bony hips falling asleep

when I turn on my side, so I flip over only to have the same thing happen on the other side. Maybe if I were exhausted, I'd be able to fall asleep despite the lack of comfort, but I've done nothing all day besides take a few cat naps and read. I'm not tired in the least.

Loki huffs in irritation and I hear him get out of bed. There's a rustling from next to the cage before I hear the jingle of keys and the lock being popped open. The door opens and I make out his shadowed form next to me. He scoops me up in his arms.

"What—" I start.

"I'm only doing this because I'll never sleep with all the ruckus you're making." He turns sideways to fit us both through the door and then lays me down on his bed.

I scoot all the way over so I'm next to the wall and roll away from him. His woodsy scent fills my nostrils and I sink into the mattress. Maybe I am tired, because being surrounded by all things Loki has me feeling comforted. Not that I'd ever admit that aloud.

Within minutes, I hear his breaths even out and become rhythmic. He's asleep and soon after I'm dozing off too. I pretend this is my life. That Loki is my man and he made me the queen he said no one would ever be. I fall asleep with a smile on my face. If only this were a different life.

"No! No! Not Ma. Not her."

I startle awake to Loki flailing in the bed next to me. He's crying out like he's in pain. I sit up and rest a hand on his shoulder.

"Loki. You're dreaming." I shake him gently.

"Huh? What?" He slowly gains consciousness, but confusion clouds his features. He looks younger like this. Vulnerable and scared.

"You were having a dream, or a nightmare," I explain.

He reaches for his pack of cigarettes from his nightstand. He lies back and lights up. He inhales deeply, but blows out slowly, casually. The smoke fills the space above him like a cloud of doom. I've never had a cigarette. I've never even been around someone who smokes. But watching him, how he visibly calms with each puff, I wish I were a smoker. I could use a little sedation.

"Do you want to talk about it?" I ask.

"No. Go back to sleep," he grumbles.

"Are you sure? It sounded—"

"I said no, Birdie."

"Okay." I lie back down, but the air feels off. He's upset and for whatever reason, it bothers me.

He turns away from me, stamping his cigarette out in an ashtray, and I scoot closer. When he doesn't object, I move nearer until I'm close enough to lay a hand on his arm. He still doesn't fight me about it, so I wrap my arm around his middle and snuggle into him. He's warm and smells even better from this close. I rest my cheek on his back, listening to his lungs expand and contract.

I don't know why I'm fighting to be closer to him. Logically, it makes no sense. But emotionally, it makes all the sense in the world. I'm not lonely tucked up next to him. He's the wrong guy at the right time.

He rolls onto his back and snakes an arm under my head, drawing me near. He combs through my hair lazily and my fingers dance soothingly up and down his torso. It feels right, being this close, no matter how wrong it is.

"My mom," he says, and then stops to think for a second. I don't rush him. I want to know everything he'll divulge. I crave insight on what makes this man tick. "She died. Right out there at the bar. The Corsettis broke in one night because they had beef with Trucker."

"Who's Trucker?" I ask gingerly.

"My dad. Anyway, they stormed in and shot the place up. They killed my mom in the gunfight. The crazy thing is, she never stayed overnight here. She and Trucker have a place. But they'd been drinking. And it's one of the rules we have around here. Don't drink and drive. So, they stayed, and she paid for that mistake with her life."

"That must make this entire thing with my dad even more difficult since it involves the Corsettis."

"Yes, and no. I feel like I'm getting the payback I didn't get back then. But yeah, it brings back memories. That's probably why I was having the dream."

"I'm sorry that happened to you. In a way, I know how you feel. That night, when Dom broke into our house, I thought my dad was dead. I heard the shot. I saw my bodyguard already dead. For over an hour, I assumed Daddy was too. When I finally got the courage to go see for myself, he was passed out in a pool of blood." I suck in a shaky breath. "I really thought he was gone. But my situation was a nightmare, and yours was a reality. I'm sorry you had to go through that."

"I expect to lose people, being in this life. I just never expected to lose her. She was innocent. It's why I never want to have an old lady. For as hard as it was to lose my mom, it was only a fraction of what it did to Trucker. I never want to be him. Have my world ripped apart and lose my mind like that. I'm only the president because he basically got voted out. He started a war with the Corsettis. We lost so many men and he didn't want to stop. He was fine sacrificing us all like lambs to the wolf as long as he got closer to his retribution. I wanted that, too. I wanted Dom to pay, but not at the cost of all my brothers. They're my family, too. You know?" He leans his head down and rubs his scruff over the top of my head. The affection makes me want to cry. Having this big, bad biker being tender and sweet is overwhelming.

"That must've been hard. To lose so many people and then to take over for your dad. I can't imagine he took that well." I wrap my arm around his middle, no longer tentative with my touches.

He chuckles lightly. "You can say that again. He blames me for not protecting my mom and for taking away his club. He doesn't come around often anymore, even though he's still a patched member. As far as I know, he stays in his house where my mom's memories live and drinks himself closer to death every day."

"My dad just works himself closer to death. My mom is why he started this company. He was successful before as a pharmaceutical rep. But her getting cancer made him turn to research and development. I can't even be upset because of all the good he's doing."

"Maybe if you were older, but you're still a kid. You need your dad still."

"I'm not a kid," I argue.

"Practically."

"How old are you?"

"Thirty-five. Almost twice as old as you. I shouldn't even have you in my bed," he says while tugging me even closer.

"Thirty-five isn't old. And besides, the only reason I'm in your bed is because I was keeping you awake. It's not like you want me in here." I'm fishing for a compliment, or an admission, or... something more. I don't know. I just want to know if he's feeling the same things I am. A connection, maybe.

"Birdie, if I didn't want you in my bed, you wouldn't be."

"Why am I, then?" I keep digging.

He rolls on top of me, forcing my legs apart to make room for his narrow hips. He brushes stray strands of hair off my brow. Our eyes meet and I look for any signs to tell me what's going through his head, but he appears to be just as confused about whatever this is.

"Have you ever been kissed?"

"Yes." Without conscious thought, I lick my lower lip. Loki tracks the motion, transfixed by it. "I'm not as innocent as you think."

"Oh, really? Then you've had a man touch you here?" His finger drags down my throat, lower to my chest, and then even lower across my exposed cleavage.

"Yes," I lie.

He quirks a brow.

"What? I have. I've been close with... men." The words sound awkward even to my ears.

"What about here?" His fingers graze one tank top covered nipple and then cross over to the other. They tighten into hard buds with the motion. He watches with lust-filled eyes and I squirm underneath his scrutiny.

"Sure. All the time." *More lies.*

"And this?" He moves to my side and slowly traces a path down my abdomen. He circles around my exposed belly button and then dips lower. He taps my clit through my yoga pants, and I gasp. My body is hypersensitive, alight with anticipation.

"Just last weekend," I squeak.

"I think you're lying to me. I don't think a boy, let alone a man, has been anywhere near you." He climbs back on top of me and I wrap my legs around him. I want him to stay right here.

"I've been kissed," I admit honestly. "A few times."

"Like this?" He presses his mouth to mine, two rigid lines barely even puckering.

"Everyone's been kissed like that." I frown.

"Well, excuse me." He smiles. "How about this way?"

Then his lips are on mine, soft and pliant. I move with him, following his lead as he sucks and nips at my lips. Too soon, he's pulling away again.

"Never," I breathe out. Too lost in the moment to keep up the charade.

"What if I use my tongue?"

I meet him halfway, holding myself up on my elbows, feeling like I may die if I have to wait to feel what he offered. We kiss, long and deep. He thrusts his tongue forward, demanding entry, but he didn't need to. I was already open for him, begging him to come inside. He tastes like danger and a cigarette, rich and addictive. He strokes and licks, exploring every inch of my mouth. I arch my back, thrusting my breasts against his chest, my nipples seeking friction against his bare skin.

His hand goes to the base of my throat and he holds me

there while we kiss. It feels possessive and claiming and even though it's a lie, I love it. I can pretend for the moment, too.

Even though I don't want to be his, someday I'd like to belong to someone. A man who makes me feel the way Loki does. Someone who turns my insides to mush and touches me like he'll die if he can't have me.

My thighs tighten around him, bringing our pelvises even closer together. That's when I feel how excited he is. A hard rod that nestles perfectly between my sensitive lips. He grinds into my center with short, slow movements. Dampness soaks my panties as my arousal heightens to a place I've never been before.

He kisses down my jaw and turns my head to the side with his thumb, his palm still flattened at my throat. He sucks my earlobe into his mouth and flicks it with the tip of his tongue. A zing of pleasure rips through me, a direct line straight to my center. He bites down and I whimper. His kisses move down my neck and across my collarbone before moving back up to my lips.

We're both panting by the time he pulls away. He rests his forehead against mine and squeezes his eyes shut, like it's painful to stop. I wish I could put a voice to my desire. I wish I could tell him I want him to keep going, but I can't. The fear of rejection has stolen my words.

"It's late, you need your sleep." His navy eyes darken, and his feature harden. The MC President mask going into place once again. He climbs out of bed and throws on some clothes.

"Where are you going?" I ask, confused about his sudden change in mood.

He ignores my question. "Can I trust you to stay in here? Or do I need to lock you up?"

"I-I don't understand."

"It's a question. Yes or no?"

"Yes," I breathe. "I'll stay here."

He gives me one last glance, grabs his cigarettes, and leaves me there. Confused, hurt, and alone.

Chapter
FOURTEEN

Loki

What the fuck was I thinking? I wasn't, that's the problem.

The clubhouse is quiet at this early hour as I make my way behind the bar. Everyone's still asleep, but there's no way I can sleep now. And if I stayed in that room, I would've done something stupid, like fucked her. I don't need some virgin getting starry-eyed because I stuck my dick in her. Like it's something special.

It's not. I lost my virginity at fourteen to a club whore. The old-timers were my age back then and thought it would be hilarious to send a girl into my room. They weren't laughing when I not only fucked the girl, but according to the gossip she spread, I was the first guy to ever give her an orgasm vaginally.

Even if she was lying, it was enough to pump my teenage ego full of pride. From then on, I made it my mission to spread my obviously natural-born skills. I couldn't tell you how many women I've been with. I've lost count. But total all the feelings I had for each bitch I've fucked, and they still wouldn't even come close to what I was feeling kissing Birdie.

I had to get out of there. She's intoxicating. And like my tequila, she clouds my judgement. She makes me want to believe in more. Makes me feel like she might be worth the risk. But I made that decision a long time ago, and I'm not about to go back on it for some inexperienced girl who doesn't even know what life is about yet.

I make a pot of coffee and take my steaming mug to the bar. I light my cig and allow the nicotine to absorb into my lungs and ease the tension flowing through my body. I roll my head on my neck, trying to stretch the tight muscles where all my stress embeds itself.

I have one more day before we carry out our plan. One more day before potentially starting another war. We'll try to get through the retrieval without Dom knowing who did it, but we need to prepare for the worst. If he comes home to all his soldiers dead and that vial missing, he'll want to know who did it and then he'll want revenge.

I have two things I need to do today that I'm dreading. First, I need to talk to Birdie about her role in our plan. If she says she doesn't want to help, we'll find another way. I refuse to force her into this. One weak link and it will risk our mission.

The second is something I should've done right after we agreed to take this job. I need to visit Trucker. If we take on the Corsetti crime family, I need to bring him in. He may be off his rocker, but no one has a bigger vendetta for them than Trucker. He could be an asset.

I sit alone with my thoughts as the sun rises slowly, filling the room with light. Four cups of coffee later, my brothers file in. First Roch. He gives me a chin lift and heads back into the kitchen to prepare his breakfast for his dogs.

Soon after, the bar is full, and Tabitha and Sissy are in the kitchen making breakfast. They live at the clubhouse, cooking, cleaning, and spreading their legs for us. In return, we give them food and protection.

Tabitha came to live with us after we were hired to kill a politician two years ago. After the job was done, we heard whimpering from inside a closet. She was barely eighteen, malnourished, and had been chained in that small room since she was sixteen. We tried to send her back to her family, but she said her dad had sold her. She begged for us to let her stay. We didn't ask her for anything except help to pick up after our messy asses, but eventually she wanted to do more.

Sissy was a whole different story. She was a waitress at a bar we frequent. She started hanging out and I'm sure she thought one of us would take a liking to her and make her an old lady, but it never happened. She gave up after a year or two and asked if she could have a job. We moved her in and Tabitha took her under her wing.

I love those girls. They're one of us, as much as someone can be who isn't patched in. I'm sure someday they'll tire of being at our beck and call and want more for their lives, but for now, we have a mutually beneficial relationship.

"You about ready to take over surveillance duty?" Khan sits himself next to me with a plate piled high with food.

"I've got some other things to do today. I'm sending Roch."

"Sounds good. What do you have planned?" He rolls two pieces of bacon together and shoves them in his wide-ass mouth.

"I've got to call up Davis to check in, then I need to bring the girl in and see if she's down to create a diversion. After that, I need to go see Trucker. If things go south, he needs to be ready."

"Cool, cool. I'll go grab Roch and head out after I eat."

"Let me know how it goes." I get up to make Birdie some breakfast, when a familiar streak of blond catches my eye.

She steps tentatively into the great room. Her hair is wet, and she has on a pair of short shorts and a tank top that barely covers her round tits and exposes her trim waist. I look around to find my brothers eyeing her curiously. They're no doubt wondering why she's not behind bars, but I know what else they're thinking.

That she's fucking gorgeous.

She tucks a strand of hair behind her ear and finally lifts her eyes. She finds me immediately and makes her way to my side.

"My little bird's being brave." I wrap an arm around her waist, letting every fucker here know she's not to be touched. I don't want to send mixed messages to her, but I also don't want anyone else sniffing around.

"I didn't know if it was okay for me to be out here, but I was hungry and smelled bacon."

"It's fine. Help yourself. I was just going to make you a plate." I motion to the buffet line laid out on the bar.

She nods and moves down the line. First adding fruit to her plate, then one strip of bacon and a piece of dry toast. It irritates me that even being held captive, she's trying to watch her weight. I take her plate from her and add two more slices of bacon and a pancake. I grab her hand and pull her to a table.

"Did you want some of this?" she asks, settling into her chair.

"No. Not hungry," I mutter.

I'm well aware of the surrounding audience. I can hear their minds spinning, the imaginary conclusions they're drawing in their heads. I don't fucking care. Let them speculate. Whatever will have them keeping their distance.

"Why did you pile it up? I can't eat all of this." She pops a grape into her mouth.

"You can and you will. You said you were hungry, so eat." I pick up a piece of bacon and bring it to her lips.

"I did, but I'm not a horse. This is too much." She takes a small bite of the bacon.

"You're too skinny."

"I'm fit, and I'd like to keep it that way. Someday soon I won't be trapped in a biker clubhouse and I don't want to go back to my old life as a fat cow."

"There's a monumental difference between being a cow and being healthy. Men like meat on their women's bones. Give them something to hang onto."

"Is that what you like?" she asks.

"It's what any real man likes."

She rocks from side to side, seeming to consider my statement before picking up her bacon and taking a healthy bite.

Good.

When she's done, I lead her back to my room for a brief chat.

"We're gonna get the vial back tomorrow." I motion for her to sit on my bed.

"Tomorrow? You're ready?" She slides back against the headboard, tucking her legs underneath herself.

"Yeah. Our plan is to storm onto the property while Dom isn't there. We've got everything figured out except how to get into the booth where a guard sits and watches the live feed from the security cameras." I sit down on the edge of the mattress, facing her.

"What are you going to do?"

"We were hoping you'd be willing to help."

"Of course. Anything to help Daddy."

I explain our plan and what her role would be. Without conscious thought, we gravitate closer and closer until she drapes her legs across my lap and my hands are resting on her thighs. She listens and asks questions. The serious look on her face is adorable. Her little nose scrunches and her muddy brown eyes narrow with intensity. She looks like a puppy trying to make it up a flight of stairs. Stoney-faced and severe, but still a cute puppy.

"Let's go over it one more time." I need to make sure she knows every single detail backward and forward.

"Not again," she argues. "We've been over it ten times. I've got it. I can do this, Loki. I promise."

"But what if—"

"No, I won't talk about this anymore. I'm ready."

"Okay." I sigh. Now that I can check one thing off my list, it's time for me to head out to Trucker's, but an idea crosses my mind and I hope I won't regret asking. "Do you wanna take a ride?"

"On your bike?"

"Yeah." I lift her legs and set them down on the bed before standing up and stretching.

"But I thought the only women allowed on your bike are the ones you're"—she quiets her voice—"having sex with."

"You mean fuckin'. And yeah, that's been the rule, but since you'll be an honorary Royal Bastard tomorrow, I'll make an exception." I help her to standing and don't miss the look of disappointment. But that makes little sense. Maybe she got a little caught up last night, but in the light of day, surely she can see why me and her are a terrible idea. "About last night—"

"No, it's cool. Seriously. We don't need to talk about it." She turns her back to me and steps into the cage. "I'm just going to put on jeans."

"Smart. I'll see you outside."

I let my brothers know where I'm headed and then hop on my bike to wait for Birdie. Ten minutes pass and I wonder if I shouldn't have left her alone.

"Swear to Christ if that girl took off," I mutter under my breath. I've just gotten off my bike when I turn around and my jaw hits the ground.

She walks toward me in strategically ripped jeans, a tank top that ends just below her ample tits, and a black leather jacket. Her hair is half up and half down with pieces framing her heart-shaped face and her lips painted a bright red.

Where the fuck did she get those clothes and that makeup? I've only seen her in workout clothes since she got here.

She smiles and takes the helmet I'm holding. She places it on her head and clasps it in place like she's been doing this all her life.

"Tabitha loaned me some clothes and a little makeup." She uses my shoulder to lift herself up and over the seat of my Harley.

I shake my head and get back on the bike. Her arms wrap around me with no prompting and she scoots so close, I feel the swells of her breasts flatten on my back. I try to think of anything else because getting a hard-on right now would not be ideal. I fire up the engine. My favorite sound in the world is my matte-black Harley Davidson Street Glide coming to life. The pop-pop-pop fills the air, and the feel of the vibrations rumbling through my body calms the chaos in my mind. To most, it's uncomfortable to feel the shaking movement and they're happy to get off. For me, what I feel when the world is quiet and I'm not in motion is what's unnatural.

I peel out of the parking lot, kicking up rocks behind us. She squeezes even tighter, holding on for dear life. I rest a hand on her thigh once we get to the freeway to let her know she's doing great. I wasn't lying when I said only girls I fuck are allowed on my bike, and even then, the ride they go on is straight from the bar to the clubhouse. This ride is different, and it makes the dread I feel about going to Trucker's not so daunting.

The roads are empty since it's a Sunday and we're able to cruise right up the mountain to the tiny cabin Trucker shared with Ma. When I was a kid, I loved living in the middle of nowhere. I could explore the woods all damn day and never see the same tree twice. Then when I was thirteen until I got my driver's license, I didn't like it as much. My friends didn't live close by and it was difficult to catch rides. The day I turned sixteen and Trucker gave me my first beat-up Softail, I didn't give a fuck where I lived because I was free.

I exit the freeway and the closer we get, the more I rethink bringing Birdie here. If that old man is drunk and belligerent, I don't want her to get caught up in our bullshit. It helps she already knows our history. She won't be quite so surprised.

I park out front and I slowly get off the bike, my eyes on the front door, looking for motion in the curtains. I help Birdie off and hang the helmet on the handlebars.

"If he gets crazy, just come out here and wait for me, okay?"

She nods and I take her hand as we walk up to the front door. I knock twice and open the door. I hear an old western on the TV, the only thing Trucker ever watches. The day he got a satellite and found the all-western, all-the-time channel was the best thing to happen to him.

We turn into the kitchen and find Trucker making a sandwich. He doesn't bother looking up.

"You hungry?" he asks.

"I brought someone," I say instead of answering, and that's when he takes his attention off the salami.

"That so?" He licks mustard off his thumb while eyeing Birdie. "Who's she?"

"That's why I came to talk to you. We took on a new job and Bridgette is the daughter of our client."

"You shouldn't be mixing business and pleasure."

"I'm not—it's not like that. We're just keeping her safe, as part of the job," I explain. "The Corsettis went after her dad. They stole something and we're going to get it back."

Trucker laughs humorlessly. An awkward, full belly, fake-as-shit laugh that has me on edge. Birdie looks from me to him, her eyes widening. I cross my arms and wait for him to finish. Just as quick as he started this dramatic production, he stops. His wolfish grin going flat in the blink of an eye. It makes him appear crazy. And maybe he is.

"That's fucking funny, Son." He pulls out his kitchen chair and sits down, motioning for us to do the same. I pull out Birdie's chair and my own. "Let me get this straight. When I wanted to go against the Corsettis for killing your mother, you turned your back on me and her memory, but when there's a little green on the table, you're all in? Do I have those facts right?"

"It's not like that, and you know it. I'm not here to rehash old shit. I'm just here to let you know what's going on and to ask if you want to help. If not, no worries. We'll be on our way." I look over at Birdie and jerk my head toward the front door.

We stand, but Trucker slams a hand on the table so hard, his highball glass full of amber liquid sloshes over the sides, creating a puddle. "Sit your ass down."

We both return to our seats fully, like children being scolded. Trucker brings the glass to his lips and chugs. His hands are shaking and his eyes close, like the only thing keeping him sane is the drink. He lowers the empty glass and when his eyes reopen, he's much calmer.

"What's your plan?" he asks in an even voice.

I detail everything out to him. In his defense, he says nothing. He listens and nods his head. By the time I'm done explaining, he's eaten his sandwich and polished off another drink.

"And this girl falls into your plan, how?" He arches a brow in question. The only part I left off was Birdie, knowing he wouldn't want to mix her up in club business.

"She'll help draw out the guard."

"Terrible idea. You don't even know her."

Birdie hasn't said a damn word since we walked through that door, likely shaking in her borrowed boots, but the second Trucker questions her motives, I know what's coming.

"No, *you* don't know me," she says. "Loki knows me. He knows I need this to go well for my daddy and that I'll do whatever it takes to get this vial back. If there's anyone we should worry about, it's you because it's one in the afternoon and you've drunk enough alcohol to put an elephant down."

Trucker's face goes red and I'm certain things'll go from tolerable to bad real fucking quick, but his mouth opens and a laugh comes out, a genuine one this time. He gets up, opens the cabinet, and comes back with a second highball.

"You're a spitfire. You deserve a drink." He pours her two fingers worth and pushes it to her. I'm certain she'll push it away, but fuck if she doesn't shoot the shit down and slam her glass back to the table. "Well, all right then. I'm in. Whatever you need."

We stand up and head toward the front door.

"Four, tomorrow afternoon. Think you can stay sober that long?"

"Son, even drunk, I'll be more prepared than you."

Chapter

FIFTEEN

Bridgette

I relax a bit as we leave Trucker's house. Maybe it's the liquor I drank, or maybe it's Loki's vibe now that his visit with his dad is over. Whatever the reason, my grip isn't as tight and I'm able to look around and enjoy the views.

Loki only drives one exit down from where we were. With a helmet on and the roar of the engine, I have no way of asking why, so I do the only thing I can: go along for the ride.

He slows our speed and turns down a dirt path. I've never been out this way, and I'm surprised when he pulls down a heavily wooded drive. I see a small cabin, not unlike his dad's, and I wonder who else we're visiting.

He parks and throws down the kickstand. I pull off the helmet and allow him to help me off the bike.

"Who lives here?" I ask, taking in the structure. It's not as nice as Trucker's. This one is older. The roof is covered in inches of pine needles, and the front window is busted out.

"Right now, no one." He takes my hand, the same way he did earlier.

I wish I didn't love the way his coarse, large hand feels around mine, but I do. It's so different from the boys I've held hands with. Theirs were soft and hadn't seen a day of labor. I doubt Loki has known anything but hard work. I picture him as a baby holding a hammer, pounding away on a Tonka truck, and smile.

"Then why are we here?" I ask.

"I own this place and I haven't stopped by in a while." He removes a key from under the welcome mat and unlocks the door.

It seems silly to have a broken picture window and still put in the effort to lock the door, but maybe it's more symbolic to him.

"Why do you own it if you don't live here?" I step inside first. The floorboards creak underneath my weight.

"I bought it a few years ago. I planned to fix it up so I had somewhere to go to get away from everything. But then I was voted Prez and I haven't had time. My cut of the money from your dad'll go to fix this place up."

The living room and kitchen are one open space. It doesn't appear to have been updated since it was built way before I was born. The kitchen cupboards that have a door hang awkwardly from one hinge. There's a thick layer of dirt on the mustard tile countertops, and saplings have risen from the ground through the wood floors. He takes me down the hall to a bathroom with a disconnected tub and no toilet. Then farther to a bedroom that also has a shattered window, but it's the view that has me stopping in my tracks. A river flows a few feet away and the lack of a windowpane allows me to hear the rush of water. As far as the eye can see, there're only trees, bushes, and other plant life. It's gorgeous.

"Wow," I say.

"The cabin is a teardown, but the layout will be the same for the new cabin. I want to wake up to this view with the windows open so I can hear the water." He shoves his hands in his pockets, looking shy about admitting his dream.

"I can't imagine anything more perfect than that," I muse.

"It's no vacation home in the Swiss Alps or whatever you fancy folks like, but it's perfect in my eyes." He shrugs.

"I've never been to the Alps." I laugh. "But I have been to Bora Bora, Hawaii, Norway, Paris, and some other pretty amazing places, and I still think this view is just as amazing."

"I can't wait until it's done."

"Thank you for showing me."

"Yeah, well. We were close by, is all." He rocks back on his heels.

He's so stubborn he can't even admit to wanting to share something about himself. I know he and I are nothing to one another but two people thrust together out of necessity. At least I can recognize we have a connection. I doubt he even admits that to himself.

"Even so, I'm glad you brought me."

He shows me a second bedroom and a screened-in porch before we hop back on his bike and head back to the clubhouse. We get there right in time for dinner and since we skipped lunch, I'm starving. Before coming here, I was never really hungry. Maybe it was mental because I knew I couldn't eat much to maintain my weight, so I just never thought about food. But the last few days, my appetite has demanded reentry into my life.

A huge Italian spread has been set out and I fill my plate. Bread, salad, pasta, and to top it off, a glass of wine. Tabitha and Sissy watch on proudly as all the men throw them compliments and come back for seconds and thirds. I had a rough start with both women, but the last two days, they've been kind. Sissy brought me meals and Tabitha brought me a new book on top of loaning me these clothes. I've never worn anything like them, but it was worth the awkwardness when I saw the look on Loki's face when I walked out. I've never felt more attractive than in that moment.

I want to feel bad for the "club whores," as they call them. I'd hate to be called that. It's so debasing. And to know my only purpose is keeping these barbaric men happy seems like such a waste of a life. But I guess I shouldn't judge because they seem content.

"You done?" Loki tosses his napkin on his plate. "I have some stuff to take care of. You good for a while?"

I know what he's trying to ask. Am I going to run? Can I be trusted? I almost laugh at the way he studies me, tries to read me, looking for any sign of trouble. He doesn't have to worry, I'm not going to bolt, but I don't tell him that. I like keeping him guessing.

"Yes." I roll my eyes and stand up. I gather our trash and toss it, planning to go back to Loki's room, but then I spy Roch standing near the hallway. I haven't seen him, except in passing, since he fixed me up.

"Y'okay?" he asks.

"I am. Thank you. How are the dogs?" I reach up and look inside the hood of his sweatshirt to see the sleeping chihuahua. "Hi, Karen."

The flat line of his lips tips up in the corners in a barely there smile. "Dinnertime."

"Need help?" I have nothing else to do today and as time ticks on, bringing us closer to tomorrow, my nerves grow. I might have jumped at the chance to help them get the vial back, but I'm nervous and anxious. I don't want to mess things up. Plus, I've been missing Sophie back home. Maybe spending time with his dogs will comfort me.

He shrugs and motions for me to follow him.

I look over my shoulder to see Loki and Khan deep in conversation. I don't want Roch to get in trouble for my disappearance, so as I pass by Goblin, I ask him to let his prez know where I've gone.

We walk back into the kitchen, and Roch takes out a stack of metal dog dishes. He opens the lid to a huge garbage can full of kibble. He scoops a measured cup full into each dish. I know he won't give me instruction on how to help, so after he scoops, I stack. When he's done, we load our arms up and walk outside.

Dinnertime must be a scheduled thing because there's a pack of sweet faces with wagging tails waiting for us. With a motion of his hand, they all sit. One by one, he points to a dog and places them in their own spot in the yard. They don't dig in; they wait. When all the dogs have their own dinner, he claps his hands once and then it's a chorus of chomping.

"That was impressive," I compliment.

He smiles shyly and I wonder how he's even in a motorcycle gang. He seems so out of place with this group of bad mannered, porn watching killers.

"What about Karen?" I ask, remembering she hasn't eaten.

He waves me to follow, and we go inside the casita. He pulls her out of his hood and sets her on the countertop in the kitchen area. It's the first time I've seen her fully, and she's even smaller than I thought. She must be a teacup variety. It won't be difficult to "lose" her tomorrow.

He takes out a small dish and a tiny can of soft dog food. He empties it into the dish and sets it in front of her.

"No teeth," he says.

When she's done, she lifts on her hind legs. Her front paws swim through the air, asking to be picked back up.

"How does she do with all the big dogs?" I'd think she would've been someone's snack by now.

"Boss." He picks her up and carries her outside.

The other dogs are done eating by now and are running around the backyard, chasing each other and barking at nothing. He sets her down and she prances around the yard. I clutch a hand to my heart as I watch the pitties gently nuzzle her or kiss her.

"This is the cutest thing I've ever seen in my life." I hook an arm through his in a friendly gesture. His blue eyes cloud over and his face hardens as he stares at where we're joined. He doesn't appear all too comfortable with the contact, so I slowly extricate myself. "Sorry."

He steps to the side, putting more distance between us. I guess he has a dark side after all.

"You know the plan for tomorrow?" I ask.

He nods once and scoops up Karen. He scratches her under the chin with one finger. She tilts her head from side to side, tongue hanging out. She really is adorable.

"Honestly, I'm scared. I don't know how much you know about me, but I don't have any experience in this sort of thing."

"Spoiled," he says.

"Rude!" I laugh. "But yes, I am—was spoiled. I can

honestly say he's broken me of that since I got here. I don't think I'll ever be able to go back to my same life."

I don't need to say who "he" is.

Roch grunts in response.

"I want to help my dad and be brave, but I heard that Dom guy in my dad's office the night he stole the virus. He's not messing around. He'll kill all of you if he gets the chance. Including me. I don't want that to happen."

"Bastards're tough." He holds Karen out to me.

I cuddle her to me, and I instantly feel better. Her small, cold, and wet nose rubs against the exposed skin of my chest and it makes me giggle. Roch and I stand in amicable silence. Occasionally, he crouches to tug on a rope with one of his dogs, or he throws a ball. With anyone else I'd feel awkward and try to fill the quiet with mindless chatter, but with him it feels like we're having a conversation with no words. He's easing my frantic mind just by being.

I care about this abrupt, near mute, slightly intimidating man. It makes no sense because we've known each other only days, but I'm sad to know after tomorrow I'll go home and I won't see him again. It's not like they want some girl hanging out and there's no way Loki will want anything to do with me after he gets paid. It brings a question to mind that I didn't know I was holding onto.

"Do you think Loki is capable of liking someone? Not me, but anyone? He says he doesn't date, but do you think he ever will?"

He exhales loudly and turns to face me. "No."

It's one word that holds the weight of everything I knew but forgot in all the moments Loki has been kind to me. In our early morning kisses, in the secrets we've admitted to each other. How could I be so stupid to think I was breaking through his steel plated walls? I let myself get caught up thinking I could be the one he changes the rules for. I'm such a dumb girl. He locked me in a cage and I'm over here with hearts in my eyes. Is it too soon to blame it on Stockholm syndrome?

I'm a paycheck. A means to an end. The money he needs to provide for his clubhouse, to renovate his cabin. He doesn't need me.

I frown. Any time we've spent together has been forced. He just wanted to keep me safe. Keep me out of the trouble I was hell-bent on being. I'm nothing but a bratty kid to him. The kissing, the touching, all of it was because he's a man who's used to having someone to sleep with every night. I put a damper on that and he got carried away.

"I'm going to head to bed." I hand Karen back to Roch. "Thank you for hanging out with me. I'll see you tomorrow."

"Night, Bridgette." It's the first time he said my name, and it comes out muddy, like he's not used to stringing so many syllables together.

I wave and walk through the clubhouse with my head down, not wanting to risk anyone stopping to chat with me even though there's only the members here today. None of the mostly naked women or the slimy guys watching pornography. Thank God.

I close Loki's door behind me and instead of curling up on his bed, I walk into the cage and lie down on the mat.

This is where I belong.

Chapter SIXTEEN

Loki

After I've gone through every detail with Sly for tomorrow, I call it a night. I saw Birdie head to bed a few hours ago. After this morning, I swore to myself I'd keep my space. Then I went and fucked up taking her to Trucker's house and fucked up even more taking her to my property.

Over dinner, I pulled away again. I let her go off with Roch. Every second she was with him, I had to fight the urge not to charge out there and bring her back. The possession I feel over her is ridiculous and I can't let it go on. She's not mine. I can't keep her.

When I walked into my room, I assumed I'd find her in my bed. I didn't expect to see her in the cage. Why the hell is she in there? It makes me wonder if something happened between her and Roch. Did he make a play for her and this is her way of distancing herself from me? Anger roils in my gut and I debate storming outside to give my brother a piece of my mind, but first, I need to get her out of there.

I should've had this thing yanked out today while I was gone. I step inside the cramped space and lift her into my arms.

"Loki?" she asks sleepily. Her long eyelashes butterfly against her cheek, but she keeps them closed.

"It's me. What're you doing in here, Birdie?" I carefully carry her out and over to my bed.

"Birds belong in a cage." She yawns, covering her mouth with the back of her delicate hand.

"You infuriate me." I lay her down and she immediately curls onto her side.

I strip down and get into bed. I'm half tempted to wake her up and demand answers, but she needs her sleep. Tomorrow is a big day for all of us. I need to keep my distance from her. I've already broke so many of my own damn rules, but the pull to her is too strong. It's one night. One more night. I'll let myself hold her one last time. No kissing, no touching, just sleeping.

Lies.

The second she's in my arms, my body relaxes. I have no idea what it is about her, but even that's a lie because I know it's every damn thing. The way she smells, the way she fights back, her innocence and the way her small body fits perfectly next to mine.

She makes me weak. I hate it and fucking relish in it. It's been so long since I've felt anything except anger, hate, and loyalty. I've been stuck in a loop. A loop that keeps me and my club whole, but sometimes I'd like to feel more.

She stirs for a second and her body goes rigid.

"Shh... I've got you." I brush her hair from her neck and place my lips there, tasting her skin.

She turns to face me. Her big brown doe eyes scan my bare chest. She looks so damn sweet and curious.

"What do these marks mean?" She traces the tally marks on my chest.

"I don't think you want to know." I place my hand over hers, halting her movement.

"I do."

"They represent each of the lives I've taken."

"Oh," she says.

"Just 'oh'?"

"I would've thought there'd be more." She shrugs nonchalantly.

Jesus fuck. This girl. Surprising me at every turn.

We hold each other's gaze, sparks flying between us, intensifying with every passing second. She lifts her head from the pillow and inches her way closer, studying me for any signs of rejection. I've been hot and cold with her, because I can't make my fucking mind up about whether she's worth the risk. She must see the hesitation because she pauses. We stay frozen like that, both of us unsure if we're ready for this step.

Fuck it.

I decide for us both and eat the remaining distance between us. I kiss the shit out of her. She tastes like a bad decision, but I'm not known for being level-headed, so I lick, suck, and explore. Taking every damn thing she'll give me. And it's a hell of a lot because she doesn't stop me when I lift her tank up and over her head, exposing her sweet tits. She doesn't tell me no when I push her on her back and climb on top of her. She doesn't stop me when I kiss a path and suck a puckered nipple into my mouth, flicking the tight bud with my tongue.

What she does do is arch into me and moan. It sounds

like music to my ears. Like the only damn thing I want to hear for the rest of my life.

I lick my way to her other breast and suck the whole damn thing into my mouth before releasing it with a pop. There's just enough light from the moon shining through the blinds for me to see the way her skin flushes. I trace along her areolas with a finger. She's so soft, such a contrast to my hard labor roughed hand.

I push a knee between her thighs and make room for my hips. She instantly wraps her legs tight around me. I know she can feel my rock-hard erection against her center, so I grind into her, rubbing against her sweet spot. Her chest rises and falls rapidly, all signs that I'm making her feel good.

I wasn't lying when I told her I didn't fuck virgins. It's too complicated, but right now I don't give a shit.

"I won't go easy," I warn.

"I don't want you to. I want to know who you are, Loki. I need you to show me," she whispers.

"It'll hurt." I smirk because I want to cause her pain. I want to fuck her up the way she's fucked me up.

She gulps but doesn't back down. "I can take it."

With those words of agreement, I crash my lips to her. This time I don't hold back. I use my teeth to tug at her plump lower lip, I suck on her tongue until she's yelping. I reach down and twist the nipple I was just barely being so tender with. She doesn't stop me. She just continues to rub her warm pussy against my shaft.

I lift up onto my knees and draw her pink panties down her legs, revealing that bare cunt I've seen but never touched. I drag a finger through her slit, reveling in how wet she is. I spread her open, staring at her juicy pussy lips and tight hole that will soon belong to me. I push a finger inside, and she instinctively clenches around me. It'll be a tight fit. It'll hurt.

I pump in and out lazily a few times before adding a second digit. I stroke her clit and the added sensation has her squirming around.

"I can't wait to feel you wrapped around my cock, but first I'll eat you until you're screaming my name."

I push my arms underneath her thighs and tug her up my body, bringing her pussy to me. I flatten my tongue and lick up her center, tasting her for the first time. It's like she was made for me. The perfect mix of sugar and tang. I latch on and eat her cunt like a starved man having his first meal in months. Her tiny little clit is swollen and ready to deliver all the pleasure I can give her. A few flicks are all it takes before Birdie explodes in my mouth.

"Loki! Don't stop. Oh my God. Please!" she shouts.

I don't have any intention of stopping. Not any time soon. I drag some of her moisture down her asshole and spread it around before putting some pressure on it. She tries to pull away, obviously not ready to be taken there either, but I yank her back to me.

"Relax. I won't be going here tonight, little bird. I'm just getting acquainted with all your holes."

I swirl my tongue around her clenched pucker and she gasps.

See? You like it.

I work two fingers back inside her, hook them to hit her G-spot, and suck her outer lips into my mouth, one side at a time. I want my mouth to have tasted every inch of her by the end of the night, just in case I never get the chance to do this again. She writhes underneath me, gripping the sheets at her side. She tenses again and I know she's about to have her second orgasm. I bite down on her clit and she explodes around my fingers.

When I know she's come down, I pull my fingers free and bring them to her lips. I paint them with her arousal before dipping down and kissing her again, knowing she can taste herself, wanting her to taste herself. She told me she wanted all of me and I'm a dirty bastard, so I don't hold back.

I stand up and yank my boxers down. My cock springs free and her eyes grow impossibly wider. She closes her legs and I shake my head. That won't do.

"I don't know if—"

"It will." I interrupt.

I pull her legs wide and kneel between them. Her cunt is puffy and red. I love how every touch, soft or hard, can be seen on her snowy white skin. I fist myself and stroke up and down a few times before placing the head of my cock at her entrance. She's so wet, she's dripping. I tease her opening, taking in the erotic sight. I press in just a little, wanting to prolong this as much as I can.

With each push in, I go a little farther until her pussy sucks my big mushroom head in.

"You're squeezing me so tight, it's almost painful."

"I'm sorry," she gasps as I press even deeper.

I chuckle. "That's a good thing."

When I've teased us both enough, I shove in, balls deep. She cries out and reaches for me. I cover her with my body, letting her sharp nails do their worst as they claw into my shoulders. The sting is such a contrast to the tingling pleasure coming from my dick. I love it. Pleasure and pain. The perfect combination.

I give her a minute to adjust. It's hard. I want to move. I want to feel the friction of my cock moving in and out. But I'm not a total jackass, and this is her first time.

"You ready?" I ask.

She nods, and it's all the permission I need. My hips piston and I fuck her hard. Her mouth gapes and I shove a finger inside. Like a good girl, she wraps her lips around it and sucks. Her moans send vibrations through me and turn me on even more.

Our eyes meet and it's the most intimate thing I've ever experienced. Her brows furrow and her hands reach around to my ass, encouraging me to go harder. She's so much more than I ever expected. My balls tighten and the tingle spreads to the base of my spine, but I want her to come around my cock, so I pull my finger from her mouth and reach between us to rub at her clit.

She meets me thrust for thrust, pushing off her heels. Her breaths get choppy and she squeezes her eyes shut. Her pussy spasms around my cock and I can't hold back my orgasm any longer. I pull out, noticing the streak of red down my shaft. It turns me on even more. I jerk myself off until thick ropes of cum spurt all over her stomach and bright red pussy. I know it was stupid to not wear a condom, but I don't fucking care. I needed to feel her raw.

I've made a mess and as much as I love seeing my seed all over her, I can't stop myself when I scoop some of it up with the head of my dick and press into her one more time. I want to cover her inside and out.

Her arms and legs fall limply to the bed. She's well-fucked, and it's a damn good look on her.

I get up and grab a washcloth from the sink. I wet it with

warm water and take my time cleaning her up. I can't tell if she's asleep or boneless, but she hasn't moved. I toss the rag in the laundry and climb in next to her. She turns into me and nestles her head under my chin. I should push her away, make her sleep in the cage. I should, at the very least, turn my back on her and make her sleep without my warmth. But instead, I comb her long hair with my fingers until I feel her drift off to sleep.

I should sleep too. Tomorrow's a big day, but my mind is spinning and won't calm. What the fuck did I just do?

I saw firsthand how opening yourself up to love ends. Trucker and Ma had a connection I never understood. He was a hard-ass, not just to me but to everyone except Ma. I never saw him fucking with a club whore. I never even saw him look. When we had parties, he'd leave when the wives and kids did. Always going home to her.

And now look at him. A has-been who can't see over his own grief. Forgetting he had an entire club and a son still alive. I miss Ma. I feel responsible for her death, but I refuse to stop living. And I refuse to catch feelings for a chick who could lead me down the same path. My brothers, my patch, my bike, those are all things I believe in. They're tangible. But love? That's a destructive emotion.

But whatever this is between Birdie and me? It's not love, it's not even lust. So, I brush stray strands of hair from her forehead, breathe in her sweet and tart grapefruit scent, and drift off to sleep knowing everything can go back to normal tomorrow.

When she's back to her mansion in the hills and I'm back to fucking random patch pussy. It doesn't sit right, but it's the way it has to be.

Chapter
SEVENTEEN

Loki

I wake up to someone climbing over the top of me. Not having my wits about me yet, my instincts kick in. I grab the narrow shoulders of whoever it is and flip them onto their back and pin them down. My eyes peel open slowly to see the wide, scared brown eyes I dreamed about last night.

"Fuck, sorry." I release her shoulders and roll off of Birdie's body.

"I was trying not to wake you up."

I rub the sleep from my eyes and sit up, swinging my legs off the edge of the bed. Blood pumps through my veins rapidly, my heart pounding. Fight or flight adrenaline still coursing through my veins.

"Not your fault. Like I said, I'm not used to sleeping with anyone in my bed."

"I don't even know how I got here." A coy smile spreads across her face as she scoots to the edge of the mattress and sits next to me.

I don't respond, I don't react, I don't play her cute little game. Lines are too blurry between us, and especially on a day like today, I need to keep things very clear.

She stands up and stretches. She's still stark-ass naked and I know she's doing it on purpose. So, I get up and turn my back on her while I put on my boxers. It does nothing to help me keep her at a distance because my dick is already hard and it's painful as I cover myself up.

I hear the bathroom door open and I know what I have to do. Go back to being a prick. Her anger with me will be the only way we can both walk away from this.

"What are you doing?" she asks when she looks in the vanity mirror and sees me behind her.

"Just making sure you don't disappear today. You're playing an important role in how things go down."

She narrows her eyes at my reflection, the scorching blaze I've grown to crave sparking to life. I want to stoke her. Throw my verbal kindling to speed up the flames. Make her burn bright. See smoke pour from her. I want to feel her fire.

"I think we're past that." She faces me and folds her arms across her chest.

"Are we? Or are you just trying to make me trust you before you fuck me over?" I mimic her stance.

"Loki. Seriously. Get out. I need to use the bathroom."

"Birdie. Seriously," I sing-song. "Go right ahead and take a piss."

"You are so messed up in the head. This kink of yours is so weird." She tosses her hands in the air. "Fine. You want to be a freak?"

She stomps her way over to the toilet and plops down, not even bothering with modesty this time. I get a flash of her bare pussy, reminding my cock of how much he liked being inside her. If I don't get some control, she'll know just how much she affects me.

Never in my life have I wanted a girl to pee or shower in front of me, but if she took a shit right here and now, I'd probably still be hard. Shit. She's right. I'm a fucking freak.

I hold her eye contact, waiting for her to tell me to turn the faucet on, but she doesn't. I'm not the only one getting comfortable with our forced closeness. She wipes and even that has me fixated. She kicks her shorts and panties to the side and yanks the hem of her tank up and over her head. Her peach-sized tits spring free. Just like her skin, her small nipples are almost the color of ivory. It was so dark last night. I couldn't see her body as clearly as I can now.

My mouth waters and I'm the first one to look away. She must be sore, but my control is slipping and instead of removing myself from the situation, I stay rooted in place. The water to the shower turns on and I hear the glass door close. With a solid surface now between us, I raise my gaze again. Her back is to me and her heart-shaped ass bounces while she angrily scrubs at her hair and body. I have the sudden urge to grab her hips, put a hand between her shoulders, bend her forward, and slam into her tight cunt.

The steam eventually clouds the glass, and it steals my view.

"You know there's a word for this. Voyeurism. I suggest seeking help," she says.

"That's the least of my problems," I mumble under my breath.

"What?" she shouts.

"Nothing. Just hurry up. I can't spend all day in here."

"No one's asking you to." She looks over her shoulder with half-lidded eyes, letting me know I'm not the only one wanting a repeat.

The water stops and she wraps a towel around her body before stepping out of the shower. I shut the bathroom door and stalk toward her. The confidence she was feeling seconds ago fades. She adjusts the knot in the towel at her breasts. I pass her and drop my boxers.

"Get back in there," I demand.

"I'm already clean."

"I'm about to dirty you back up." I flip the water back on, rip the towel from her body, and pull her under the warm spray.

I lift her up to straddle my waist and being the dutiful girl she is, her legs wrap around me. Like a beacon in the night, my already hard cock nestles itself between her puffy pussy lips. I groan into her neck and suck her flesh into my mouth. I want—no, I fucking need to mark her. When I send her home, I want her to remember me. If I could scar her with my teeth, I would. Marring her forever so every single stuck-up cocksucker who comes after me would see she was mine first.

I slam her against the wall, and she grunts when the air is knocked from her lungs. I reach between us and position my cock at her entrance, then I slam home.

"Loki," she cries.

"This'll be fast and hard," I say through gritted teeth.

I grind into her with each thrust, making sure my pelvic bone rubs against her clit. I take her mouth and for everything I give her, she gives it right back. She uses her legs to pull me harder into her. She takes what she needs from me, and it's the hottest fucking thing I've ever seen.

I pinch her nipple, tugging and twisting. She cries out and her head falls back in ecstasy. She spasms around me with such a force, my own orgasm builds. When I'm certain I've wrung every ounce of pleasure from her, I lower her to her feet. She looks at me questioningly as I push down on her shoulders, forcing her to her knees.

Confusion crosses her features, but when I bring my cock to her lips, she catches on. She grips the base of my cock and tentatively pumps up and down.

I'm blocking most of the spray from the shower, but tiny water particles collect along her long eyelashes that she's batting at me. I burn the image to my memory, knowing after she's gone, I'll be calling on it every time I jerk off.

"Suck me," I order and trace my cock along her kiss-swollen lips.

"I don't know how," she admits.

"Wrap your mouth around me and suck, Birdie. It's not complicated."

She does as I ask and hollows her cheeks as she bobs up and down my dick. I groan in pleasure. Her hands find the globes of my ass and she squeezes. She doesn't know she's just given me permission to fuck her face. I grip her head and press her farther down my cock. She gags and tries to pull away, but I won't let her go that easily.

"Relax your throat. Let me do the work."

I expect her to fight me, but she doesn't. She nods with her mouth still full of me. Jesus fuck. She'll be the death of me if I'm not careful. I squeeze my eyes shut, letting myself enjoy every second of this. She still gags when I shove down her throat, but she recovers quicker each time.

When I know I'm seconds from exploding, I yank free of

her mouth and jerk myself off. Hot, thick spurts of cum shoot all over face and tits. She gasps in shock, allowing some of my seed to make it into her mouth. She doesn't cringe or make a show of pretending to love it, her expression just goes curious. Her pink tongue peeks out, and she licks her lips. The sight prolongs my orgasm, making me feel like it'll never end.

I release my dick and gently pull her to standing. I move out of the way so she can rinse off. I press my body flush against her and wrap my arms around to her front. I caress her tits and allow myself to explore every part of her I can reach. When she turns around, I kiss her sweetly and take my time washing her clean again.

I turn off the water and pat her warm skin dry. It's gentler than I've been with anyone, but she's been such a good girl, I want to reward her. I want to show her I'm not all hard lines and angry words.

"Can I please go get dressed now?" she asks, reminding me she still thinks herself a prisoner.

Good. Now that our shower is over, my mind clears from the lust fog she had me in. I keep losing focus and as much I love fucking her, I can't forget why we've been forced together in the first place.

"Sure."

I follow her out and we both dress quietly with only a few stolen glances.

"So, what now?" she asks, hands on her hips.

"I've got shit to do."

"Can I come?"

I growl in frustration. This bitch thinks this is playtime. Like it's *bring your birdie to work day*. "No, go play with the dogs or something."

Instead of arguing, she grabs her book from the cage and lies back down on my bed. I hate it when she goes into defeated mode. It makes me feel guilty, and I don't feel guilty for shit. Ever.

"Fine. Put on your shoes. We're going outside."

She jumps off the bed and hurriedly pulls on a pair of sneakers. "I'll stay out of your way."

"I don't believe that for a second," I mumble.

We grab a bite to eat and go outside. Moto's tuning up his bike and I find my toolbox to do the same. With as hard and often as we ride, our bikes require constant maintenance. We've got shit to do to prepare for later this evening, but for now, I need the distraction. We've made a plan A, B, C, and D for tonight so now it's just a waiting game before it's time to load up.

"What are you doing?" Birdie asks.

"Changing the oil on my bike."

"Can I help?"

"You said you'd stay out of my way." I remind her.

"I am. I will. I've just never worked on a car, let alone a motorcycle. Thought I could learn something." She juts her chin up.

"Why? Because you'll go home tonight and buy yourself a Harley?" I laugh.

"I could."

"You'd be dead in a week. This is a man's machine." I set the tools down in the garage and walk out to get my bike. When I've rolled it into position, I grab a new filter and a couple quarts of oil.

I pull on a pair of latex gloves and get to work. I unscrew the oil cap and start my engine to warm the oil so it's easier to drain. Birdie watches like she's studying for a test later. Her nose scrunches in concentration. After a couple minutes, I turn the engine off and squat to pull the drain bolt.

"Will you pass me that drip pan?" I point to where it is.

"Sure," she chirps.

I remove the oil filter and watch as the thick, murky oil runs out. While I wait, I take out my phone and check my messages. I reply to a few of them and then tuck my phone away.

"Everything all good for tonight?" she asks.

"Yup." I open up the new filter and a quart of oil. I rub some oil into the O-ring.

"Why are you doing that?" She leans over my shoulder to get a better view. She's so close that intoxicating grapefruit scent fills my nostrils.

"It'll give it a better seal when I put the new filter on." I turn my head. She's so close I'd barely have to lean forward if I wanted to kiss her. And I want to. The way our lips fit together is like two puzzle pieces finding their place together. I clear my throat and get back to work.

I install the new filter, making sure it fits properly.

"Grab me that funnel."

"Please," she says.

I'm not about to be her trained dog, so I walk over and grab it myself. She scoffs, but I ignore it. I set the funnel in place and take the drip pan over to our oil disposal can.

"Can I pour one in?"

I look over my shoulder to see Birdie with an open quart of oil, tipping it, ready to pour.

"No!" I yell, but it's too late, she's already filling the funnel with oil, which goes into the engine and promptly falls out of the bottom because I haven't screwed the drain bolt back into place.

I set the drip pan down and rush over, taking the plastic bottle out of her hand.

"What did I do wrong?" Her lower lip trembles.

I point to the ground where a puddle of oil grows by the second. "That."

"I'm sorry. I didn't know."

"It's fine. Go grab some paper towels and some rags on the shelf."

We work together to clean up the mess with her apologizing every two seconds.

"Come here," I order when we're done. She comes over to where I'm standing. I lift her up from under her arms and plant her ass on the workbench. "Stay here."

She folds her arms across her chest in a fucking adorable pout, but she does what I say and watches from a safe distance as I tighten the drain bolt into place and then pour oil into the engine.

Despite myself, I keep an eye on her too. She's so attentive, like she'll need this information in the future. Which is ridiculous, because this girl doesn't look like her hands have ever gotten dirty. But her curiosity is cute and makes me strangely proud. Like she values my talents and knowledge. I want to feel more of that, as dangerous as it is.

I finish cleaning up and putting the tools away before moving my bike back to where it was parked.

I stalk back over to Birdie and lift her up again. As I lower her to the ground, I go slow so her body lingers against mine because fuck it. The temptation is too strong. She sucks in a sharp breath that has me smirking.

"All done," I say.

"What's next?" she asks, following me back into the house.

"Now you'll go with Tabitha and Sissy and get a bit of a makeover."

"What?"

"We're pretty sure Dom knows what you look like, which could blow your cover. So you're going to get a club whore makeover," I say with a pleased smile on my face.

"No way. I can't dress like them."

"You can, and you will. It's the only way this will work."

She mulls it over, chewing on the inside of her mouth. "Fine, but I get final say on what I wear because a fishnet dress is not a good look on anyone."

"You can have veto power." I agree because I don't want anyone seeing her naked besides me.

"Fine. Let's do this."

Chapter EIGHTEEN

Bridgette

Loki knocks on a bedroom door and I shift uncomfortably from foot to foot, trying to relieve the ache in my core. I was sore after we had sex last night, but I didn't let it stop me from allowing him do it again in the shower. I always assumed my first time would be with someone tender and kind. Instead, it was with Loki and he's nothing but rough and aggressive and absolutely perfect.

I didn't know my body could come alive like that. He filled me with so much desire and yearning. I felt like I'd dissolve into a puddle of need. Instead, I exploded like a rainbow. Colorful and full of life. It was raw and dirty. He did things to me I didn't even know were possible. Things I didn't even know I wanted. The only problem is I worry about how anyone else will compare. There's no way I could settle for sweet and gentle now. Not after what he's done to me.

"Hey, baby." Tabitha answers the door with a huge smile plastered on her injection filled lips.

I step out from behind his hulking form and the smile she was sporting falls. *Good.*

"Hey, darlin'. You ready to work some magic on this one?" He hooks a thumb toward me.

"Right. Sure." She sighs. "Come on in."

I peer into the room, seeing two beds, a dresser, and a couple nightstands. They've decorated half of the space in colorful Hawaiian flowers and the other in brown and gold cheetah print. Sissy sits cross-legged on the flowery bed. She's dressed in a slinky black nightie, scrolling on her phone.

"I'll leave you to it." Loki turns to leave.

"You're not going to stay?" My eyes go wide with panic and I grab his arm, stopping him. While these women have had kind moments, they also have made sure I know I'm not their friend. I absolutely don't want to be left alone with them.

"Not my scene, Birdie." He leans over and kisses my cheek. I'm so stunned at the sweetness of it, that I drop his arm and cover the spot his lips touched, as if I'd be able to feel it.

Before I can argue again, he's gone, and I'm left in the lionesses' den. I rock back on my heels awkwardly as they both stare, gaping. Clearly, they're just as surprised by the kiss as I was.

"I like your room. It's… unique." I compliment.

"I'm sure it's nothing like what you're used to, but it's home."

"It's lovely," I say, looking at the pictures on the wall. I recognize a photo of a hut sitting over crystal blue water. "Oh, this is the Maldives, right?"

"Yeah." Sissy jumps off the bed and stands next to me.

"It's so pretty there. I went with my girlfriends for our senior trip."

"I'd love to go someday," she says wistfully.

"You haven't been?" I look over at her. I assumed since she had a picture that she'd been there.

Sissy's eyes fall, and she goes back to her bed.

"No, princess. She hasn't been there." Tabitha yanks me over to the closet. "Let's get this over with. I was thinking something like this."

I gawk at the neon orange wrap dress with cut-outs down the sides.

"No," I deadpan.

"Why not? It's hot."

"Neons are for bathing suits, not for dresses." I shake my head.

"That's my favorite dress." Sissy rushes over and steals it from Tabitha's hand, clutching it to her chest.

I've offended her again. If I were back home, I wouldn't care. If Sissy were one of my friends, I'd make fun of her. But it feels wrong with these women. I care what they think about me for some stupid reason. I want to be their friend. I want their approval.

"Maybe something in black?" I ask hopefully.

"Black is my signature color," Tabitha says, moving to the darker section of the closet. "How about this?"

The dress she shows me is pleather, sleeveless, and form-fitting. I don't know why anyone would be walking their dog in a dress like this, but it'll definitely attract attention. It'll probably give me a rash with the plastic material, but if I'm trying not to look like myself, it fits the bill.

"I like it." I hold it up over my body and look into the full-length mirror.

"Okay, we have wardrobe. Now let's do makeup. You and Sissy have similar complexions, so I'll let her take over."

"Come sit." Sissy offers me a wooden chair in front of a vanity occupying a corner of the room.

I lower onto it and look at myself in the mirror. I look the same. The fresh highlights in my damp blond hair don't need a touch-up. My flawless skin glows despite not having my normal products. And my eyes are the same earthy brown. But I'm not the same. Not even a little bit. The fake, plastic expression I've perfected over the years is gone and in its place is something real. Someone who has seen some things. I like it.

Sissy dabs and smooths, contours and highlights. She lines my upper lid with a liquid black eyeliner and fills the crease of my eyelid with a neutral color. I let her do whatever she wants. Even when she asks for my opinion, I don't give it. I'm curious what she'll do on her own.

"Going to have to cover this up." She lightly traces a spot on my neck.

"I might've burned myself." I blush and cover the red and purple blotchy skin. Even without looking, I know what it is. Remembering the sting from him sucking my skin into his mouth has me tingling all over again.

"I've seen a lot of burns in my life. None of them were a hickey." She dabs my neck with concealer and sets it with powder.

I drop the subject, knowing she'll see through any lie I tell.

Her face pinches with focus as she applies a set of false lashes. I don't know how old she is, but I'd guess mid-twenties. She's pretty and I can tell why the guys keep her around.

"How did you end up here?" I ask when the curiosity overwhelms my ability to stay quiet.

"In Reno?" she asks, blowing on the strip of eyelash.

"No, here. In the clubhouse."

"I was a waitress at the biker bar. I'm an orphan and didn't have anyone except the guys when they came in on the weekends. I got to know them and started hanging around. They became my family. I wanted to be here all the time, so I asked if I could stay." She clamps down on the lashes with a set of tweezers and pushes them into my lash line.

"Do you like being a… club whore?" I ask hesitantly. The guys use the term like it's nothing, but I don't know if it's derogatory to them.

She grins. "I do. I'd like to be an old lady. I'm not getting any younger, but even if it never happens, I'm happy. What other girl can say she has a gang of hot bikers taking care of her? Plus, look at them. It's not a hardship having sex with them."

I frown, an image of Loki and Sissy together running through my mind. Despite my better judgement, I ask, "Have you and Loki…?"

Her head tilts to the side, confusion in her beautiful features. "Well, yeah. I've been with all the guys except Goblin and Roch. They have more discriminate tastes."

I nod and tuck my hair behind my ears. It's what I expected, and it shouldn't even matter. He's not mine. He doesn't even want me, except to terrorize and have sex with. And I don't want him. He's not my type at all. I mean, he's attractive and intense, but he's a self-proclaimed murderer. It's ridiculous for me to care who he sleeps with. And yet—

"Of course. I don't even know why I asked."

"You have a thing for Prez." She waggles a finger at me.

"I don't," I say adamantly, shaking my head.

"You do. Girl, don't do it. He's not the kind of guy for you."

"I swear, I don't. I was just curious is all."

She makes a *humph* noise in disbelief.

"What? I don't," I say.

"If you say so." She motions to the mirror. "You're done."

I glance up at my reflection, not even prepared for what I see. At eighteen years old, I'm used to being fresh-faced. I wear little makeup and what I do use is only to enhance subtly. There's nothing subtle about the way I look. My bright red lips scream for attention. My thick lashes are sultry and sexy. My face has a whole new shape from the contour. I look like a woman.

"I can't believe this is me." I turn from side to side, looking from all angles.

"It's you, boo." Sissy reorganizes all of her cosmetics.

"Now let's do something with that hair." Tabitha steps behind me, pulling my hair back. "I think up will work better. Show off those snatched cheekbones."

I watch as she sections my locks off. She puts a loose French braid down the center, then moves to do the same on either side.

"How did you end up here?" I ask. I'm a little nervous to ask more questions, but it would be rude to not inquire.

She blows out a breath. "I was sold off by my parents when I was sixteen to a politician."

I gasp. I wasn't expecting that.

"My dad had some gambling debts. And it was either pay them off with me, or they'd come after him and he was too selfish to die, so… yeah. I spent two years locked in a closet, only taken out when—well, anyway. I don't want to dirty your little head with the details. The Royal Bastards were hired to kill the politician out for something unrelated and they found me. They took me in." She presses her lips together, her eyes watering a little.

"Didn't you just trade being a slave to him to being a slave to the club?" I slap a hand over my mouth.

"You've got the wrong idea about us. We're not prisoners. We want to be here. All of those guys out there? I love them. Like brothers, except not, because we fuck." She laughs.

I look at her, horrified. Where am I and how did I have no idea people like this existed?

"Don't get all uppity," she scolds. "You have no right to judge me. Until you've walked a mile in my shoes, you can wipe that look right off your face."

I think about it. She's right. I'm not completely ignorant. I know I've lived a charmed life. I watch the news. But hearing about humans being trafficked is one thing and looking into the eyes of someone who had that life is another.

"I'm sorry. I didn't mean it disrespectfully. I'm genuinely curious."

"Yeah, well. My life isn't a science experiment for you to study." She takes the three braids, pulls all of my hair into a sleek ponytail, and fastens it with a hair tie. "There you go."

I like it. It's edgy and matches the makeup. I stand up and move to Tabitha's bed where the dress is lying.

"I only brought sports bras," I say, only now realizing my undergarments won't work.

The girls laugh hysterically. I turn to them questioningly. I wasn't trying to be funny. I really don't know how I'll make this work.

"You don't wear a bra with a dress like that. It'll be so tight, you'll be good," Sissy says. "Plus, guys like to see movement. They like to know how soft you are so they can picture what you feel like."

The look on my face has them laughing all over again. I circle back to the dress and sigh. When in Rome, I guess? I go into the bathroom and peel off my yoga clothes. Before I dress, I take in my nudity. I bounce a little, watching my boobs jiggle.

Do guys really like that?

I roll my eyes and pull the dress over my head.

They were right. It fits like a second skin and a bra would just stand out. When I turn and look over my shoulder, I see panties will be a mistake too. Especially the boy cut ones I have on now. I slide them down my legs and tuck them into my folded clothes.

If my friends could see me now. I can't even recognize myself. The person reflecting back at me is a bad bitch. Isn't that the term for a woman who looks like she doesn't take crap from anyone? I feel more confident, more alive, more like the person I feel I really am than I ever did in the designer outfits I'm used to. Who knew all it took was some pleather?

I slink out of the bathroom, not wanting to make a grand entrance. But Sissy and Tabitha had their eyes peeled to the door, waiting.

"Holy shit balls," Sissy blurts.

"You look sexy." Tabitha nods in approval.

"Are you sure? I feel a little overdone." I smooth down the dress even though there are no wrinkles.

"Men never wonder why a woman is dressed up. They're too stupid. They'll just see your ass and tits and stumble all over you." Tabitha hands me a pair of heels. "Hope size six and a half will be okay. It's all I have."

"I'm a seven, but I can make it work." I slide into the

shoes that appear to have been repaired with a sharpie, but from a distance no one will know.

"Go get 'em!" Sissy cheers.

I smile tightly. Butterflies fill my belly thinking about what I'm about to do. Or is it because I'm worried Loki won't like my makeover? Either way, I'm nervous.

load my Five-seven pistol with the hollow point cartridges. Commonly known as a "cop killer," it's one of the guns we hoarded during our weapons trading days. I tuck extra rounds in my pocket and slide the pistol into my waistband. Then I load my Mossberg shotgun and set it in the back of the van. My brothers all load their guns of choice and Sly brings out his backpack full of the computer equipment he needs to take down Dom's security cameras.

Since we're trying to be discreet, we'll be riding in cages. I hate not having my bike with me, but the roar of our engines would clue the capo and his crew guarding Dom's property in that we're coming.

"Hey, Sly. Where's Dom at?" I ask.

"He left for that club he owns, like he does every evening. Nothing out of the ordinary," he reports.

"Good." I'm glad everything is going as it should. The

last thing we need is for any kind of deviation in the plan. "Have you seen Trucker?"

"No, man. Is he supposed to be here?"

"Yeah, said he'd be. Probably passed out drunk." I should've known he'd be a no-show.

"Where's the girl?" Khan asks, sidling up next to me.

"She's inside getting dolled up." I take a seat on the rear bumper of the van.

I couldn't tell if Birdie was nervous about today or not. I didn't ask because it doesn't matter. Frightened or not, she has to do it and sometimes talking about it can only enhance those feelings.

I remember the day I turned eighteen and Trucker sent me on my first job delivering a shipment of guns to a cartel in Los Angeles. It was terrifying. I was scared we'd get caught or things would go sour. But the second I straddled my bike, I had to shut that shit off. There's no room for self-doubt when you're in this life.

But Birdie isn't in this life and I don't know how to prepare her. The girl is so fucking naïve, there's not enough time to bring her around. So, I just treated it like it was every other day since she's been here. Hopefully, she's got her shit straight in her head, so she doesn't ruin our cover.

Khan lets out a wolf-whistle and I follow his gaze to see the sexiest bitch I've ever laid eyes on.

I swallow. Hard.

Her tits are spilling over her short black dress. Her heels make her legs appear miles long when I know it's not true. Her lips are cherry red and appear just as juicy. She's adorable in her comfortable clothes and fresh-faced, but like this, she's a fucking goddess.

She stops in front of me, placing her hands on her hips. "Will this work?"

"At making my dick hard? Yeah. At distracting the soldiers on Dom's property? Hell yeah." I yank her close, making room for her between my legs. I have the primal urge to make sure my brothers know she's not theirs to ogle.

"I don't care about your penis," she sasses, but I see how being close to me affects her. I know that look because I have the same lust filled eyes, parted lips, and heaving chest.

"That right?" I smirk.

"I don't." She turns her head, focusing everywhere but on me.

That won't do.

"Eyes right here." I grip her at the base of her throat and turn her head back to me with my thumb and forefinger. "Always give me those eyes, Birdie."

Her pupils are blown, swallowing the brown of her irises. She bites down on her bottom lip, scraping her teeth along the flesh until it springs free. I'd kill to be the one biting down on her sweet skin. I wrap an arm around her waist and pull her even closer. My cock lengthens down my thigh and I know she can feel it. Her palms flatten against my chest, so I flex my pecs and smirk when she sucks in a sharp breath.

I turn her face to the side and press my lips to her ear so I can whisper, "You can pretend you don't like me, that I don't turn you on. But I know the truth. I know if I reached under your dress, my fingers would be coated with your sticky sweetness. I think it would only take one pinch of your swollen clit, and you'd be screaming my name."

I suck her earlobe into my mouth, flicking it with my tongue. Then I press a kiss to her neck and release her. She stumbles a bit, gripping my leg to steady herself. She straightens and smooths down her dress.

"You're wrong. I'm dry as the Sahara Desert," she says, but her body betrays her with every word.

"I'd love to sit here and prove what a liar you are, but we don't have time right now. But if you're a good girl today, I'll reward you later." I push off the bumper and look around. My brothers are actively trying to not pay attention, but the snoopy fuckers heard every word. I focus back on Birdie. "Are you ready? Do you have questions?"

"No, I'm good." She steels her spine, exuding confidence.

"Okay. Let's do it then." I give her a smack on the ass and finish loading the last of our weapons.

Roch approaches and hands over a sleepy Karen to Birdie. She barely wakes as she's transferred between them. Roch strokes the dog's head. I know this is hard for him. I may not know what trauma he suffered in his past life, but I know his dogs are what keeps him human. Without them, he'd be the coldblooded killer he turns into when we're on a job and he wouldn't be able to turn it off.

We load up in the two vans. Khan driving one, and Sly driving the other. I sit on the middle bench seat next to Birdie. She quietly coos to Karen as we make the twenty-minute drive. We park two blocks away to let Birdie out, and Sly parks on the north side of the building so he's close enough to hack into their system.

"If you get any weird vibes, get out. Don't worry about getting Karen. Just get the fuck out of there. Once you hear the gunshots, find somewhere to get low and out of the way. We'll find you." My words are sharp and stern. Birdie has a hard time listening and following orders, so I want to make sure she knows the seriousness of the situation.

"Okay. I will."

I watch her walk down the street. Something in my gut is doing cartwheels, something I've never felt before. I hope it's not my instincts telling me something is off. Every part of me wants to go after her. To not use her in this way. But it's too late. We have a plan and we're running out of time.

"Come on." I pull the sliding door of the van shut. "Game time."

Khan drives us closer. We pass Birdie as she crosses the street. Once she gets to the other side, she'll be able to send Karen between the iron fence. We park across the street from the compound where we can watch from a safe enough distance to be ignored, but close enough to watch.

She gets to the fence and crouches to let Karen down. The dog stretches and sniffs. Birdie gives her a pat in the right direction and like she understands the plan, she goes between the fence posts and into the lush landscape of Dom's property. Birdie scans the area until she sees us. She takes a deep breath and walks around the corner to the front entrance.

I wait five long goddamn minutes, my insides churning more and more with each passing second before I call into the radios, "Sly, you guys good? Ready?"

"Ten four, Prez."

We pile out of the van. I open the rear door and we all take a long gun, doing one final check on our weapons. It's sunset, dark enough to hide, but not so dark we can't see what we're doing. We split off in different directions, all knowing where our individual stations are.

I climb the fence, my spot being near the security booth, and in my direct line of sight is Birdie. I watch as she shamelessly flirts with the rat bastard who approaches her at the gate. She talks her way to the booth and in no time, it's being opened and she's in.

Then things go bad. Fucking horribly bad. I watch as they manhandle her and soon it's clear they plan to take things much further.

"Cameras are shutting down in five, four, three, two, one. Move in." Sly's voice chirps in my ear.

Over my dead fucking body. It's go time.

Chapter
TWENTY

Bridgette
Ten minutes earlier...

My hands are shaking, so I fist them at my sides. I walk through the entrance and within seconds, a man in all black approaches me. His hair is greased to his head, and he's big. Like body builder big. I internally shudder, but outwardly I relax my body to play the role of helpless woman.

"What are you doing?" the man calls out. "This is private property."

"I'm sorry to bother you, but I lost my dog." I jut my lower lip out in a pout. "She ran right between the fence and won't come to me. I was hoping you could help me find her?"

I keep walking farther into the property, scanning the area, looking for Karen. I pray she doesn't pop out and run to me. But she doesn't. There's a cement path that meanders around the houses on the compound and trees, bushes, and flowers lining it.

Lots of hiding places for a small dog.

I turn to my left and see the guard station Loki told me about. I walk that way, ignoring the guard.

"You can't be in here. Turn your fine ass around." He circles a finger in the air.

"She's my baby. You have to help. Please," I plead. I bend forward and pull up on a bush, both to make a production of searching, and to give him a shot of my chest.

He chokes and clears his throat. "Fine. I'll help you look."

"Really?" I jump up and down, pretending to be excited, when really, I'm cringing at how stupid these men are. "Thank you so much!"

"But if we don't find it in five minutes, you're leaving. With or without the dog."

"Okay. I'm sure she's around here somewhere." I make a dramatic show of looking around before pointing to a camera. "Do these things work? Karen is a teacup chihuahua. It'll save us a lot of work if we can see the entire property."

He mulls it over, eyeing me with hesitation and suspicion as he sizes me up. I strut over to him, swaying my hips. He bites down on his lower lip and I know I have him.

"Please? The sooner we find her, the sooner I'll be out of your hair." When I'm close enough to see the whites of his eyes, I put my hands in a praying position in front of me and say, "I'll repay you for your kindness."

It's a lie. I won't be doing anything for this asswipe, but I have to make him believe he'll be getting something out of it.

"What kind of repayment are we talking about?" He flicks my ponytail off my shoulder and traces my collarbone with the tip of his finger.

"I'm sure we can agree on something. But we need to

find Karen first." I wink. I've never winked before in my life and I hope it looks sexy and not like I have dust in my eye.

"Come on, the camera feed is in here." He places a hand at the small of my back, leading my right to the guard station. "What's your name, baby?"

"Birdie," I say. I don't know why I give him Loki's nickname for me. I guess I've grown used to it and maybe even like it. No one has ever called me anything but Bridgette. "What's your name?"

"Name's Ricardo, Ricky for short." He knocks twice on the door to the booth.

My confidence grows. This was way too easy. The door opens to another large, greasy man. He's sitting in front of a desk with ten TV screens stacked two deep. He could be Ricky's twin with his dark, Italian skin, and deep brown eyes.

"Who do we have here?" A sly grin breaks out on the man's face. He creeps me out, even more than the first guy.

"Carlo, this is Birdie." Ricky introduces us. "Her dog ran onto the property and I thought we could check out the feed and see if we can find the poor thing."

Ricky motions for me to step inside. The three of us crowd into the cramped space.

"That so?" Carlo leers, his eyes traveling over every inch of my body until they stop at my boobs. He sucks on his teeth. The disgusting sound has me wanting to gag.

It suddenly hits me how vulnerable I am in here with them. The door is still open, but with both of them in the way, I'd never be able to get out. I should've stayed outside. I pray the Royal Bastards show themselves soon.

"I don't see her," I say, hoping to turn their attention to the screen and off of me. "Maybe she ran out looking for me. I should go check."

I try to edge past them, but Ricky puts himself between me and the exit. Carlo wraps an arm around my middle, putting a punishing grip on my hip.

"Hold on. Why don't you come sit on my lap so you can get a better look at the feed?" Carlo pulls me between his legs and with powerful hands and forces me down onto his lap. I feel his arousal digging in my ass and panic overtakes me.

Where is Loki?

"What does your puppy look like?" Carlo noses behind my ear, turning my stomach.

I lean forward as much as I can, but all it does is grind my butt against him. I realize my mistake instantly. I try to sit up, but he places a hand between my shoulders, keeping me in position.

"You've got a great ass," he says, running his other hand down my spine and to my ass.

"I don't want this. I just want to get my dog and leave," I protest with a shaky voice.

"Except we had a deal. Just because we didn't find your mutt, doesn't mean you can just leave without paying up," Ricky says.

Carlo spins the office chair. With me still folded in half, it puts my face at crotch level with Ricky, who tips my chin up, forcing me to make eye contact. The same fear I felt when Dom was in my house fills me again. My body trembles and a hard lump settles into my stomach. If he puts that wretched penis anywhere near my mouth, I'll throw up.

"What do you say we show Birdie here a pleasurable time?" Carlo asks.

"I think that's a brilliant idea." Ricky undoes his belt and pops the button of his black jeans.

Tears blur my vision. I'm trapped. If I move forward, I'll be closer to Ricky and the near exposure of his manhood. If I lean back, I'll feel the godawful, lust filled, heavy breathing of Carlo behind me. The thought crosses my mind that maybe Loki found the vial and is just going to leave me here. He could tell my dad I ran off. He could wash his hands of me and not put the club's safety at risk by getting me out of here, too. He's ruthless enough to do it, but despite everything, I thought he was starting to—maybe not like me—but at least not hate me. Not enough to abandon me here.

Carlo tugs at my dress, lifting it higher and higher up my thighs. I try to pull it back down, but he grabs my hands and pins me by my wrists at the base of my spine with one hand while the other goes back to expose me.

"Stop it. Stop. I don't want this!"

"Fuck, man. She's not wearing panties," he hisses. "I think there never was a dog. I think she came here just for this." He grabs handfuls of my ass and rocks me back and forth on his erection.

This can't be happening. Where's Loki?

Loud popping fills the air, halting Carlo's movement. So many I can't count. I blink away the tears just in time to see Ricky's wide eyes before his head jerks to the side and blood sprays all over everything. Including me. I scream until my lungs burn as the warm liquid drips down my face.

"What the fuck!" Carlo shouts and jumps to his feet, sending me flying forward. My head slams into a monitor hard enough to shatter the screen, sending searing pain through my skull.

Carlo runs out and I fall to the floor. I make myself small under the desk. Gunshots still fill the air. Loud bangs and softer pops. With each one, I jump. Terror has me unable to move, think, or do anything except curl around myself and hide with my eyes squeezed shut.

A hand winds around my arm and rips me from my hiding spot. I'm certain it's Loki. That this is all over. But as my eyes slowly open, it's not my sexy captor I see. It's Carlo. Every bit of relief is doused instantly. Blood spills down his cheeks and his face is contorted into a sinister sneer. He looks utterly insane.

"Get up," he orders, his eyes jumping around, looking for danger. "Do you know them? Is that why you're here? To distract us so your buddies out there can take us out?"

I'm frozen. Paralyzed in fear. Even if I wanted to go with him, I couldn't. My body isn't my own right now.

"Bitch, I said get up." He yanks me to standing and holds me flush against him with my back to his front. Something cold and hard digs into my temple. "You think you can set up Dom? Dangerous move. Now you're going to help get me out of here. Don't be stupid and you'll make it out alive."

He shoves me from the booth. I trip and stumble with every step. My feet don't want to do what this man says and neither does the rest of me, but I also don't want to die. I look around for any signs of the Royal Bastards, but they're nowhere to be found.

I see dead Italian men splayed out on the ground.

I see blood.

I see gore.

But I don't see them.

He jerks me from side to side, using me as a shield from the unseen threat. Movement catches my eye near the front gate and Khan steps onto the cement walkway, standing in-between us and the black SUV I'm assuming Carlo is trying to get to. The giant biker has a gun pointed in our direction. I plead with him with my eyes, begging him to get me out of this situation. His expression softens the tiniest bit before hardening once again.

"Let her the fuck go and we'll let you leave with your life," Khan demands.

"You think I'm stupid? No. She's coming with me, or we both die. Your choice." Carlo presses into my temple with what I can only assume is a gun. "Toss your gun and lift your shirt so I know you're clean."

We stand there for what feels like a lifetime before Khan curses and tosses the gun into a bush and spins in a circle, holding his shirt up.

"Now lie face down in that bush." I see a flicker of steel as Carlo gestures with the gun at the side of my face.

"Fuck!" Khan shouts and does as he's asked.

I hear another pop and a whoosh of air whizz above my shoulder. Carlo jerks back, but doesn't let go.

"Shit," he curses and makes himself smaller behind me. "Move, bitch."

He shoves me from behind, all the way to the car. He climbs in the driver's side first and I'm certain he's going to let me go, but he keeps a firm grip on my arm as he climbs over the console. Then he pulls me into the driver's side.

"Shut the fucking door," he says.

I take another glance around, wondering where everyone is. When I don't see help, I do the only thing I can; I pull the door shut.

"Start the car and pull out. Now." His arm hangs limply at his side and I realize they've shot him. But the other hand presses the gun into my neck painfully. "Do it now, or we'll both end up dead."

"I don't know how to drive," I shriek as I press the ignition button. Technically, I have my license. I took Driver's Ed in high school when I was sixteen and passed. But I haven't driven myself anywhere for a long time.

"Well, you better figure it out fast. Get us out of here, now." He grunts in pain as his limp arm puts the car in reverse.

I back out of the long driveway cautiously, slowly, biding more time for the Bastards to get here. Khan reemerges, his shotgun aimed at the car. Then I see Moto and Sly appear at his side. They yell back and forth. I see the confusion on their expressions as they debate how to handle this.

They open fire at the passenger side of the car. I scream and hold my hands over my ears. The windshield bends with the momentum of the bullets, but it doesn't break.

Oh my God. It's bulletproof glass.

"Fucking drive. Now!" He slaps me across the cheek with the gun still in his hand. I hear a crack come from the bone breaking under the force of the hit. Then the pain. Excruciatingly sharp pain sears through my face. "Swear to God, if you don't move this car now, death will be a better option for what I'll do to you."

I press down on the gas, bullets still hitting the SUV. In my rearview, I catch sight of Loki. He's standing between the street and the driveway. He has some kind of handgun aimed at us, but that's not what scares me. His eyes focus intensely on me, his features are hard as stone, and his body is rigid, unyielding.

"Hit him if you have to, I don't fucking care, just get us out of here," he barks.

But I can't. My up and down feelings for Loki have morphed into something I can't explain even to myself. There's no way I can do what Carlo says. Hurting Loki is an impossibility in my mind.

But Carlo doesn't care. He presses down on my thigh, forcing my foot to shove down hard on the gas. The car lurches back at a speed that sends me flying forward and into the steering wheel. I quickly right myself and try to lift my foot, but he has it pinned down. I crane my head over my shoulder. Loki stands stoic, his gun firing in rapid succession. Each second brings us that much closer and I will him to move. To get out of the way.

At the very last moment, Loki dives to the side, rolling along the sidewalk. Carlo lifts up on my foot and turns the steering wheel, so we end up on the street.

"Drive. Now," Carlo demands.

With shaky hands, I grip the steering wheel and drive us down the road. In the rearview mirror, I see the guys running to the vans. But they're too late. They'll never catch up.

"Where am I going?" I focus on the road ahead. The compound is way on the outskirts of town and there's only one road connecting this area to the city.

"Jump on Veterans. Do not go less than seventy. If I see that speedometer go any slower, I'll start shooting you in places that won't kill you but will hurt you. Badly." He presses the gun into my shoulder.

I accelerate until I reach seventy. The speed limit is forty-five on this road, so I have to weave around slower vehicles. My movements are jerky, making the tires squeal since I'm not used to being behind the wheel.

Carlo presses a button on the touchscreen on the dash. A phone ringing sounds over the speakers.

"What," a stern voice clips.

"Boss, we got a problem. A huge fucking problem." Carlo runs a hand through his hair. "That motorcycle gang, the Royal Bastards, they raided the compound. They took everyone out."

"What?" the voice roars, making me jump. "How did you get out?"

"There was a girl. I grabbed her. I'm sure she was with them."

"Bring her to me. I'm sending a crew to the compound." His deep, raspy voice turns threatening. "And, Carlo?"

"Yeah, Boss."

"If I find out your carelessness has anything to do with this breech, you'll be paying for it with your life."

The line goes dead and Carlo lets out a string of curses.

"This is your fucking fault." He punches the dash with his good hand.

A hot tear runs down my aching cheek.

How am I going to get out of this?

Chapter
TWENTY-ONE

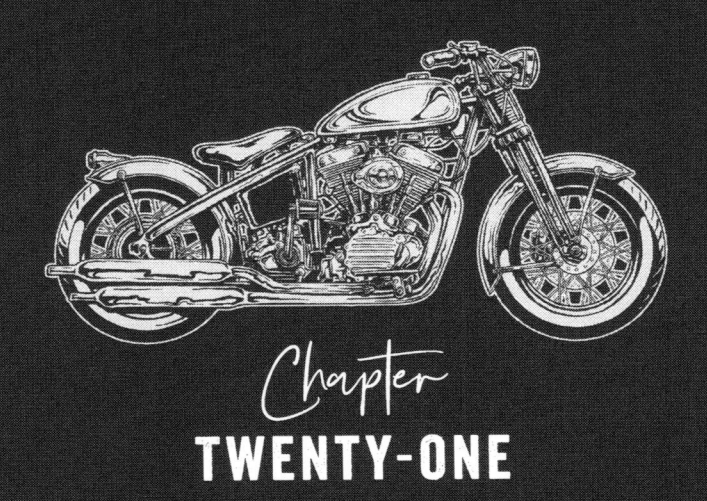

Loki

"**W**hat the fuck?" I roar, watching the blacked-out SUV speed down the road. That car is armored to the max. We couldn't even pop a tire. I should know better than to expect anything different from Dom. "Are we whole?"

I look at each of my brothers, who nod.

"And the virus?" I ask, my eyes on Sly and Moto.

Sly pulls the glass vial from the pocket of his cut. He jiggles it around. At least something went right.

"Chase," Roch roars and motions in the direction Birdie headed.

We sprint to the vans, separating into the same vehicles we drove in.

"Where did he go?" Moto asks when he notices the empty seat next to him in the back.

"Christ. He went to find Karen." I open my door, but I don't even step out when I see Roch running toward us with the tiny, tan dog.

When he's inside, Khan turns over the engine and speeds toward the highway.

"Where am I going?" he thunders.

"If I had to guess, I'd say the club. Where else would he go?" Moto suggests.

"I agree," I say.

As we make our way down the highway, my mind runs through what just happened. Everything was going as planned until it wasn't. Khan, Roch, and I took every single one of those fuckers while Moto and Sly breeched the house.

It was me who missed the kill shot on that last goon. But he was being blocked by Birdie, and I didn't want to clip her. I bend forward, yanking my beanie from my head and tugging at the ends of my hair. I don't know what this emotion is. Yeah, I'm fucking angry he got away, but it's something else. Fear maybe. For her?

Yeah, the bitch was taken, but the vial is where the actual money is. Twenty Gs is nothing compared to the bigger payday. Yet, I already know I won't stop until I have her back. Money or not, she doesn't deserve this. She was only trying to help. And her father? Fuck, he's going to be pissed. He said he didn't want to know the plan, so we didn't bother to check with him. But I seriously doubt he would've been okay with his baby girl being involved.

I dig my cell phone out of my pocket and dial up Sly.

"Yeah, Prez?" he answers.

"I need you guys to go back to the clubhouse. Put that shit in the safe. Bring in the old-timers. Bring the kids and wives in. We're going on lockdown," I order.

"Got it."

I click the end button and turn in my seat. The second van falls behind and turns off the next exit. With the vial safe,

I can at least breathe a little easier. Except why is there a fucking fist around my throat?

Because of Birdie.

I think about what they could be doing to her right this second and I want to break something. It makes it hard for me to sit in this van and not be doing anything. I'm anxious and jittery. I need her back. Even though she'll never be mine. I won't rest until she's free.

"What's the plan when we get there?" Khan asks.

"I don't know. There aren't enough of us to storm in there. Besides, it's in the city. That means there'll be cops. And those cops are most likely on Dom's payroll. Let's just get there and see what we can find out," I say, looking out the window. It's pitch-black out, which might work to our favor.

Minutes later, we pull into the club's parking lot. Feroce is one of the many nightclubs the mafia owns. It's also Dom's home base. He likes to take care of all his business there while being surrounded by beautiful women. But there's also a basement. It's where he takes care of a whole different kind of business. It's where people go to disappear. I've never seen it, but I've heard rumors. We have enough contacts around the city to hear the whisperings of everything Dom does.

The thought of Birdie being down there, being subject to his wrath? It infuriates me more. She may have gotten a glimpse of how the other half lives, but it was just that. A glimpse. I know Dom will delight in showing her all the dark corners of the world. He's a sadistic son of a bitch.

We step out of the van and scan the area. I need proof she's in there before we can proceed.

"Look," Roch says, pointing behind the row of dumpsters. The top of a black SUV is barely showing.

We casually make our way over there. Khan and Moto keep an eye out as Roch and I open the gate behind the club. It's the vehicle we've been looking for. It's littered with dents from the bullets. That means Birdie's inside.

"Shit," I curse.

We walk back to the van, standing behind it so we're hidden from the crew who protects this place. I guarantee they are on guard right now.

"How do you want to handle this?" Khan asks.

"We can't go in, just the four of us. They'll drop us the second we step foot inside," I vocalize the obvious. "But we can't leave her here. We promised to protect her."

"We need to get back to the clubhouse. We can regroup and think this through. Reach out to some of our contacts. We need to be smart about this," Moto says.

Roch and Khan nod, but I can't bring myself to do it. She's in there. Scared and possibly hurt. I can't just walk away.

"I'll go in. Alone. I'll talk to Dom. Figure out how to make this right. If he wants that vial back, he can fucking have it. I don't give two shits if that'll mean jail time for Davis or if Dom uses it for his own benefit. Either way, it doesn't fucking matter, as long as we get her back." I pull out my gun and check how many bullets I have left. Not many. I pull out some ammo from my pocket and reload.

"That's not how this works, bro." Kahn rests a hand on top of my gun. I glare at him for questioning me and he lets go but doesn't stop trying to talk me out of this. "You go in there after we just killed fifteen of his men? You'll be dead before you hit the ground. Let's go back to the clubhouse. Maybe we can call in some nomads and Tonopah. We need to do this the right way if we all want to stay whole and get the girl out alive."

He's right. I know he's fucking right, but it doesn't make the thought of leaving her here any easier.

"Fine. But call our brothers on the way. We need backup," I say to Moto.

We get back in the van. I bring the screen on my phone to life. While Moto is making his calls, I bring up the phone number to the man I am dreading calling the most. Davis' name flashes across the screen and I mash the green button.

"This is Martin," he answers.

"We got your vial back," I reply.

"Thank God. Can we meet tonight? I need to destroy it before it does any more harm."

"Well, there's been a complication."

"What kind of complication? Is Bridgette okay?"

I say nothing, but I hear the moment he knows his daughter's life is in danger. His breath hitches and I hear the thud of him falling to the ground.

"They've taken her," I say.

"No. I gave her to you to protect. I thought she'd be safer…" he trails off.

I explain everything to him. By the time I'm done, the man is crying. Full-on sobs and it's awkward as fuck.

"She's all I have left. I've ignored her for so long and now she's gone," he blubbers.

"Davis!" I snap. "She's not gone. We'll get her back. In the meantime, we're keeping the vial. I don't know if it'll come in handy later, but I don't think we should destroy it just yet."

"No, Loki. You don't understand what that is. A micro drop is all it takes to infect a person. After that, all bodily fluids can spread the virus and within twenty-four hours, they'd be dead. The devastation is unimaginable. We can't let it get into the wrong hands again."

"We won't. But if we destroy it, we lose all of our leverage. Anything that could help us get Birdie back," I argue.

"Birdie?"

I'm so used to calling her by my nickname for her, I didn't even catch my mistake. I don't know how to explain this. I tossed Birdie's cell the day she moved in. She's had no contact with her dad in days. Christ. Has it only been *days?* It feels like she's been under my roof for a lifetime.

"I'll call you when I have an update." I press on.

"Please. Just get my baby girl back," he begs.

I end the call. I'm not into making promises, and I've had enough of him spewing his emotions all over. I'm not his therapist, or even his friend. I'm just the man who got his daughter abducted. And by the end of all this, I'll be the man who rescues her, too.

Let's just hope she's the same person after I get her back.

Chapter
TWENTY-TWO

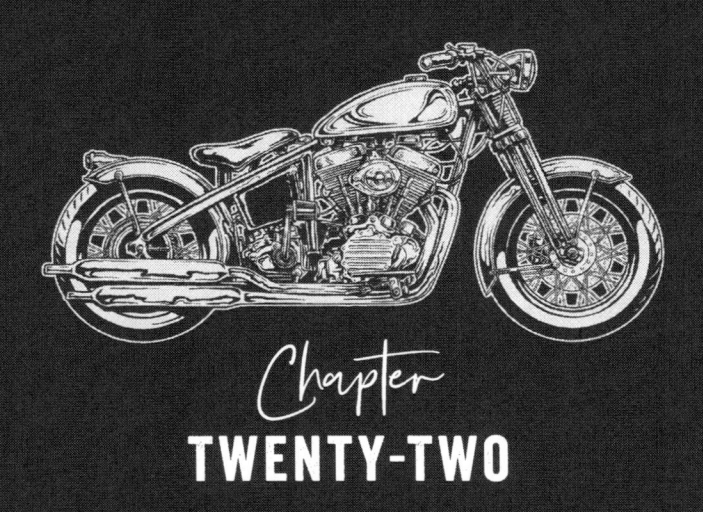

Bridgette

Carlo drags me by my arm through the back door of Feroce. I've heard it's the place to be, but I've never been here. Ruby and Lindsay have both been clubbing here. Using their money and status to gain them entry despite their age. Dance clubs just aren't my thing. I'd much rather be at home with a tub of popcorn and Netflix.

He leads me through a dark hallway and then down an equally dark set of stairs. There are dim red LEDs lining the ceiling, but it's barely enough light to see where you're going. It's cold, both in temperature and feeling.

"Where are you taking me?" I try to jerk from his hold unsuccessfully. I brush a strand of hair off my brow and am reminded I'm still covered in blood. Ricky's blood, my blood, Carlo's blood. I suddenly feel nauseous and desperate for a shower. I have a feeling that won't be happening anytime soon.

"The boss wants to see you."

"Who's the boss?" I ask, but I already know.

"You'll soon find out."

There's a door at the bottom of the stairs and Carlo releases me long enough to bang on it. His other arm hangs limply at his side. I see where the bullet entered his shoulder from behind and I wonder which Royal Bastard shot him and why they didn't aim for his head.

The door opens a crack and a cynical eye topped with a bushy eyebrow peeks out. It disappears, and the door opens fully. We step into a cement box of a room. Off to one side, there are chains hanging from a beam in the ceiling. Off to another is a crude shower head coming off an exposed pipe, a wound-up hose, and a metal grate for a drain. In the center of the room sits one lone chair.

Only one other man is in here, the one who opened the door. He motions for us to move farther inside.

"Boss'll be down in a minute." He leaves us, the door echoing in the empty room when he slams it shut.

"Carlo, there's still time for both of us to escape. I heard Dom. He'll kill you. Why don't we leave right now? Maybe the Royal Bastards will protect you, too," I plead.

"Stupid girl." He lowers his head and shakes it, laughing sardonically. "If you think there is anywhere either of us can hide, think again. My heart may be beating, but I'm already dead."

"If you're already dead, then let me go. It's the same outcome, but you won't be responsible for my murder."

"You want to know the difference? I let you go, and I'm tortured for months without being killed. I keep you here, and he might make it quick. Painless." He pulls a gold chain from under his shirt. It's a rosary. He kisses it and makes the sign of the cross.

I wrap my arms around myself and sink to my haunches. This can't be how I die. Where's Loki? Why hasn't he come for me? I was so stupid. He's larger than life, with more confidence than I ever knew a man could have. Never did it cross my mind he wouldn't keep me safe. He talked me through plenty of scenarios. Every single one ended with him rescuing me and I was so naïve, I believed him. I thought I was brave enough to live in his world. I thought we'd do this one thing and he'd see he wants me. He'd rethink his stance on never having an old lady. He'd want to keep me in the cage of his heart for a lifetime.

For a while he had me thinking I was missing something by staying locked up in my castle. Living a simple and spoiled life. But if this is the alternative, then send me back to my lonely and shallow life. At least I was safe there. Except I wasn't. Not really. Dom broke into my house. He killed Angelo. He shot Daddy. Maybe nowhere is safe. Maybe we all teeter along, never knowing when our time will be up.

The door opens and I stand up, not wanting to look vulnerable when I meet the man who has so thoroughly ruined my life.

A gorgeous man in a custom three-piece suit walks in. It's an Armani. I'd know that fabric and cut anywhere. He has an easy, almost delighted, expression on his face. His hair is cropped close on the sides, longer on top, and swooped back. He looks more like a model than a gangster. He flashes me a blindingly white smile. It's fake. Everything about him is a carefully constructed facade. I only know this because I have one too. One I've spent years perfecting.

"Miss Davis, I presume?" He lifts my hand and brings it to his cold, stiff lips. The second they touch, I jerk back. "You're a spirited one."

"Why am I here?" I ask.

He ignores me, turns to Carlo, and gestures for him to sit in the chair. "You guys fucked up. I watched the video before it cut out. You let her inside, you allowed her to distract you from your only job. But you brought her to me, so for that you'll be rewarded."

I don't even see it coming. One second Dom is lifting Carlo's chin and the next, he's slicing across his throat.

"No!" I cry out in reflex. I have no feelings for Carlo, but I still don't want to watch him die.

Dom releases Carlo and he makes a sickening choking sound I doubt I'll ever be able to scrub from my mind. His pained eyes meet mine. He reaches up to his neck, gripping it as if he can stop the river of blood from leaving his body. I try to look away. I don't want to see this. But I can't. Even as tears blur my vision, I still see.

Dom paces around the room, pulling a cloth from his pocket and wiping away the blood. Once cleaned to his satisfaction, he tosses it onto the dying man's lap.

A gurgling noise comes from Carlo, and then he falls off the chair and onto the floor. Although his eyes remain open, he stares blankly in front of him and I know he's dead.

"Why would you do that?" I yell, wiping at my eyes. The hands come back with black smudges and dried blood. I know I'm a mess, but I couldn't care less.

"This is what happens when I'm betrayed. I thought it was important to see because you, my dear, top a lengthy list of people who betrayed me today. The only reason you aren't lying there next to him is because you're worth more alive than dead. For now, anyway." He stops in front of me, placing his hands in his pockets casually. "But that won't be the case forever."

He walks away, whistling, through the door and back up the stairs. The bushy eyebrow man reemerges holding a stack of clothes.

"Boss wants you to shower." He thrusts the clothes at me.

"Wh-where?"

His head jerks at the rusty shower head on the other end of the room.

"But what about him?" My eyes land on Carlo's dead body.

"Someone will come for him, eventually."

I take the clothes and he leaves. I hear the lock engage before he stomps up the stairs. Leaving me alone with a dead body. I'm trembling, cold and afraid. There are no windows in this room to give me hope of escape. Only a locked door I have no hopes of getting past.

I skirt past Carlo and over to the shower. My need to wipe away the blood and gore is too strong to deny. I turn the dial and ice-cold water sprays in all directions. I twist the knob in the opposite direction, searching for hot water, but it's still glacial. I can't shower in this. The room is already like a freezer. My teeth chatter and gooseflesh covers my skin.

Instead, I scoop handfuls onto my face to rinse the blood and makeup. I'm sure I look something like a drowned raccoon, but it's better than catching pneumonia. Besides, the only soap is a shriveled old bar that has cobwebs and dirt crusted into it. I'm not putting that on my skin.

When I'm done, I sit down in the farthest corner from Carlo. My feet are throbbing from the cheap heels, so I yank them off and stretch my toes. I look through the clothes bushy eyebrows brought me. A short, thin cotton dress and a pair of panties. That's all. I ignore the dress since it's skimpier than the one I have on, but since the panties appear to be new, I pull them up my legs. Going commando seemed like a good idea earlier when I wanted to look hot for Loki. Now I feel too bare, and I need all the barriers I can get from anyone who comes into this room.

I use the dress as a pillow and curl into a ball on my side, facing the wall so I don't have to look at Carlo. Last week I was lying out by the pool, sunning myself and feeling bad I was all alone but not wanting to call my fake friends. Three days ago, I was locked in a cage, feeling bad I was being treated like an animal. Today, I'm trapped in a room with a dead body, quite possibly hours from being killed myself.

How the mighty have fallen. Except I was never mighty, was I? More like a pathetic sheep who hoped for more but never attempted to achieve it.

I wish Loki had let me keep my cell phone. Then I would've been able to call him. Tell him where I am. An idea pops into my head. They didn't search me or Carlo when we came down here. He had a cell phone on him. And a gun.

I crawl slowly over to him, my body trembling from the cold and really not wanting to touch a dead body. I pull open his suit jacket and see his gun tucked into his waistband. I've never handled a gun before, but I must learn fast. It might be the only thing to keep me alive. I pull it out, feeling its weight, and practice pointing it. I set it down on the ground to look for his phone.

Carlo's eyes are still open, and it creeps me out. I really don't want to touch him, to root around in his pockets, but I also need to call Loki. I hold his pant pocket open and reach in. Keys. A wallet. Bingo, a cell phone. I tug it free and take it and the gun back over to my corner.

Shit. His phone is fingerprint protected. I crawl back

over and stare at Carlo's limp hand. I don't know if I can do it. Touch his dead skin. But then I look around and see just how dire things are. I have to. I take a calming breath and on an exhale, I grip his thumb. It's cold and… dead. I drop it and shoot up onto my feet.

"Ew. Ew. Ew." I dance around on my tiptoes in disgust. A shudder shoots up my spine and I force myself to still. I have to do this, and I need to be quick. I don't know when they'll be back.

I will myself back over and crouch on my haunches. I lift his thumb and place it over the sensor on the phone. Nothing happens. I bring the phone to life by touching the screen and try again. Still nothing.

What the heck.

Then I realize his thumb is too cold with the lack of blood flow through his body. I remember on a ski weekend in Aspen, I had a hard time getting my phone to recognize my thumb. I know what I have to do next, I just really, really don't want to. I hold his thumb in my hand, hoping despite how cold I am, it will be enough. Seconds feel like hours as I try to warm him.

I close my eyes and picture my last good memory. Riding on the back of Loki's bike, pressed against his muscular back, the warm summer air breeze through my hair, and the hint of promise that maybe we could be something to each other.

I press Carlo's thumb to the sensor again, and it unlocks. I scurry back to my corner and bring up the dial screen.

"Damn it!" I shout to no one. I don't have his phone number. Actually, I don't know anyone's number by heart. I've become reliant on the pre-programming of my phone. The only number I know by heart is Daddy's.

I reluctantly dial the numbers. I haven't spoken to him in so long and so much has happened. I blink back tears as it rings. He answers on the fourth ring.

"Hello?" His voice is rough and raspy, as if he's been shouting.

"Daddy?" I croak out, emotion clogging my throat.

"Bridgette? Is it really you? Are you safe? Where are you?" He doesn't even pause before throwing out an additional question.

"Daddy, stop and listen. I'm at a club downtown. Dom has me. I need Loki's number. Right now. They'll be back any second and they'll take this phone away."

"I'm so sorry, honey. I never meant for this to—"

"Daddy. Stop. There'll be time for this later. Please, just give me Loki's number," I beg.

"O-okay."

He gives me the number and I repeat it over and over in my head so I won't forget.

"I love you. I have to go."

"Wait!" He stops me before I can hang up. "Just tell me. Are you okay?"

"I'm okay for now, but I don't know for how much longer. I need to go."

"I love you. Be brave. We'll get you out of this and I'll take you on a vacation. Wherever you want to go. You can have the credit card and shop until you drop," he says. A month ago, this would've made me happy. Now it just reminds me of my inconsequential existence.

"I love you. Talk soon." I end the call before I can get any more worked up. It's not the time or place to have an existential crisis.

My nose runs and I wipe it with the back of my hand before mashing in Loki's number.

"Yeah," he answers on the first ring.

Just the sound of his voice floods me with emotion, and tears fill my eyes. My voice catches and a sob breaks free.

"Birdie? That you? Talk to me," he soothes.

Chapter
TWENTY-THREE

Loki

"Loki, I need you," Birdie says through a wail. It tugs at my heart and fills my soul with even more rage than I've been feeling since I saw her leave in that SUV.

"I know, darlin'. I'm coming. I just need you to hang on for a bit longer, okay?" I snap my fingers, gaining Khan's attention. We've been holed up in the Chapel for hours now, reaching out and gathering everyone we can. We need numbers because Dom doesn't fly solo. Those Italian pricks are like cockroaches; you kill one and ten more come out of the woodwork.

"I can't. I can't do this. I can't be locked down here with a dead body. Please, come now," she pleads.

"Whose dead body? Tell me where you are in the club."

Khan sits down next to me, handing me a piece of paper and a pen so I can write down as much information as I can get from her.

"Carlo, the man who took me. Dom slit his throat. I'm in the basement. It's a concrete room." She sniffles and I throw my fist into the wall, breaking clean through the sheetrock. I can't fucking stand to hear her crying, not when her tears aren't for me.

"Fuck. Okay. I've got my brothers from the Tonopah chapter coming in. One night. That's all you have to do. Just hang on, Birdie. Be brave."

"I'm not brave. I'm just a dumb, rich girl. Remember? I wasn't built for this." Her cries turn into sobs. I want to wrap her in my arms, protect her from the world, but that's not where we're at right now. I need my fiery little badass to come out. It's the only way she'll survive this.

"Stop your fucking pity party right now, Birdie," I bite out. It kills me to not comfort her, but I can't allow her to be vulnerable, not when the sharks are circling.

The line goes quiet and for a second, I think she's hung up. I pull the phone from my ear and see it's still connected. I wait for her to speak.

"Are you kidding me right now? You're safe in your clubhouse and you think you have the right to tell *me* to be brave?" Gone is the crying and I know I'm playing this the right way.

"I didn't stutter," I say.

"You're unbelievable. You know that? I hate you so much," she grits out. If she were here, I know I'd see color creeping up her cheeks, her round eyes would narrow and turn stormy, and those perfect rosebud lips would be pursed. Fuck, I wish I could see that.

"There's my girl. Now keep that. Don't show your weakness, Birdie. He'll use it against you. Stay mad."

"That'll be easy. I'll picture your stupid face."

I smile. She doesn't mean it, but it's good to hear her backbone back in place.

"Don't lie. You love my face." I flirt.

"Not right now, I don't. And I swear if you don't get your ass—"

I hear a man's voice and then Birdie screams. There's a thump and then a blood-curdling, terrifying scream. My stomach hits the ground and I want to throw up. I rip my beanie from my head and throw it across the room.

"I'm assuming this is Trucker?" Dom's deep voice fights to be heard over Birdie's shouts.

"No, dick. This is Trucker's son, Loki. I'm also the guy who'll string you from your toes and allow our dogs to rip your flesh from your bones."

"That right?" he asks. "Your dad couldn't take us on, why do you think you can do any better?"

"We weren't prepared before. We're ready now. And this time, we'll win the fight, motherfucker," I growl. "And if you touch a hair on her head, I'll make you pay in ways you can't even imagine."

"You guys did a suitable job at slutting her up, but I did a lot of research on Mr. Davis. I think having his daughter in my possession might be an even bigger motivator than the vial. But your reaction has me curious. This your girl?" he asks.

"She's not my anything, but she's under my protection and I will get her back."

Dom laughs, a dark and sinister sound that only further pisses me the fuck off. Then I hear something I will never forget. Something that will haunt my nightmares for the rest of my life.

"No! No! No!" Birdie cries out followed by a loud thud and then nothing. No sound.

"Sorry, had to shut the bitch up. If you want to see her

alive, I suggest you bring me my money. Only the price has doubled. Let Davis know for me, would you?"

"You can quadruple the price. It makes no difference. By the end of the day tomorrow, you'll be dead."

"You know, your dad said the same thing to me after I killed your mom. That didn't work out either, did it? I got the gun business, and you all ran away with your tails between your legs. So excuse me if your threats aren't taken seriously. You have twenty-four hours. I'll be in touch with where we'll do the trade-off."

The line goes dead and I hurl the phone across the room, shattering it to pieces. I hate that he won the last time we went to war, but this time is different. I swear with every fiber of my being, I will kill that motherfucker.

"Sly, grab an extra phone and swap SIMs," Khan orders.

"Sure," he says, leaving the room.

"Brother, what happened? What did he say?" Khan asks.

"She's at the club, but we already knew that. In the basement. A cement room." I list off all the details she gave me. "Dom wants double the money, or he'll kill her. I don't even know how Davis would get that much money in cash. But I don't want it to get to that. We bowed down to that shithead once and we can't do it again. He needs to be taken out."

My brothers bang their fists on the table in solidarity. This is why I chose the life of an MC. Who else would put their lives on the line for you? Who else would stand next to you in a firing squad out of loyalty? All these mindless fuckers who have thousands of friends on social media think it means shit. Sure, their "friends" will click a button to like a post, but will they be there for you when shit gets real? Fat fucking chance.

"So where are we at?" I ask.

"Tonopah's on their way. They're sending Mammoth, Rael, and Diablo. I've also called in some Nomads. Dunk, Mac, and Coyote answered. They've been riding down the coast, so it'll take them a little longer to get here. We can probably be organized by tomorrow afternoon," Moto says.

"Good." They're all brutal motherfuckers, perfect for what I need.

"Trucker called. Said he got the day mixed up. Said he's around if we need him," Goblin says cautiously.

My dad is the last person I want to see right now. He talked a big game, but when it came down to it, he was missing in action. I don't have the time or energy to deal with his bullshit, so I push him to the back burner. I'll have a lot to say when this is over, but he's more of a liability at this point.

"Roch, how are we looking with ammo and weapons? We'll need every fuckin' thing." I turn to my Sergeant at Arms.

He gives me a thumbs-up. I quirk a brow and he sighs, leaning forward and resting his arms on the table.

"M82s, Five-sevens, Mossbergs, ammo, all good."

"Thanks, bro."

He's torn up about Birdie. All my brothers are. Somehow that little thing snuck her way into the hearts of everyone. Even Tabitha and Sissy are cut up about it. But no one more than me. I can't fucking stand the thought of her being there, Dom doing fuck knows what with her, while I sit here and do shit. We've got to be smart, though. We're taking him down, not just for now, but for forever. By tomorrow night, Hades will have another soul to burn.

I head off into my room, needing some time without prying eyes. I'm fucking raw, battling why I feel this tightness in my chest. I can't even remember the last time I cried, but hearing Birdie's voice almost caused that forgotten emotion to surface. Even when Ma died, I didn't shed a tear. She knew our life and knew it was always a possibility that we'd piss off the wrong people and suffer retaliation.

But Birdie, she had no fucking clue about my world. Sure, she'd gotten bits and pieces while she was living under our roof, but she didn't see the underbelly. The place where even the dark things get darker. Where black goes pitch and ain't no one who didn't grow up this way can prepare for that.

I pull out my kit and set it on my nightstand. I've got another two tallies to make for the Italian assholes I took out earlier. In ritualistic fashion, I sterilize, load the ink, and mark my flesh. Staring down at the crude lines, I visualize where Dom's will go, but I won't allow myself to ink my flesh with it yet. I won't deserve it until his soul has left his body.

I've just tucked away everything when I hear the roar of motorcycles outside. I find my Tonopah brothers sitting at the bar when I've finally composed myself enough to step out of my room.

"Loki, brother, how the hell are you?" Rael stands and gives me a shoulder pounding man hug. I take in the three of them with their skull painted faces. It's creepy as fuck.

"Thanks for coming, man. We need the manpower."

"No problem. Been meaning to make a stop in Carson City, anyway. Kill two birds with one stone."

"I've asked Dunk, Mac, and Coyote to join us. As soon as they get here, I'll explain everything." I sit down at the bar and Jake sets a shot of tequila in front of me.

We have a few drinks, catching up until the nomads show. Then I call everyone into the Chapel. I'm about to shut the door when I notice the prospects cleaning up after us.

"Clint, Jake, get your asses in here."

Their eyes widen, and grins appear on their faces. They're good kids and they've done a lot to prove themselves. It's only right to bring them in on this. If they hold their own, I'll patch both of them in.

My brothers cheer and bang on the table as the dopey prospects enter. The only jobs we've given them are cleaning and guarding the property. Soon, we'll see if they can take lives too.

I spend the next hour breaking down everything that's happened and everything I know about Dom's operation. Then I go over the plan for tomorrow. After everyone gives their feedback and they've taken my plan from a house on stilts to a fucking fortress, we call it a night.

"I just want to thank Tonopah and the Nomads for being here. It's not your mess to clean up, and I'm honored you were so quick to be at my side. Cheers." We clink our beers and go in separate directions to get some sleep.

Tabitha and Sissy prepared the spare bedrooms for Mammoth, Rael, and Diablo. But Mac, Dunk, and Coyote head outside to pitch their tents. All three are retired military and can't stand to be in-between enclosed walls for too long.

As I pull back my covers and climb in bed, I get a whiff of grapefruit and pull the pillow Birdie'd been using just last night to my chest. I don't know what she's going through right now, but I pray she can hang on a little longer.

Chapter
TWENTY-FOUR

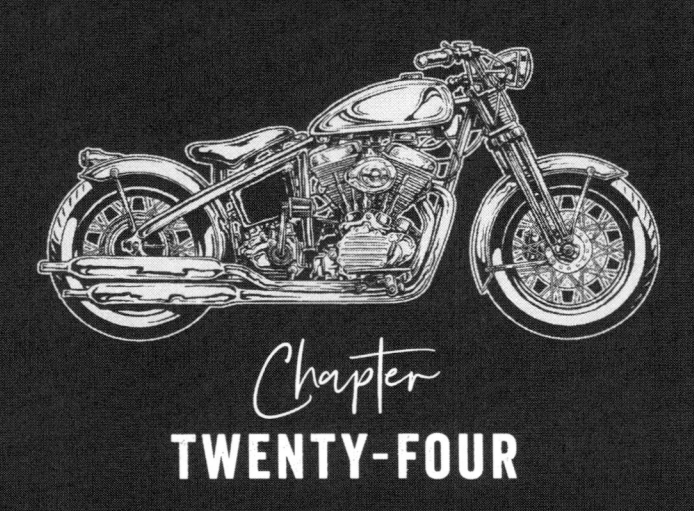

Bridgette

I wake up with my head throbbing and chilly water pouring down my face. I look up and see I'm now under the shower. I taste something metallic and brush under my nose. My hand comes back with bright red blood on it. I look around, still trying to focus, but my head is pounding, and my vision is blurry. My teeth chatter from the ice-cold spray. I try to crawl away, but a firm foot presses into my lap.

"Welcome back," a deep voice says. I turn to my left and see Dom. "You don't take directions very well, do you?"

"What?" I ask, confusion fogging my mind.

"You were told to shower and get dressed," he says.

"T-the w-water, it's cold. There was no t-towel." I stumble over my words from my uncontrollable shivering.

"Loki must be soft if he hasn't broken you." He removes his foot and drops the disgusting bar of soap on my lap. "Now remove your dress and wash."

I stare at him in disbelief. It wasn't long ago Loki had

demanded the same thing from me, but with him, I didn't feel dirty. I didn't have the same fear I have with Dom. I don't want to show this man my body. I don't want his wandering eyes on me.

"Maybe you need encouragement to obey." He rears back and kicks my hip. I fall to the side and cry out. "When I ask you to do something, you do it. It's simple."

I push myself to sitting, then to my knees, then finally to my feet. My whole body trembles. My bones hurt and my lungs feel like they're going to explode. I've never been this cold in my life.

Dom watches me expectantly while motioning for me to speed things along. I reach for the hem on my dress and pull it over my head. The panties I put on earlier cover my private parts and I hold my arms over my breasts. I rub the withered and dry soap across my belly, trying to ignore the smear of dirt it left on my skin.

Dom reaches over and tugs my arm down. My head lulls back and I stare at the ceiling. I'm humiliated and I can't meet his gaze. I don't want his leering gaze etched into my memory.

"Mmm. Look at what you were hiding. Bellissima, my pet." He cups one of my breasts before sliding down to my nipple and clamping down on it with his fingers. He tugs hard, sending even more sharp pain through my body.

I bite back the urge to scream and cry. Loki told me to be brave. He told me I'd only make it out if I was strong. I can do that for him. I can survive this.

He gives my other breast the same treatment before his roaming hand skirts down my belly and to the band on my panties. I should've known they wouldn't stop him.

"Now let's see what you're hiding under these." He doesn't

pull them down like a human being, no. He rips them from my body.

Still, I look up. There are tiny cracks in the gray cement, spidering in all directions. I follow each path, trying to focus on anything but the hums of approval coming from Dom.

"Such a pretty pussy. I'd ask if you're a virgin, but I don't think Loki would fight so hard for you unless he's been between these thighs." He smacks my thigh. Because my skin already feels like tiny needles are repetitively stabbing it from the icy water, the strike feels like bee stings. "Spread."

I don't. He may violate me any which way he wants because of his size, but I won't make it easy for him. I can't. I keep my legs squeezed tight despite the weakness in my muscles.

He grips my chin and moves it down. I pinch my eyes shut. "You're so defiant. Some men like girls who bend to their will from the get-go, the ones who check out mentally when put in a stressful situation. But I love strong-willed women. It's so rewarding when I finally break their will. Now, open your eyes."

Again, I leave them shut. I won't give him what he wants. He thinks he can break me, but he doesn't know me. If I've learned anything since the day I left my sprawling mansion, it's that I'm a survivor. No matter the situation.

I feel Dom's deep rumble of laughter against my cheek, making me aware of just how close he is. Then the sound stops abruptly, like it was never real to begin with. He slams me against the hard concrete and wraps a muscular hand around my throat. Not in the way Loki did it, with possessive hunger and barely-there pressure. Dom's intentions are to choke me, to cut off my air, to hurt me. I cough and sputter, my windpipe completely depressed.

"You want to be a brat, you'll be punished like one. Now open your eyes and I'll let go," he grinds out.

I try to rip his hand away from my throat, but it's no use. He has a death grip on it. I keep my eyes closed. I'm no good to him dead, making me semi confident he'll let go before I die. But with every second he denies my lungs the air they need, the more my body screams for me to listen until my legs spread on their own. Immediately, he releases me. I bend over, gasping loudly until I can breathe normally. He waits until I've regained control of myself before gripping my shoulder roughly and shoving me back into the concrete.

"See? This relationship can be so easy. I ask. You obey. You stay alive."

My eyes meet his and what I see has me wishing he'd just kill me. He's vacant. A shell of a human. No soul living behind his brown depths. His features are all sharp. A pointed noise, a strong jawline, and a dimple in his tapered chin.

"Now spread your fucking legs." He's losing his patience. I need a new tactic.

I slowly step my legs out. The cold water sluices between my legs. I watch as Dom's eyes lower to the apex of my thighs. His lips part as he takes me in. I almost welcome the flush of embarrassment as it heats my body.

"Now wash," he demands.

I take the bar I've been squeezing in my hand and wash down below. I better not catch an infection from the soap. That would be the icing on my craptastic cake. To live through this and catch a flesh-eating bacterium on my vagina.

He spreads my outer lips open, exposing my clit. "Such an adorable little button."

"Such a weird compliment," I mock.

"Your fire's back, I see." He shoves a calloused finger into my dry opening, scraping my insides along the way. The intrusion has me trying to pull away to remove the penetration. "Nice and tight. Just like I thought."

He abruptly pulls out and turns the water off. He wipes his wet hands on his pants and then pulls his cell phone from his pocket. He types something out while I stand there frozen in place. My toes and fingers are blue, and I'd do anything for my steam shower right now.

He watches me for a minute before the steel door opens, and another large Italian man walks in. He scans my naked form, but only briefly. He hands Dom a towel and then he's gone.

"Come here." He holds the towel open.

Out of sheer desperation for any kind of cover, I go to him. He wraps the towel around me, and I secure it in the front and cross my arms to ensure it'll stay put. It's threadbare and stained with God knows what, but I don't care.

"Dry off and put on the dress I gave you earlier. I'll be back in a while. I need to go get out of my wet clothes. When I come back, the fun can really begin." He leaves the room without a backward glance.

I stumble to my corner and collapse, my frozen body not able to hold me up any longer. I draw my knees to my chest and curl into myself. I don't know when he'll be back, but I figure I have time to warm myself up. I rub roughly up and down my arms, trying to work blood through my limbs.

Carlo still lies dead in the center of the room. It's a stark reminder of where I am and the people I'm dealing with. I can't test Dom anymore. I need to stay alive until Loki gets here, even if that means being agreeable. Swallowing my pride will be a bitter pill but allowing this narcissist of a man to steal me of my life is worse.

With that thought in mind, I remove the towel from my body and wrap my hair up in it instead. The dress, if you can call it that, barely covers my behind and dips dangerously low in the front. I still don't have a bra, so I'm sure the look is obscene.

I towel dry my hair and finger comb it the best I can. My hair is naturally kinky, so I'm sure it will be a frizzy disaster, but what do I care? I'm definitely not here to impress anyone. Actually, the worse I look, the better. I rub the towel over my eyes to remove the makeup and then I wait.

My mind spins with a hundred possibilities about what he means by "fun." Judging by his violating touches, I'm sure I won't like it. Will I be able to let him use my body just to stay alive? The thought of that greasy man's penis inside me makes me want to vomit. But there are worse things he could do. I've seen *Dateline*. I've read the newspaper. I shudder, wondering what he's into.

My eyes become heavy, exhausted from the events of the day, when the door flies open. Dom appears, dressed immaculately in a three-piece charcoal gray suit with a navy-blue tie. The large man who gave him the towel is two steps behind. He has a black bag and some kind of saw in his hands. It's circular and big.

My eyes flitter from Carlo to the man as he kneels down and opens the black bag. Dom approaches me and holds out his hand to help me up. I stare at it a moment, but the second I hear that ominous looking saw turn on, I obey the unspoken demand. He places my hand in the crook of his elbow and walks me to the door.

Right before he leads me up the stairs, I see the man cutting clean through Carlo's shoulder and placing his arm in the bag. I gasp and my bare feet miss the first stair. Dom saves me from falling and huffs in irritation at my clumsiness.

We make it to the dark hallway and instead of turning left, where I know the exit is, he leads me right. Toward the loud music. We step out into the club. There's over a thousand people crammed into the space. Strobe lights flash and the house music I hate so much is at ear piercing levels.

We walk around the edge of the dance floor until we get to a roped-off section that leads up to a balcony. A man holds the rope open and gives Dom a chin lift. He scans me and I use my eyes to plead with him. Hoping he can see I'm in danger. I don't have shoes on, my hair is a tangled mess on my head, and I'm certain there's still streaks of mascara staining my cheeks. But he doesn't look at me any differently than he would a speck of dirt on his shoe.

On the balcony, there are a slew of women in all states of undress. Some are slumped into the velvet sofas, some are sitting on the ground, leaning over a table covered in a white powder, and some sit perched on men's laps, grinding down on them. I've only seen scenes like this in movies. In my gullible mind, it was overdramatized theatrics. Not something that exists in real life. Tears prickle and I roughly wipe them away.

Dom leads me over to a high-back, tufted chair. He sits and yanks my arm violently until I'm forced to the ground at his feet. He surveys the club, situated like a king on his throne. I tuck my knees under me and tug the short dress down my thighs as far as it will go.

A woman saunters over and steps between Dom's legs, her hands going to his thighs. She's in a silky red dress that hangs torn from her shoulder, revealing an enormous fake boob. Her eyelids are droopy and there's a white film under her nose.

"Dom, it's good to see you," she slurs.

He reaches up and pinches her nipple. He pulls and stretches her flesh until she winces and lets out a hiss. With his other hand, he slaps the drawn out skin hard. Instead of jerking away and trying to escape, she moans like he's making her feel good.

"On your knees," he orders, and she complies. Sinking down so she's next to me. She turns her head briefly and sneers at me like she thinks I'm her competition. Dom rustles around, unbuckling his pants. "Pull me out and suck me."

Like a kid digging into a bag of candy, she excitedly unzips his pants and reaches in. She pulls out his penis. It's already hard and the head of it is purple and angry looking. She lowers her lips and kisses it almost sweetly. I can't watch anymore, so I turn to look at the crowd below. So many fortunate people, dancing and partying, unaware of what's happening above them. Or maybe they are. I feel like I know nothing anymore. Like good people are a rarity.

Wet slurping and gagging noises come from inches away next to me. I cover my ears with the palms of my hand, trying to block it out. I don't want to be here. I don't know how I'll get out. I'm trapped in a nightmare, desperate to return to my cage in Loki's room. What I thought was my prison was really my protection.

I catch movement in my periphery and when I peer over next to me, Dom is tossing the woman to the side. She hits her head on the coffee table and falls limply to the ground.

"Dumb bitch doesn't know how to suck cock." Dom stands up and yanks on my hair. The sting from my scalp makes me flinch and I scramble to my knees. "Open your goddamn mouth. And I swear to God, if your teeth even touch my cock, I'll blow your brains out all over those people down there."

He grips the base of his penis and I come face-to-face with it. My stomach turns just thinking about putting that vile thing inside any of my orifices and bile tries to make its way up my esophagus, but I swallow it down. If just having my teeth touch him has that kind of consequence, I don't know want to know what he'd do for having vomit get on him.

"I said fucking open, my pet." He thrusts toward me again and shame washes over me. This is what he's reduced me to. The beautiful and upcoming socialite, Bridgette Davis, is now being forced to perform sexual acts on the leader of the mafia.

My lips barely part, but it's enough to have him shove inside. I relax my jaw, trying to accommodate his size, but it's hard and the joint instantly aches. I don't know how I'll do this. I have the urge to bite the offending object clean off and as much as I want to stay alive, death might be a suitable alternative to this.

With a fistful of my hair, he jackhammers into my mouth. He hits the back of my throat with such force, I'm positive he'll bruise me. I try to let it happen. I try not to gag. But I do anyway. Acidic bile fills my mouth and leaks down my chin. I squeeze my eyes shut and try to push him away, but he holds tight. I gag again, causing even more vomit to flood my mouth.

He notices the flood of liquid and pulls out. He wipes my chin and shoves his fingers into my mouth. I wretch and fall forward, catching myself with my hands. I've never felt so disgusting, so used, so repulsive. Everything about this is wrong and I wish it would just be over. Be done with. I can't take much more.

With another yank of my hair, I'm back to my knees. I don't look up at him, scared of what he'll do next. What horrors I have yet to experience. I don't want to find out.

"Such a repugnant whore. I don't know what Loki sees in you. Can't even suck cock." He tosses me to the side, and I tumble to the ground. I roll into a ball, covering my head and tucking my knees in.

It's then I check out. My brain's done trying to process everything that's happening. I stare unseeing, my awareness drifting into a state of oblivion. Things are better here. No Carlo being chopped into pieces. No Dom trying to pound a hole into my throat. No club full of whores and drugs.

Just peace and quiet in the dark corners of my mind. No one can touch me here. No one can violate me. I'm safe.

Chapter
TWENTY-FIVE

Loki

I'm going out of my mind wanting to leave this clubhouse and find my girl. I've spent the day pacing the floors, watching as the seconds and minutes and hours pass by, just waiting until it's time to ride. My brothers take care of any lingering details, only approaching me when it's necessary to get my opinion on something.

I'm a fucking dick when I answer, not holding back my barely controlled rage. Not knowing what Birdie's going through, what that fucker is doing to her, has me riding on the edge of sanity. I need to know she's okay, need to know she's safe. It doesn't help that her stupid-ass father texts me over and over, demanding answers. Answers I can't give him. Not yet. So, I ignore the constant vibration coming from my pocket.

I step out back, needing some fresh air. I'm instantly surrounded by wagging tails and lulling tongues. I reach a hand down and give each one a scratch behind their ears. I'll admit, just being around them lowers my blood pressure. I feel the noose around my neck loosen slightly, making it easier to breathe and think.

"Prez?" Roch pushes his way through the dogs and stands next to me. For as excited as they were to see me, they're even more excited when their owner arrives. He crouches down and pays each one attention.

"Yeah?" I reply.

"Y'okay?"

"I'll be better when this is over. I need her back." I'm not an emotional person, but Birdie makes me stupid. She has me all twisted up inside. I hate feeling out of control and irrational. But at the same time, I won't ever let her go again. She might want nothing to do with me after this, but I don't give a fuck. I've gone insane.

"Okay," he deadpans like it's just that easy, and maybe to him it is. He works in absolutes. Either things are or they aren't. And to him, just based on my declaration, she will come back to me.

I nod and pound him once on the back, thanking him in my own way. His eyes close for the briefest of seconds and I'd fucking kill to know what goes on in his head. To know his story. But it's not my business. I know the second we step off this property, he'll turn into the beast he tries to hide from the world, doing anything to bring my girl home. That's all I need to know.

Fucking finally, the time comes for us to leave. It's risky storming into the club when it's packed full of partygoers, but it's also the best option. The crowd will make it easier to come in unnoticed. The chaos that'll ensue will help us get out of there.

We hop onto our bikes, not giving a fuck if they hear us coming. Only the prospects ride in a van, and that's because I didn't know what kind of shape my little birdie was going to be in. If she'd be fit to ride. Our plan is to go hard and go fast. Two-by-two we speed through the streets of downtown, people stopping and staring, some ducking into stores out of fear.

I let all my anxiety flow out my limbs as the road passes under my tires. Now that we're here, now that she's almost mine again and I'll soon be sending Dom to Hades, it's excitement that fills my veins. I dream of all the ways I can kill him. All the ways I can make him pay. But at this point, I won't be picky. As long as I can watch the life drain from his eyes, I'll take it.

It's dark out and we pull up to the Italian restaurant next to the club. It's also owned by Dom, but there aren't as many cars, so we can park together. We don't waste time. We tuck our weapons into the back of our pants and make our way to the back door. Bass from the music rattles the latch and when I try to turn the knob, I find it locked.

Sly jumps in front of me and crouches down. He takes all of three seconds to pick the lock before he swings the door open. We pull out our guns and storm through the door. The huge-ass motherfucker guarding the exit catches a bullet between his eyes before he can even reach his gun. He falls with a thud to the ground, blocking our path down the narrow hallway. Khan pushes to the front of the line and drags his ass out of the way.

"Time to party," he says, leading the way.

Knowing Birdie's in the basement, the second we get to a set of stairs going down, Khan stands by to let me go first. Something feels off, like there should be more men around guarding the basement. The door at the bottom is locked. I rear back and kick it. It budges but doesn't open. It takes two more tries before the door flies open. With my gun raised and ready, I walk into the room. It's just as Birdie described. An empty cement box. In the center is a chair, and under it is a large dark stain. Blood. It's otherwise empty.

"Fuuuuuuck!" I roar.

"Prez," Goblin says, and I turn my gaze to him. He's holding Birdie's black dress. The one she was wearing yesterday.

"Where the fuck is she?" I ask.

"Couldn't be that easy." Khan sighs and racks the slide on his gun. "Guess we'll do it the hard way."

I take the steps two at a time back to the main level. Going farther down the hallway will dump us into the club, but we have no choice. If Birdie's here, we have to find her. The dance floor is full of people grinding on one another shoulder to shoulder. I scan the room. It's a standard club with a couple bars along the walls.

Goblin pats my shoulder and points to a set of stairs being watched over by another one of Dom's goons. I look up to see a balcony. There're a few women leaning over the guardrail, drinks in hand.

"Maybe they're up there," I yell to Khan, then turn to the crowd of men behind me. "Tonopah, stay here and make sure no one else comes down this hallway. Mac, Dunk, Coyote, stay at the bottom of the stairs and watch our backs. Jake and Clint, mix in down here and be ready for whoever needs you."

Kahn lifts his chin and we head that way. He sneaks up

behind the fucker blocking the stairs, wraps his arm around his throat, and presses metal into his head. The man holds his hands up in surrender. Khan walks him to the wall and slams his head against the hard surface. He collapses into a heap on the ground. No one even so much as glances over, too absorbed in their dancing and drinking. Oblivious to the danger that's come knocking on the door of the club.

I slowly make my way up the stairs. The second I can see the entire top level, I stop and scan the area. Deep purple sofas and chairs are scattered throughout. A large glass-top coffee table has mountains of coke on it and half naked bitches take turns sniffing the shit up their noses.

A few dudes sit on the furniture while girls dance and grind on their laps. In the center of the fucking room is Dom. A girl bounces on his dick and another stands to his side with her legs spread while he finger fucks her roughly. Both look fucked up and probably don't even know where they're at right now, let alone what they're doing.

I don't see the girl we came for, though. It worries me. If she isn't down there, and she isn't up here, where the fuck is she?

Two of the girls snorting dust stand up to make way for two more to take their place. It clears the area in front of Dom for a split second. Long enough for me to see a tiny girl sitting on the ground at Dom's feet. She's practically naked, her dress torn, and she's barefoot. I'm not even sure it's Birdie until she looks in my direction for the briefest of seconds. She looks hollow and blank, but I'd still recognize those deep brown eyes anywhere.

I take a deep breath and take the final five steps. We fan out undetected until a gunshot rings out from down below.

Dom jumps to his feet, sending the girl on his lap flying forward and into the railing. He tucks his cock back in his pants and looks over the edge. He must see my men because his eyes make a wipe sweep before looking to the side and seeing us.

The gunshot has made the partiers aware something's going on and they need to get out. Everything happens all at once. A riot breaks out downstairs from the sound of it, the bass thumping music comes to a screeching halt, and it's not much better up here. The girls scream and run toward the stairs, only to see us and run the other way. Dom uses the chaos to grab my girl to use her as a shield. Her head flops to the side, and she looks unable to stand on her own. Wrath like I've never felt burns deep in my belly, trying to claw its way out. All the possibilities of what he's done to her flood my mind. Whatever Dom reads on my face causes him to pale.

That's right, motherfucker. I'm coming for you.

There's a hallway against the far wall and with a gun to Birdie's head, he drags her toward it. Her eyes may be open, but she isn't there. Part of me is glad she doesn't know what danger she's in and part of me is fucking enraged he caused that blank stare.

For everything he's done to her, I'll do it to him ten times over.

My brothers and I shove people out of the way, not giving a shit what happens to them. By the time we get to the hallway, I see there are a couple places Dom could've escaped to. There's an elevator to the right and the left side is lined with doors. I'm certain at least one leads outside.

"Moto, run downstairs and have Tonopah block the side exit in case Dom tries to escape that way," I yell, and he pushes people out of the way to rush down the stairs.

My brothers and I split up, kicking in doors, looking for the bastard. The door I kick in is Dom's office. I check in the attached bathroom and behind the door, but there's no sign of him. Back in the hall, Khan, Sly, and Goblin have come up short too.

"Stairs," Roch says, poking his head out of the place he was checking.

"Let's go," I yell. There's a landing with stairs going up and down. "Roch, Kahn, let's go up. Sly and Goblin, you go down. Tonopah should be down there. If they saw anything, call my cell."

"Got it," Sly says.

We take the flight of stairs up, which kicks us out onto the roof. It's a flat open space, but it's dark and I can't see a goddamn thing. I spin a finger in the air, motioning for us to fan out. With quiet footsteps, we go in separate directions. I take the area behind the door we just came out of.

I creep forward until I get to the edge and then walk along the short lip that makes up the perimeter. They're not fucking here. My phone vibrates in my pocket and I tug it out.

"Yeah," I answer.

"Prez, we got a problem. By the time Tonopah got out here, they saw a black SUV leaving. The good news is they're following them. The bad news is, he knows he's being tailed and there's no telling where he's going. It could be a trap," Moto says.

"Where are they?" I wave my brothers over and we head back the same way we came in.

"Heading out of town, west toward Truckee. Before I called you I hit up my boy who works for Dom. He said he's got a storage facility out there. It's where he stores his guns. Must be where he's going."

"All right. Let's all head that way. Don't approach him until we get there." I press the end button and shove my phone back in my pocket.

The club downstairs is a ghost town. The only people down here are the nomads, prospects, and the body of a bouncer one of my brothers must've put down. That explains the gunshot. We get out the back door and run to the restaurant parking lot. We hop on our bikes, Jake and Clint jump in the van, and we all take off down the road. In no time, we catch up to Goblin and Sly. Like bats out of hell, we roar down the road. My focus is laser sharp. Get to Dom, get my girl, blow his fucking head off his shoulders.

My phone rings and I answer it through the Bluetooth in my helmet. "Yeah?"

"Dom's stopped at some warehouse. Not sure what it is. There're at least seven cars parked here. Assuming there's at least that many inside. We fell back before they turned into this place. He probably knew it was intentional, but he might assume he lost us." Mammoth's deep voice rumbles through the speakers.

"All right. We're almost there. We can come up with a plan then," I say.

"K." Mammoth disconnects the call.

Ten minutes later, we creep down a dirt road until we get to where the Tonopah men are waiting. This is where being the prez becomes tough. Asking your brothers to go into a building full of weapons, not knowing what we could run into brings the weight of the world on my shoulders. If someone doesn't walk out alive, it's on me.

"My guy says they've got all kinds of weapons in there. AKs, fully automatics, you name it, it's in there. All the ones we used to traffic, plus explosives," Moto explains. "It won't be easy to take them. We have to assume they're armed to the max."

I scan the face of every man while lighting up a cigarette and taking a deep drag. "If any of you don't want to go in there, I'm giving you an out right now. Get on your bike, ride away. This is my fight, and I can't expect any of you to risk your life for me. That's my girl in there. It started off as babysitting, but it's not that anymore. I'm claiming her right fucking here and now. I need my brothers, but—"

"Gonna stop you there, Prez. We're in. If she's yours, that means she's family and we protect what's ours," Kahn states vehemently, staring daggers into each one of my brothers, daring them to say any different.

"Fuck yeah. We got your back," Rael agrees.

Even the prospects nod their heads. If I weren't so stressed about Birdie, my black heart might warm with love for all these guys. But the only thing I feel right now is fury. I'm fucking ready to get this over with.

"Moto, Sly, you guys do a perimeter check, let us know what you can see. The rest of us need to suit up. They may be armed to the max in there, but we're stocked too. Grab whatever you're most comfortable with out of the van," I say.

We split up. I sent Moto and Sly because they're like fucking ninjas. Moto is trained in martial arts and does fucking yoga. It makes him spry and quiet. Sly is like a fox. It's how he got his road name. He's a sneaky fucker who can creep into any room unnoticed. Plus, the two are joined at the hip and work well together.

Ten minutes go by and we're strapped to the max. This is war for men like us, it's what we prepare for, what we hope to avoid, but when it comes down to it, we're prepared.

"Couldn't see much," Sly says. "But there's about fifteen of 'em in there. You were right, they've got some nice equipment and they're ready to use it. There's a front, a back, and a side entrance. I say we try to draw at least a few outside. The rest of us can split up and go in through each door. If we come at 'em from all sides, we'll have an upper hand."

"Sounds like a plan. Why don't you and Moto work on making them come outside? We'll wait for your call and then breech the building. Got your cell?" I ask.

"Yep. And I have just the thing." The corners of Sly's mouth tip up in a devious grin. He runs to the back of the van and collects God knows what, then he and Moto run down the hill to the side of the warehouse like giddy little boys.

We stand and wait. Five minutes later, an explosion goes off on the corner of the building. It erupts in flames, thick black smoke billowing into the air.

"Fuckin' Sly," I mutter. "Let's go."

Chapter TWENTY-SIX

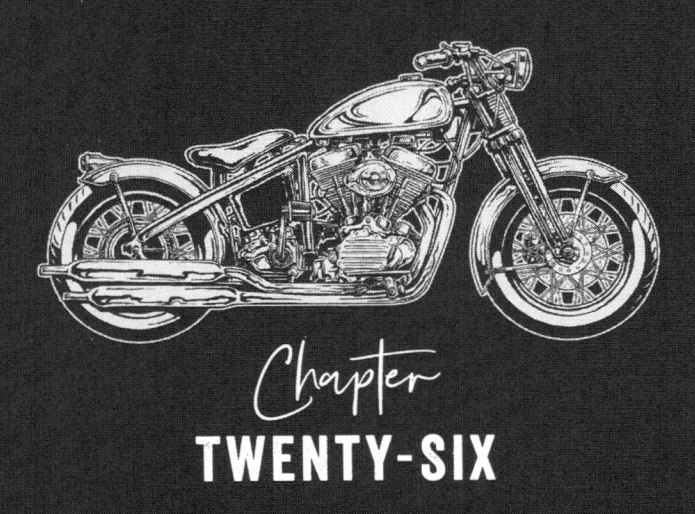

Bridgette

A loud boom jolts me awake. My head throbs and doesn't feel like it's attached to my body. I try to lift my arms, but they're tied around the back of the chair I'm on. I look around to gather my bearings, but I don't recognize the world around me. The room is small and so dark, I can't see more than two feet in front of my face.

My entire body aches, like I've been in a car accident. For all I know, I have been. My eye is swollen and throbbing, and muscles I didn't even know I had, feel like they've been used to the point of abuse. Each shift in the chair brings on a fresh round of pain and stiffness. I jog my memory, searching for answers lost in the depths of my mind.

I remember waking briefly after being tossed into that cement room. Last night, maybe? The floor was hard and unyielding, but I curled up and fell back asleep, anyway. Then I remember being woken up to a bucket of icy water dumped on my head. I was forced by one of Dom's men to shower yet again, and he brought some food and a new dress. After that, the details are blurry.

There was another night of being toyed with, called ugly names, made to do things I didn't want to. So, I checked out again. I don't know how long I've been unconscious for this time. But every time I woke up, something horrifying was going on around me, so I let the serene darkness suck me down under. In a way, I'm thankful. There're some things you can't unsee or undo. But if your mind isn't present, do those things even really happen to you? I'm not sure.

The smell of smoke fills my nostrils and I wonder what's happening outside of this room. I wriggle my hands around, trying to free them from the rope holding them together, but with each twist, they tighten and cut into my skin more. I push my feet in the ground and stand up. My hands were only bound together, not to the chair. Using my flexibility from years of yoga and Pilates, I fight through the burning pain and step through my arms, bringing them to the front of my body. The exertion makes me dizzy and I lower to the chair until it passes.

When I'm certain I won't topple over, I take small steps and feel around. I run into a wall of cardboard. Boxes, I realize. The entire wall is stacked high with them. I keep going until I reach the end and then follow the perimeter. I've traced along three full walls of boxes when I reach an empty wall. Then I feel it. A door handle. I try to turn the knob, but it's locked.

I debate banging on it, but what would that accomplish? Having one of Dom's idiot guards barge in and shut me up? No, I don't want that. The room is slowly filling with more smoke. It permeates my lungs and I cough. Wouldn't it just be my luck to live through what Dom has done to me, only to die in a fire? I find a corner and sit down.

I startle when a series of loud pops fills my ears. Gunshots. I'd recognize that sound anywhere now. I don't know if this is a good or bad sign. Maybe Loki has finally found me. Maybe he's here to save me.

If you pray for a dark angel to save you, does God listen? Or is it the devil I should ask this favor from?

Loki's not a good man, definitely not getting into heaven, but he's my savior, and that's all I care about. If he goes down, I want to go down with him. Wherever his life takes him, I want to be his ride or die. I'd gladly burn in the fires of hell if it means we'll be doing it together.

If he gets us out of this mess, I know he'd never put me at risk again. He'd protect me. He'd keep me safe. I felt the change between us probably before he even knew it happened. I saw the look in his eyes when I drove away from him with Carlo's gun on me. That was the look of absolute desperation. It matched what I was feeling inside.

A wave of determination washes over me and I can't sit here like a pathetic, sitting duck. I reach over and feel my way to the top of one of the cardboard boxes. I yank at it until it falls to the ground. I peel up the corner of the tape with my fingernail. It's difficult with my hands bound and not being able to see what I'm doing, but I keep working on it until I have enough leverage to yank the tape off the top.

Lifting the flaps, I feel around inside. It's full of something gritty and somewhat powdery but smells woody. Sawdust maybe? I find a smaller box inside and pull it out. Everything I do takes three times as long with my hands stuck together, but I'm persistent.

More gunshots ring out and I jump at the sound. I don't know what's going on out there. I can only hope it means the Royal Bastards are here.

I shake the box and hear tinkles of something metal and small inside. I rip the thin cardboard and find that it's a box of bullets. They're useless without a gun, so I keep digging but only find boxes and boxes of ammunition.

I reach for another box. This one is heavier and takes a lot more effort to get off the shelf. Especially when I have to constantly stop to rest so I don't pass out. I'm dehydrated, hungry, and my nervous system is on the fritz. But eventually, I get it to crash to the ground.

I peel back the tape and reach inside to find more sawdust. But underneath the top layer is something metal and long. I wrap my hands around it and lift it out. It's a gun. A long one with a skinny barrel and a smooth, wide base. Even if I could see what I'm doing, I'd have no clue how to load and fire it. I trace my fingers over every inch, but it's no use.

I still clutch the thing to my chest like it'll save my life. It's the first time I've had access to anything but water and a tuna sandwich since I left the compound, and I'm not about to let it go. If anything, I could hit someone with it.

More gunshots sound, but this time closer. Maybe even right outside the door. I bring my knees to my chest, a death grip on the gun.

I can't believe I'm in this situation. I can't believe this is my life. I smell horrible. I've only bathed with a dirty, crusty soap. My hair is greasy and matted. My dress, what's left of it anyway, is torn from God knows what. I've endured the most heinous of acts, and it's not over. My eyes well with tears and I don't even bother to fight them.

I wish this could be all over with. If I'm going to die, just fucking kill me already. If I'm going to be rescued, just let it happen. Right now. Right this second. I can't take much more. I know I keep telling myself this and I know I've taken it all and more, but I can't anymore. I've reached my threshold.

I hear the door handle jiggle right before a bullet pierces the door and hits the box right above my head. I scream and jump to my feet. A pinhole of light shines through the wood. My body trembles in fear, and I cover my ears. Another hits to left of me and there's more light. Then another. I jerk back. Only, I didn't hear where that one hit. The others were thuds into the boxes all around me. I see the third hole in the door, but not—

I feel something wet trickling down my body. Pain registers when I press my palm to my side and it comes back wet. I don't need to see it to know it's blood. White hot, searing agony shoots through my stomach. I've been shot. Sweat breaks out across my brow, a wave of nausea hits me, and I grow lightheaded. I lose consciousness before I can lower myself to the ground.

And here I am, taking even more. Will I never break?

Chapter
TWENTY-SEVEN

Loki

We go running for the building after Sly's explosion. It's part genius because it'll make them come and inspect, but it's also fucking stupid because he set the building Birdie is in on fire.

A few men in suits materialize and run over to the fire. Sly and Moto are quick to draw and drop them before they even knew what was happening. We split up, each of us taking an exit. Khan, Roch, and Clint are with me. Time to see what this prospect is made of.

We walk in the front door and men go scurrying, hiding behind huge pallets of what I can only assume are guns or ammunition. Except Dom. He's in the middle of the room. He aims and fires right at me. I duck behind a pallet, thankful it absorbs the bullet. A fire fight breaks out, indicating my brothers have now entered the building.

I look to my left and see Roch. His eyes shift wildly, his chest heaves, and his normally calm demeanor is gone. We've lost him to his demons and his bloodlust won't be satisfied until he's made his kills.

"I want Dom alive," I yell to him and he nods in understanding.

I peer around the corner. Dom's gone. I creep in the direction I saw him last, keeping my eyes peeled. Kahn is to my right and has his arms propped up on a pallet, a gun in hand. He's laser focused and shooting to kill. From my periphery, I see an ominous figure pop up behind my VP. I aim and fire, watching as the back of his head explodes. Kahn jerks around and I see the body fall. His eyes find mine and he nods in appreciation.

I keep moving forward. Dom has nowhere to run. All exits are being blocked and his men are dropping like flies. This'll only end one way, with us sending him to Hades. With one of the Reapers dragging his soul into the fiery depths of hell.

Royal Bastards are everywhere, but I see no more Italians. Until one pops up from in-between the high-stacked boxes and fires.

"Shooter," I yell and follow the trajectory of the bullet to see what he's shooting at, but I'm not fast enough and I see Jake's eyes go wide before his body drops to the ground.

Motherfucker.

"Goblin! Jake!" I yell and he runs to the prospect and holds him under the arms, dragging him outside.

Fuck this shit, I'm done playing games and I'm sure as shit not watching any more of my men be injured or worse. I walk, uncaring, through the rest of the warehouse. Anyone with greased back hair in a suit, even if they're already dead, catches one of my bullets. I'll kill the motherfuckers twice.

The smoke from the rapidly spreading fire is getting thick. I pull my bandana over my face to keep from taking as much in. I don't know where Birdie is, but if I were to guess, she's wherever Dom went. When I see him pop up and run toward the far corner, I know I've got him. Kahn and Roch show up by my side and we continue on our path that way.

I don't bother trying to shoot at his retreating form. I need him to lead me to my woman. Then I see it. A door. Dom turns the handle, but it's locked. He digs through his pocket and I aim for his arm. I fire and miss. The bullet going right through the door. I can't kill him until I know for sure where Birdie is. Kahn and Roch open fire in his direction.

Then I hear it. An ear-piercing scream and it's definitely Birdie's voice.

"Wait. Don't hit that door. Birdie's in there," I yell out. It's too risky hoping she gets low to the ground. She doesn't have good instincts, and I can't trust her to be logical right now.

Dom sees our hesitation and uses it to his advantage. "Don't come close. I'll kill her myself." He aims a shotgun at the door. The pellets from that gun will send a fiery spray at Birdie if he fires. "Turn around and leave."

"We're not leaving, Dom. I think you already know that. There's only one way for this to end. Either you hand her over or we all blow up in this building. You've got grenades in here? Bombs? Ammunition? That fire's moving quickly. Won't be long now." I challenge, stepping even closer.

"I don't think you'll let it get that far," he says over his shoulder. "This girl means something to you. I mean, I can see why. That mouth… that tight pussy… man, we had some pleasurable times. At least for me."

Fucking red. I see bloody fucking red. I see his brain on the end of my knife after I carve it from his skull. I see his flaccid dick being thrown to the dogs while he watches them devour it. I see my knife being shoved up his asshole, over and fucking over until there's nothing but a bloody, gaping hole.

Roch grabs my arm, halting me from moving forward. He shakes his head slowly. My chest heaves and I rip my arm from his hold. I sure as shit am not letting him walk away with Birdie. Especially not after what he's done to her.

"Guys, we gotta get out of here. Everyone else has evacuated. The fire's spread—" Sly doesn't finish his sentence because an explosion sends all of us flying through the air.

I land in a heap fifteen feet to my left. My ears are ringing and there's a shooting pain in my leg. I look down. A large shard of wood has impaled my calf. It doesn't even look real. I can almost dismiss it as fake because my jeans are covering my skin. I can't see the wound. But the searing pain convinces me I'm not seeing things. I cough from the thick, black smoke that's filling the air. The jostling has me falling back onto my side and clutching my leg.

Sly crawls his way over to me. He's bleeding from his head and his right arm.

"Fuck, man." He sits up when he makes it to my side and runs a hand through his long hair.

"Birdie," I say, gripping my calf to hold it steady. Even the smallest movements are excruciating.

"I think she's okay for a minute. Dom was blown off his feet too." He looks around the wood from every angle.

"Yank it," I demand.

"Prez. I don't know. There could be nerves or an artery. Shit, man. I don't know. You need a hospital."

"Fuckin' yank it now. That's an order." I don't pull the President card often, but it's necessary right now.

Sly blows out a breath and wraps his hands around the wood just above the entry wound. "I'm going to count to three. One." He yanks it out in one swift motion.

I grit my teeth and moan. "Fucker. You said three."

"I didn't want you to be flexing your muscles when I did it." He tosses the wood to the side and inspects my leg, ripping my jeans open to see what we're dealing with. "It's not spurting blood, so I think we're safe."

"We need to get to Birdie. Help me up."

Sly climbs to his feet slowly, painfully. He's in worse shape than I thought. He helps me up and I scour the ground to find my gun. I must've dropped it in the blast. I find it and do a quick inspection, making sure nothing was damaged. It looks fine.

Ten feet in front of us, Roch is on his back, unconscious. There's no obvious injury, no pool of blood. He's black with soot and probably hit his head.

"Get him out of here."

Sly nods and drags him to the side door, the only exit not blocked by fire. I hobble closer to the closed door. Dom's unconscious body lies feet away from it. I ignore him for now and press my ear against the wooden door. I can hear faint coughing and moaning coming from the other side.

"Birdie." I pound on the door. She doesn't answer. "Get low, darlin'."

I step back and aim for the doorjamb, right next to the handle. I fire a single round, splintering the wood. I ram my shoulder into the door. It pops open easily. It's hard to see anything in here between there being no light and the smoke. I pull my pen light from my pocket and shine it into the room.

There, curled into a ball, is my birdie. I rush over to her, ignoring the pain in my leg. I brush her hair from her face. Her face is bruised and bloody, and her eyes are closed. I scan down her body and that's when I see the pool of red. I shove off my cut and yank my shirt over my head. I press it to the wound, earning a pained groan from Birdie.

"It's okay. I've got you." I lift her into my arms. My calf is screaming at me, threatening to give way, but I won't let it. I'm getting her out of here if it's the last thing I do.

I've only made it two steps when the doorway fills with a shadowed figure. Fucking Dom. The double barrel of his shotgun is pointed right at my head.

"All this"—he gestures around us with the gun—"and you still don't win. You're just like your dad. A weakness for a woman is your downfall. There isn't a cunt out there worth all this. I should kill her and let you live like I did with him. That way you'll be reminded of what pussy you are every single day of your miserable life."

I look down at the angel in my arms. "I tried," I whisper and lift her higher so I can kiss her parted lips once more. "I fuckin' tried."

Her eyelids flutter open only a fraction, but enough for our eyes to meet. An entire conversation takes place within a few seconds. All the regret that we won't get the life we deserve together, long summer night rides on my bike with her plastered to my back, me putting a property patch on her, a blond-haired daughter and dark-haired boy who will never be born, and all the kinky fuckery we'll never have.

Her eyes shut, and relaxed resignation softens her features. I can't go out like this. I can't let this be our end. I want that life. I want a forever. The burning fury fills me once again, fucking pissed this asswipe thinks he can take it away. I drop Birdie's legs and hook under her shoulders, so she doesn't fall to the ground. I reach behind me and wrap my hand around the cold steel of my gun.

I'm too late, though. A series of loud *pops* ring out and it's over.

Done.

Chapter
TWENTY-EIGHT

Bridgette

I imagine death to be a freedom. Freedom from pain, freedom from emotion, freedom from every human suffering. That's not how it is, though, because the stabbing pain in my side is still smarting. The heartache from knowing Loki and I won't ever see where our connection would take us still throbs. Even the pressure of his strong arm holding me up is still very much there.

"Birdie, open your eyes," a gruff voice pleads. I feel myself lower onto the ground. None of this makes sense. "Darlin', give me your eyes."

God sounds a lot like Loki.

I try to force them open. I really do. But I know the second I do, my almost life will be over, and I don't want it to be. I'm not ready. Then someone smacks my face and my eyes pop open in shock.

"Ouch." I reach a hand up and rub at my cheek.

"There you are," the same voice says.

I blink. And blink some more. God looks a lot like Loki. There's a halo of light around his head and a smile brightens his ruggedly handsome face. He strokes a finger along my jawline gently. Then I see the black streaks across his forehead, blood dripping from his head, and I smell smoke.

I'm not dead. We're not dead.

"Did you slap me?" I croak.

"Had to make sure you were okay." He chuckles.

"But you hit me."

"Let's argue about this later. We've got to get out of here. This building is about to blow."

He scoops me back up, and I let out a pained groan. I look around and see dead bodies everywhere, but my eyes catch on one body in particular. Dom. I wouldn't be able to even recognize him if I didn't know his custom-tailored suit so well. He's covered in blood and his body lies contorted awkwardly. I quickly tuck my head into Loki's chest.

"She okay?" another voice asks.

"We've got to get her to a doc, but I think she'll be all right." Loki limps out of the burning building. "We're minutes from this building exploding. Take care of him, would you?"

I don't ask questions. Not right now. There'll be time for that when Loki and I are alone. When I feel healthy enough to know more. I'm emotionally drained and exhausted.

Loki walks me through the dirt and up a hill. His leg is dragging, and I know he's injured.

A van speeds past us, back to the building, but I still don't ask. I don't even have it in me to worry. They know what they're doing. Loki stops next to his bike. His eyes fixate on the building. Not even a minute later, the van is back. It stops suddenly and Clint jumps out. The prospect throws open the side door and Loki lays me down on the bench seat, climbing in after me. It's only then I notice his pants torn open and blood stained.

"What happened?" I ask.

He lifts my head and rests it on his lap. "Shh. We can talk about all that later. Right now, we just need to make sure you're okay."

The tires squeal as Clint drives away from wherever we were. We haven't even driven two full minutes before I hear a loud, window rattling explosion. I try to sit up, but Loki holds me down.

"Just rest. You're okay now," he coos uncharacteristically.

He's being nice. I don't like it. When he's gruff and rude, it makes me feel tough. Like he knows I can withstand his temper. This gentleness and coddling make me feel as though he thinks what I've been through is enough to break me. And it isn't. I won't let it.

"At least there won't be any evidence," Clint notes.

Loki grunts and combs his fingers through my hair soothingly. It's a tangled mess, but he patiently untangles it without tugging. I know I must look horrible, but the only thing I see painted on his features is concern. It's weird. The only two looks he shows me are annoyed or turned on.

"What about Jake?" Loki asks Clint, who doesn't respond verbally, but must've indicated something terrible because Loki's face falls and his grip on a strand of my hair tightens. "What did you do with him?"

"He's in the back. Khan said we'll take him to the graveyard."

Loki curses and lowers his head.

My heart aches. Jake was just my age. He had his entire life ahead of him. He died saving me, and he didn't even know me for more than a week. So much has happened in such a short amount of time. It feels like I've known all these men forever. Fat tears spill from the corners of my eyes. I make a vow to do something special in Jake's honor.

The ride is longer than what's comfortable. Every pit in the road or turn we make takes me to a whole new level of pain. By the time we stop, I'm sweating and grimacing, desperate for some relief.

"Stay here a second." Loki lowers my head to the seat. I don't have it in me to argue.

He climbs out of the vehicle and disappears from view. I hear muffled voices, all of them male, except for one woman's voice. I wonder where we are and why we're here. I need a doctor. I'm certain I've been shot.

Moments later, Loki reappears. "Roch's friend is going to help you, okay? I just need to move you inside."

"No, please don't. It hurts so bad," I whine.

"I know, but she's a doc. She'll fix you up."

I cry silent tears as he helps me sit up and then lifts me in his arms once again. He takes me inside of a sterile smelling building and lays me down on a stainless steel table. A large machine appears above me with a bright light that has me squinting.

"Hold still, darlin'. We need to take a picture of your side," Loki says.

I hear a buzzing, and a moment later, he's back with me. He lifts me up again and takes me to a different room and lays me down on yet another hard, stainless steel table.

"Where are we?" I ask.

"Somewhere safe where we can get you help. Don't worry. I'll be right back."

I shiver with the loss of his touch. I look around, trying to get my bearings, but it's no use. I've never been here. Hanging on the wall is a picture of a beautiful Native American woman kneeling next to a German shepherd. There're glass jars on the counter to my right holding cotton balls and swabs. Ugly mint green cabinets line the wall and the rest of the room is empty.

A soft hand lifts mine, and I turn to see who is holding it. The woman from the picture stands over me. Her eyes are black as night and her long stark hair is braided over her shoulder. She brings my hand to her chest, and she gives me a comforting smile.

"Hi, Bridgette. My name is Aiyana. I'm going to hook you up to some machines so I can monitor you and give you some medicine that'll make you sleepy, but it will also relieve some of the pain you're feeling. Would that be okay?" I don't know this woman, but her soothing tone and calm demeanor have me nodding. "Before I do, I need to ask you some questions."

"Okay." Something clips onto my finger and a cuff slips over my arm. A steady beep sounds from next to me.

"I'm not well versed in"—she pauses, looking uncomfortable—"women's health. But before I operate on your side, I need to know if I should look for injuries in other places on your body."

Ah. She wants to know how far the sexual abuse went. I don't want to think about it, and I definitely don't want to talk about it. And honestly, I'm not even certain what all they did to me. But I think I'd know if whatever happened tore me or hurt me more than emotionally. I shake my head.

Her features soften. "Okay. I'll still take some blood so we can make sure you didn't contract anything."

"Yeah, okay." I wasn't even thinking about STDs or anything else while Dom was abusing me. Fear constricts my lungs and the beeping from the machine speeds up. What if he gave me something? What if I lived through this, just to die from a disease?

"Bridgette, I need you take some breaths for me," Aiyana says while putting a mask over my face. Cool air blows into my nose and mouth. I breathe it in. "You'll feel a little sting, okay?"

She looks over, and I follow the path of her gaze. A younger version of Aiyana stands to her side holding a long, thin needle. Aiyana gently lowers my hand to the cold table and then I feel the stick. It's nothing compared to the pain in my tummy.

"You'll start feeling tired. And as soon as you're comfortable, I'll remove that bullet that's lodged in your side. It doesn't look like it's hit anything major, so it should be simple. You'll wake up feeling much better."

"Where's Loki?" I croak.

"I'm here." Loki appears above my head. He trails his fingers down my forehead, across my cheek, and then swoops down along my collarbone. My eyes grow heavy and soon I'm drifting off, thankful for the reprieve and happy that the last thing I see is Loki's beautiful smile.

Chapter
TWENTY-NINE

Loki

"She's out," Aiyana says. "You can go in the next room. My daughter will stitch you up."

"I'd rather stay," I argue. I don't know this woman, never even heard of her until Roch suggested bringing her here. To a fucking veterinarian. I can't believe I'm putting Birdie's life in the hands of an animal doctor. I've been second-guessing myself since we pulled in, but our options are limited if we want to keep the cops out of our business.

"I need a sterile environment." She looks me up and down pointedly. "And you're a mess. You're bleeding all over my floor."

I look down and see the fresh droplets of blood at my feet. My open wound had closed in the van, but the second I started walking again, it reopened. I take one last look at my girl, covered in bruises, cuts, and scrapes. I did this to her, but I can't be the one to fix her. I place a parting kiss to her forehead.

"Take care of her," I plead.

"She'll be fine. Tell my daughter to send Roch in when she's done stitching you both up. I'll need the help."

Without a choice and feeling fucking helpless, I hobble out of the room and into the next room over. A young girl I don't even think is old enough to drive a car is opening a suture kit.

"Take off your pants and hop up on the table," she says without taking her eyes off what she's doing.

"It's customary to know someone's name before you ask them to take their clothes off, darlin'." I'm not flirting. It's just awkward as fuck to undress in front of an underage girl.

"Trust me, I don't care what's under your clothes. I'm just trying to get you all fixed up and out of my mom's business before cops show up and haul us both to jail for aiding and abetting."

Reluctantly, I drop trou and hoist myself on the table. It's silent as she cleans up my leg. It stings like a motherfucker, but I don't complain.

"So, how do you know Roch?" I ask.

Her brown cheeks tinge pink, but then she clears her throat and sits up straight. "He's been bringing the dogs in for years."

"Oh, right. The dogs." I don't know why I didn't solve that equation on my own, but something tells me there's more to it. Both these chicks look to Roch like he means something to them. More than just a customer. I don't pry. It's none of my fucking business, and if my brother has kept something from us, I know he must have a damn good reason.

"This'll sting." She pokes a needle and depresses the plunger a little before moving down the wound and doing the same. She continues until she's gone around the whole six-inch gash. Then she rotates my leg and does the same on the other side. "You really should have an X-ray. Make sure there's no tendon involvement, or a chipped bone."

"I'm fine. Just stitch me and my brothers up and fix my girl. Then we'll be on our way," I say.

Ten minutes later, my leg's bandaged and I thank the girl. I send in Roch and give him Aiyana's instructions. He has a blood-soaked towel pressed to the back of his head. I watch as he steps into the room. The kid runs to him and wraps her arms tightly around his middle. She sobs loudly into his chest. He doesn't return the hug, but he reaches behind him and slides the pocket door closed.

Who the fuck are these people to him?

I step into the waiting room where Sly, Khan, Moto, Goblin, and Clint are sitting stoically, all of them staring at the ground. Their eyes lift when I take a seat next to my VP.

"How is she?" Goblin asks.

"The doc said she'll be fine. It didn't hit any organs or arteries, or whatever. She just has to remove the bullet." I lean forward, resting my arms on my thighs.

"What about…" he trails off, but I know what he's asking. We all saw those girls up in the club's loft. It was obvious what was going on, what most likely happened to Birdie.

I shake my head, stopping my mind from going there. I can't. Not right now. If I do, I'll lose it. I'll fucking tear this office apart in a blind rage. I'll fucking go to the van right now and tear Dom's almost lifeless body limb from limb. I'll fucking lose any shred of sanity I have left after our day from hell.

"Birdie said she was fine. We haven't talked about it, though," I say. "What about the nomads and Tonopah?"

"They headed out. They were a little nervous that the building explosion and a bunch of out-of-towners might be pieced together."

The room goes silent again, all of us lost in our thoughts. My mind drifts between my girl and Jake. The kid would've been voted in after this. He held his own up until his last breath. I'll do right by him. I'll bury him with his patch. I'll hang his picture in the chapel. He'll be part of our history.

An hour passes. Roch hasn't come back, but the girl called in Sly to stitch him up. A few minutes later, he returns. Another hour goes by before Aiyana walks in. We all stand abruptly.

"She's okay. The bullet grazed her kidney, causing a slight hemorrhage. But she'll be fine." She hands me two unmarked pill bottles. "One is an antibiotic. Make sure she finishes these, even if she's feeling better, so she doesn't develop an infection. The other is for her pain. I trust you'll make sure these go to her and not anyone else."

"We're not druggies." I huff.

"I don't know what you are. And I don't want to. I don't feel right about any of this, and if it weren't for Roch, I never would've let you in my doors."

"Understood. Thank you." I pull out a wad of cash and hand the entire thing to her. There's about ten grand in there and it's not enough, but it's all I have on me. But then my brothers step up and thrust wads of bills at her, too.

"I don't want your money. I don't know how you earned it and I want nothing traced back to me." She holds her hands up, refusing the cash.

"It's clean, ma'am. I promise," Sly says. He's our money guy. Every dollar we come across is thoroughly cleaned by him.

"Excuse me if I don't trust a gang of bikers who drop a sweet girl on my doorstep with a gunshot wound."

I stiffen at the accusation I'm responsible for Birdie's injuries. *Except, I am.* This entire thing was my fault. I'm the one in charge. I could've shot down the idea at using her as a diversion. I was too arrogant to think anything bad would happen to her.

"We'll leave it here, do whatever you want with it. Throw it away for all I care. But I don't carry debts and it's the only way I can make things even between us," I say and drop the cash on the counter. Everyone else follows suit.

"Fine. Bridgette was just waking up when I left her. I don't have a wheelchair, so you'll have to carry her out. But be careful. She'll be quite sore." Aiyana gives us one last look and then disappears down the hall.

"I'll meet you guys at the clubhouse. Will you have Sissy change my bedding before I get home? I want everything to be clean for Birdie," I ask Khan.

"Sure, bro. On it."

"Oh and call her dad. Let him know she's safe and she'll call him soon."

He nods and walks out the door.

I make my way into the room I left my girl in. Roch is holding her hand, his eyes downturned and sad. In any other situation I'd bristle at their closeness, but I know they're friends and if he can comfort her right now, the only thing I can feel is grateful for his efforts.

"Hey, darlin'. Feeling okay?" I ask.

Roch straightens and releases her hand. She slowly turns her head toward me. Her eyes are half-lidded and she's pale. She looks nothing like the ray of sunshine she was when I took her from her dad's house.

"Hey," she slurs. "Can we go home?"

"Which home do you want to go to?" I ask and hold my breath. I wouldn't blame her if she wanted to go back to her daddy. She's probably safer there now that Dom's threat's extinguished.

She looks at me blankly, like she doesn't understand the question. "I thought I'd be with you, but if—"

My stone-cold heart pounds in my chest. I eat up the two steps it takes to reach her side and lower my lips to hers. I kiss her sweetly, trying to convey how happy she's made me by choosing me.

"I want you with me," I murmur against her mouth.

"Me too."

"Let's get you home, then." I lift her as carefully as possible, cringing when she groans in pain. "Just a few more minutes, then we'll get you in bed."

Her arms wrap around my neck, and I carry her to the van. I lay her on the bench seat and rest her head in my lap like before. Clint climbs into the driver's side and guides us home. I can tell he's taking it extra slow, being cautious not to jostle Birdie. It makes me proud to have him on my side. I can't wait to hand him his patch. He's more than earned it.

Birdie's asleep by the time the tires crunch over the gravel parking lot at the clubhouse. She doesn't wake when I carry her inside. She still doesn't wake when I rest her in my bed. I remove the white blanket Aiyana had covered her with. She's in a bloodstained and dirty bra and panties. Her abdomen is wrapped in a sterile bandage.

I remove her underwear. I'll fucking burn that shit later. Sissy brings in a bowl of water and a couple of washcloths. I cover her breasts and pussy. Then Sissy helps me wipe her down. It feels wrong to do this while she's not conscious, but I have a feeling she wouldn't want to wake up covered in dried blood and who knows what the fuck else. I wish I could wash her beautiful blond hair that's matted and crusty, but that'll have to wait.

"Thanks," I say.

"Need anything else?" Sissy whispers, collecting the bowl and wash rags.

"Maybe some water and crackers for when she wakes up and needs to take her meds?"

"Sure. Be right back." She squeezes my shoulder and then disappears out the door.

I cover Birdie with the sheet and comforter. I wish I could pull her into me. Hold her close. But I don't want to hurt her further. So, I settle for sliding in behind her and resting her head on my lap once again. It's early morning, the sun's coming up, and it's been a long-ass twenty-four hours. I lean against the headboard, light up a smoke, and stare at the ceiling, my mind going through everything that's happened.

The club. The warehouse. Dom seconds from killing both me and Birdie. Clint appearing out of nowhere and saving my ass. I don't even know how he knew where we were or what was going on, but there'll be time to put it all together.

The door opens and Sissy sets two bottles of water and a sleeve of crackers down. "Let me know if you need anything else. The guys are taking care of all the loose ends. Khan wanted me to tell you."

"And him?" I ask.

"He'll be waiting for you when you're ready." She steps back out, silently closing the door.

Jolts of excitement charge through me knowing what I have left to do. The last piece to this fucked up puzzle waits for me. But I force myself to relax. There'll be time for that after I'm sure Birdie's okay.

Chapter
THIRTY

Bridgette

I blink my eyes open and startle. The basement. The club. Dom. But when I focus, I'm not there anymore. The rest of it comes back to me. The Royal Bastards saved me. I'm in Loki's room alone. And my cage. I never thought I'd miss it, but I do. I'm safe in there. I might've felt helpless and small when Loki forced me in there the first time, however now I know what's out in the world. And it's so much worse than what goes on under the roof of the clubhouse. I'd so much rather be under Loki's lock and key than where people like Dom can use and abuse me.

I pull the blanket off, and cool air conditioning hits my nude body. My only covering is a bandage wrapped around my middle. The bedspread moves beside me, and I lift it to reveal a sleepy Karen. My heart warms, knowing Roch brought her in here for me. I scratch behind her ears as she stretches. I scoop her up and sit up slowly, wincing at the throbbing ache from the wound. I use the nightstand as leverage so I can stand. I'm weak. Both from being starved and the trauma my body has been through, but I need to feel safe right now.

I struggle to move my feet, each step taking more effort than the last. I open the door, walk inside, and collapse onto the thin mattress. Everything hurts, but I feel better in here. I wish Loki were around to lock me in. Then I'd really be protected from danger. Karen snuggles into me and I cover us both up with the thin blanket. I try not to fall asleep, but my eyelids are so heavy.

"Goddamn it, Birdie." A loud voice booms, waking me.

Standing outside the bars of the crate is a furious Loki. His scowl is adorable. The way his eyes wrinkle in the corner and his brow furrows is my favorite look on him. Especially when I'm the one who's made him mad.

The door swings open, and he ducks down to enter. He grumbles unintelligibly as he lifts me up and returns me to the bed. It's not where I want to be, but when he's with me, I feel almost as protected.

"Why would you go in there?" He steps out of sight, but is back in a flash, this time with a tiny chihuahua in his hands. He lays Karen next to me. She complains from being moved, but quickly settles next to me.

"You weren't here," I say.

"I'm going to get this thing out of here." I hear him jostling the cage.

"Please don't."

"Bitch gets abducted, tortured, shot, and then comes home only to crawl into a fuckin' dog crate," he mumbles to himself.

"Loki," I call out.

"What?" he snaps.

"Can you get me an ibuprofen?" My side is almost unbearable at this point. I need something.

"Fuck. I'm sorry. The doc gave me some pain pills. Hold on."

I close my eyes and take deep breaths, trying to keep from tightening up. Seconds later, I hear a pill bottle opening. Loki kneels down beside the bed and holds a large white pill to my lips. I open and he places it on my tongue.

"Let me help you sit up a little so you can drink this water. You also need to eat a couple crackers, so you don't get sick."

I struggle through the pain and swallow the pill down. Loki breaks the crackers into fourths and hand feeds them to me. He watches me with rapt attention. He's so gentle, it's maddening. Irritating, even. This isn't him.

After four crackers, I purse my lips tightly. "No more."

"But—"

"My stomach is off. I wasn't given much to eat or drink while I was… away," I say.

Loki rips his black beanie from his head and throws it across the room. I reach over and tousle a strand between my fingers. I smile at having my angry man back.

"This is serious, Birdie. I lost my mind while you were gone. I couldn't stand to think about what he might do to you."

"I know, but I'm okay now. You saved me."

"I put you in Dom's path. Whatever happened is my fault." He climbs on the bed next to me and wriggles his arm under my head.

"I could've said no. You didn't make me help."

"I'm so sorry, Birdie." He brings my hand to his black T-shirt covered chest.

"I know you are. But I'm okay now."

"Are you? Because you don't look okay. You look like shit," he says, and I flinch. I try to pull my hand away, but he tightens his grip. "I didn't mean it like that. You're beautiful. You'd be beautiful no matter what but seeing what he did to you on the outside and not knowing what he did to you on the inside, it's driving me crazy. I need to know everything."

I look into his pleading eyes and think over my options. I don't want to talk about it. I don't want to think about it. But I know his imagination must be going wild and the not knowing is hurting him. Besides, he's right. He needs to know it all. Not just because I need time to heal, but also because I might've contracted a disease.

"I don't remember everything. I think between whatever drugs he forced on me and my self-preservation, I spent most of the time not really there. But I know he did things to me. Things you probably don't want to talk about."

"I want to talk about it. You can't keep it all in, it'll eat you alive. You need an outlet. Let me be that fuckin' person."

I take a deep breath and spell it out slowly. "Well, you already know he kept me in that room. He made me strip and shower in freezing cold water. He made me dress up and took me upstairs but wouldn't give me shoes. I'm assuming so I didn't try and run. He beat me for not doing what he said and not wanting to sniff the drugs. I think that's where this came from." I lightly brush my cheek. "He forced himself on me, both orally and although I don't remember it, I know he raped me."

"Motherfucker!" he roars and jumps off the bed. He paces next to me and runs his hand through his hair, making the curls stand up on end.

I don't cry. I don't react at all. I'm numb to the whole

encounter. It doesn't feel real. Maybe one day it'll hit me, but right now, the entire thing feels like a nightmare. Like something I made up in my head. Like something I saw happen to someone else. Definitely not Bridgette Davis, wannabe socialite with a perfectly charmed life.

"I saw you," he hisses. "At the club, I mean. That's where we found you. You were on the floor. At *his* feet. He dragged you out of the building, using you as a shield. You looked out of it. I saw the drugs. Figured he forced them on you. We followed him to the warehouse. We killed every single one of his fucking men. He ran to that back office and I knew you were in there. I think it was one of our bullets that shot you. It all happened so fast. It wasn't until I realized the bullets were penetrating the door that we stopped shooting at him."

"I was awake. That room was full of guns, but I didn't know how to load one, let alone fire it. I knew you were there. I was so scared something would happen to you and I'd be left with him." I look down at my dirty fingernails and absentmindedly try to clean the blood and grime from under them.

"I wasn't going to let that happen. I know I was kind of an asshole to you—"

"Kind of?" I smirk.

"Okay." He rolls his eyes. "A colossal asshole. I was so caught up in making sure I didn't end up like Trucker, I didn't realize I already had until you were gone."

"I like your asshole tendencies," I admit, hoping he quits it with all this coddling.

He strides over to the bed and sits down at my feet. He pulls them onto his lap and rubs circles into them. I want to tell him to stop. I don't need his kindness. But it's soothing and my body sinks further into the mattress.

I can see the wheels in his brain turning as he studies me, but I say nothing. Any conclusions he comes up with he has to make on his own. He's not a man who can be influenced by others. He's arrogant in his self-confidence, and that's okay. I wish I believed in my judgement as much as he does. I wish I were as strong in my convictions as he is. It's something I admire in him. I want to learn from him and better myself by taking his lead.

He tugs on one of my toes, seemingly finalizing his thoughts. "I want you to stay here. With me. I can't give you a mansion on the hill overlooking the city. I can't buy you all those fancy clothes and take you to five-star restaurants. Not because I can't afford it, but because I don't believe in that lifestyle. I'm a simple man, Birdie. We live a dangerous but unassuming life here. I'm not saying I won't spoil the fuck out of you, but it won't be what you're used to."

"We don't know each other very well," I point out.

"I know. We can get there."

"Maybe we'll hate each other."

"Maybe. I might drive you as crazy as you drive me." A teasing smile creeps up on his beautiful lips.

"Trust me. You already do." I grin back and it splits my lip back open. I feel a trickle of blood drip down my chin. It's a stark reminder of where I'm at and how long it will take me to feel like myself again. "I'm not who I was two days ago. I might never be her again."

"I know that, too." He scoots closer and reaches up to wipe the blood away.

"I won't be ready for… you know. Maybe not for a long time." I have to say it. I know he's not used to going without female attention and even the thought of going there, even with him, makes me sick to my stomach. I won't soon forget how it felt for Dom to force himself on me.

"Fuck, Birdie. You don't think I know that? The last thing I want to do is fuck you right now. I want you here because I want to take care of you. I want"—he shakes his head—"no. I *need* to make sure you're okay. And only when you're ready will I want anything more from you."

"I don't understand how things could change so quickly. You were counting down the minutes before you could send me packing. You told me over and over you want nothing to do with me. I'm not your responsibility anymore. You don't need to protect me. I'm not a charity case for you to take pity on."

He sinks to his knees at my side, cupping my bruised cheeks with reverence. He leans in and softly kisses each hurt he can get to. It's so tender and sweet, it makes the dam on my emotions break. Tears leak from the corner of my eyes and he kisses those too. I patiently wait for him to finish. This is for him, not me.

He rests his forehead against mine. "I do pity you, but that's not why I want you here. I want you, Birdie. Not just your body. All of you. Your sass, your fire, your bitchy attitude and also your kindness, your heart, your fucking soul. I'm a man who gets what he wants, so quit arguing and give yourself to me."

"What if Dom gave me a disease?" I ask because ever since Aiyana suggested blood tests, it's infected my mind and maybe my lady bits.

"We'll cross that bridge when we get to it. But not even that will make me want you to go."

"Okay," I whisper.

"Okay?" he asks, pulling back to look me in the eyes.

"But you have to do something for me."

"Anything, darlin.'"

"You have to tell my daddy."

Chapter
THIRTY-ONE

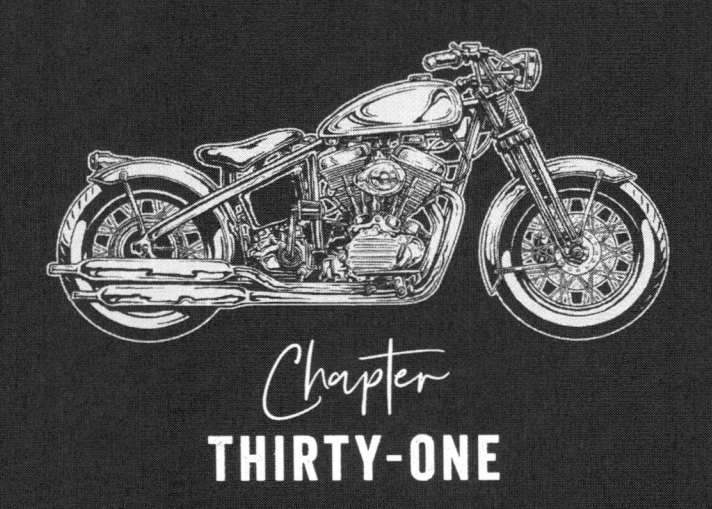

Loki

"You have to tell my daddy," she says, like it's a deal breaker. Like telling an old, rich guy I'm keeping his daughter scares me.

Fuck that.

"I thought we agreed I'm your daddy now."

Her eyes go as wide as saucers as she tries to decipher if I'm telling the truth. I keep a straight face, not giving her any hints. Honestly, I've never had a daddy kink before. But fuck if I don't want her looking at me with those big brown eyes and make me the most important man in her life. There's time for all that shit later, though. Much, much later.

"How about I help you shower?" I ask, ignoring the questions running through her mind.

"Can I? With this?" She points to her bandage.

"Doc said it was fine as long as it mostly stays out of the water and we pat it dry after."

"I'd love to feel clean after..." she trails off. I hate that in her mind, there'll always be a before and an after that'll make her think about that jackass every time.

"Let's do it then. Do you want to walk, or do you want me to carry you?"

"Walk. I want to stretch my legs."

"Gimme a minute to start the water." I step into the bathroom and make sure the shower is the right temperature. I set the shower seat I had Tabitha pick up inside the stall. I figured it'd be some time before Birdie would be strong enough to stand, and I wasn't sure she'd want me to see her naked right away. Or ever, for that matter. It fills me with pride that she's trusting me to take care of her.

I help her sit up and then stand. She's wobbly, so I keep an arm around her, letting her put her weight mostly on me. I suck in a breath, looking at her naked body. There's not an inch of skin unmarred, but she doesn't need my emotions right now. She's dealing with her own.

I tenderly sit her down, out of the spray, and strip my clothes. Nothing about this is sexual. Even my dick understands as it hangs limply between my legs.

I unwrap the white bandage wrapped around her middle, leaving the gauze taped over the bullet wound. I take the shower head off the holder and switch the settings until it's a gentle flow and not a harsh spray. I stand behind her and ease her head back. I wet her hair and wash it with the grapefruit scented shampoo I've been dying to smell again. I massage into her scalp until I press into a lump and she jerks away.

"I'm sorry," I say.

"It's okay. I don't even know where all the bruises are. Everything hurts, so it's hard for me to tell."

The angry demon I've been actively suppressing threatens

to rear its ugly head, but I keep it tamped down below the surface. As I rinse Birdie's hair, my mind spins with all the ways I'll get revenge. All the new and ugly ways I can kill. How every man I'm sent to extinguish will take on Dom's face from now on. If I was considered ruthless before, it's nothing compared to what I feel capable of now.

After I'm done taking care of Birdie's hair, I help her stand. She leans forward on the glass enclosure to hold herself upright. I squirt body wash into my hand and with featherlight touches, I soap up her back. She has black and blue bruises everywhere. Some small and some big. Each one feeds the fire within me, but I swallow it down so Birdie can't sense it.

She turns around and I do the same to her front, staying clear of the bandage. Even when I clean her breasts and between her legs, my dick doesn't take notice. Birdie's face flames in embarrassment and her split lower lip wobbles. Fuck, I hate seeing her like this.

"You're beautiful," I tell her, and she huffs. "I'm serious. Even like this, you're the prettiest girl I've ever landed eyes on. All the bruises and cuts are temporary, but what's in here"—I place a hand over her heart—"and here"—I tap my finger on her temple—"that beauty is forever."

She glares at me like I just said something wrong. I thought that was a damn fine speech. I'm proud of myself for coming up with it. I chalk it up to her pain and move on.

I take a washcloth and wet it. Turning back to her, I don't even know where to start. Her eye is almost swollen shut and there's a gash on her cheek. Her lip is split and there's a bruise on her forehead. Instead of wiping at her face, I pat it, clearing the dirt and dried blood the best I can.

"I'm tired," she says, her body swaying slightly.

"Pain pill must've kicked in. Let's get you out." I toss the washcloth on the ground and turn the water off. I grab a towel and wrap it around her before walking her back to my bed. "Let me get you something to wear."

I could open her backpack, choose clothes from there, but I don't. I open a drawer and pull out an RBMC T-shirt. It'll be baggy on her, comfortable. I pull away the towel, exposing the bandage, and take out the supplies the doc sent home with us. She hisses as I slowly tug the tape away. It honestly doesn't look as bad as I thought, but the skin is being held together by stitches and there's red, angry skin around the wound.

I clean it and wrap it, then slip my shirt over her head. Her eyes are droopy; she's seconds from falling asleep. So I lay her down and pull the comforter over her. Karen stretches, stands up, and snuggles back into my girl's side. With both of them sleeping, I decide I can step away for a while.

I lock the door from the inside and tuck the key in my pocket. I don't want anyone in there poking around. My brothers have good intentions, but Birdie needs to rest so she can regain her strength.

"She okay?" Roch asks when I sit down next to him at the bar. Clint pours me a shot of tequila and I toss it down my throat. It's afternoon and I still haven't slept since the warehouse. I'm wiped, but I can't calm the chaos in my mind.

"I think so. She's sleeping. Thanks for Karen. Birdie was happy to have her there."

"S'okay." he mumbles around his beer.

"Clint," I call out to the other end of the bar where he's made himself scarce. He's good about shit like that, knowing what he's privy to and when to disappear. Not anymore, though. He's about to get his patch. "Can you call Church for me?"

"Sure, Prez. On it." He pulls out his phone and starts texting.

The guys are probably all on the property but being respectful of the noise they tend to make. I grab a bottle of beer and make my way into the Chapel. There's a new framed picture on the wall. I took it during a charity ride at Christmas time. Jake stands proudly next to his bike, handing a little girl a gift at the Children's Hospital. I press my fingers into the frame, remembering earlier when we buried him on some land the club owns. It's where all of our fallen men are laid to rest. It was quiet and simple, but respectful.

The guys file in shortly after that and all take their seats. Clint pulls the door to close it, but I stop him. "Clint, get your ass in here."

Shock and nervousness paint his features, and I can tell he thinks he's about to have his ass handed to him. I shouldn't get enjoyment out of it, but damn if we don't all need a little comic relief.

"What'd the kid do?" Goblin asks dramatically. He knows where I'm going with this.

"That's the thing, he didn't do shit." I lower my head and shake it.

"What do you mean?" Clint asks.

"You didn't do shit *wrong*, man." I smile. "You fuckin' held your own in that shootout. You protected your brothers, you didn't hesitate to shoot, and you got my girl back to the club safe. But most of all, you saved my girl's life. You made us proud."

My brothers and I pound fists on the table and clap. The

kid's cheeks pink in embarrassment. He's got some growing up to do if he wants to be taken seriously outside the club, but he'll get there.

I stand up and walk to the sideboard. I reach in the cabinet and pull out the patch. I set it on the table and sit down, pounding the gavel to regain control of the room.

"Let's take it to vote. All in favor of patching in our boy, Clint, raise your hand."

"Hell yeah," Khan says, his hand shooting in the air.

"No doubt," Moto says, his lifting too.

The rest of my brothers' hands rise with words of encouragement. I knew they'd all vote this way. We don't take in new members often, but when we do, we're all on board.

"It's unanimous. Welcome to the Royal Bastards!" I toss the RBMC and 1%er patch to him. "Now cut that prospect patch off."

Clint has a huge-ass smile on his face as he tugs his vest off. He cuts the patch off with a pocket knife and sets down the RBMC logo in the center. "I don't know how to sew. Think Tabitha'll do it for me?"

We all let out a series of curses. Stupid kid.

"No, man. Sewing that shit on is an honor. You do that yourself. If you don't know how, pull up a YouTube video," Sly scolds.

"Right. Okay."

"Now that's settled. Let's get down to business. What's the word on the street? Any blowback?"

"Not from the cops. I think they're letting the Corsettis handle their own business. Anthony, as you all know, was absent at the warehouse. Apparently, he'd been out of town when we raided. But he's back. And he's pissed. He knows it was us.

There were plenty of witnesses at the club that night and we weren't subtle," Khan says.

"But my guys say it'll take some time to rebuild. Literally every guy close to the family was killed." Sly grins devilishly. "We have time."

"Okay. That leaves one thing and you all know what I'm talking about. I know we're all pissed about what happened, but don't be taking it out on our prisoner. We do just enough to keep him alive," I say.

"When?" Roch asks.

"Tonight," I say, and Roch nods in understanding. He's on my side with this one. "Sly, has the money hit our account?"

"Sure did. But her dad won't fork over the twenty Gs until he's seen his daughter in person."

"Honestly, I don't give a shit about the twenty, but I know he must be losing his mind. I'll talk to Birdie tomorrow." I turn to our newest member. "One last thing. Now that you're in, Clint, you need to do two things. Number one, quit being so fuckin' boring so we can give you a road name. And number two, find us some more prospects. It's your first assignment. You'll be vouching for them and you'll be training them, so choose wisely."

Clint's jaw drops like I just asked him to climb Mount Everest. I bang the gavel, and everyone stands up, giving Clint man hugs to welcome him in. He's still a runt and I can see the wince as each one of my tough as shit brothers pound on his back.

"Roch, can I steal you away from the party?" I ask and get his signature nod. Whenever someone's patched in, there's a huge-ass party and I've already put Sissy and Tabitha in charge of getting the girls and hang-arounds over tonight. It'll be loud and chaotic and a fucking good time. Too bad I'll miss it. Except

I'm not really bummed at all. I'll be with Birdie, right where I want to be.

I lead Roch to my room and unlock the door. My girl's right where I left her. Karen's nose sniffs into the air and when she gets Roch's scent, her eyes pop open and she runs over to him. He scoops her up and stuffs her in the hood of his sweatshirt. She pops her head out to lick him a few times before settling back in like the lazy bitch she is.

"I need to step out, but I don't want to leave her alone. Think you can watch over her?" I ask, observing him. Yeah, they're friends, but my brother is a better man than I am. He's calm and gentle with my birdie. And she trusts him. I don't know if she trusts me all that much yet. I'm a jealous fucker and seeing the way they interact drives me mad. It's not about me right now, though. It's about her.

"K," he says, keeping his eyes on me.

"I'll be gone a few hours. She needs to eat and take her antibiotic and pain meds in an hour." I point to where the bottles are on my nightstand.

"K."

I walk over and kiss Birdie on her forehead, whispering I'll be back soon.

I clasp Roch's shoulder and walk out.

I hop on my bike and ride out of town. The sun is setting, and it's my favorite time of day. Everyone's home from work for the day, but it's before the night crowd comes out, so the roads are virtually empty. The sun glows burnt orange and casts colorful hues on everything it touches.

I barrel up the freeway until I reach the exit to Trucker's house. I'm relieved to see his hog in the driveway. Would've sucked to come all this way and him not be here, but I'm sure he's on his third whiskey by now. Hopefully, he's not too tanked to ride. I don't bother knocking; my bike isn't quiet. I find him at the kitchen table, staring out the window.

"Thought you'd be by," he says without lifting his gaze from outside.

"I've got a present for you." I take a seat across from him.

"Oh yeah? What kind of present?"

"The kind you need to come back to the clubhouse to see."

"Been drinking." He holds up his lowball.

"Sober enough to ride."

"How do you know?" he asks, finally giving me his attention.

"You're not slurring and you're still sitting up straight."

"Been studying me, kid?" He quirks a brow. "You're right. This is my first."

"Wow, old man. Must be a record for you and this time of night."

He blows out a loud exhale. "I'm sorry I bailed on you the other day. I lose my days sometimes."

"I know. Maybe if you put down the bottle—"

"I don't want to let you down again."

"Don't you? Because past behavior says otherwise," I grumble.

"Don't be a little bitch over it. You've loved nothing like I loved your ma. You lose someone like her, then you come talk to me." He takes a healthy gulp of his drink. I need to get this back on track before his first drink turns into his fifth.

"I lost her, too."

"Yeah, I know. I'm sorry. It's just different when you're old and looking forward to things quieting, spending more downtime with the person you dedicated your life to. Then poof. She's gone and you're alone."

"I get that, Trucker. I do. But you still had a son. You still had your club. You about got us all killed."

"I see that now. I was just so laser-focused, I couldn't see anythin' other than my dead wife." He lets out a pained choking sound that hits me right in the gut.

"That's where your present comes in. Come on. Let's ride." I stand up and walk out to my bike. I know he'll follow. He's too curious about what I've got for him.

And I'm right. Minutes later, he has his cut on and he's straddling his bike next to me. It's been a long-ass time since I've ridden with my dad. It feels right, like it always should've been this way. If only Dom hadn't fucked our lives up.

Hopefully Trucker's revenge will bring him back to us.

Chapter
THIRTY-TWO

Bridgette

"Roch, you're here," I say, covering my yawn.

"Y'okay?" he asks from the corner of the room where he's leaning against the wall, as far away from me as possible.

"Actually, I'm hurting," I admit. If it's not the pain that drags me from my slumber, it's the nightmares. But this time, it was the deep ache in my side.

Roch pushes off the wall and hands me a sleeve of crackers. I scoot up the headboard only enough that I'll be able to eat and drink. I open the crackers and nibble on one, but I still have little appetite.

"Eat." He sits on the bed and pushes my hand up to my mouth until the cracker smashes into my lips.

"Fine. Sheesh." I take a bigger bite, but it turns to paste in my dry mouth and I cough.

Roch holds a bottle of water to my lips and tips it slightly. I drink the cool liquid, washing the cracker down. After I've swallowed half the bottle, he takes it away and thrusts another cracker at me. I eat in silence; the only sound in the room is the low bass from music in the great room and the sound of my chewing. It's comfortable, though. Since Roch never has a lot to say, it doesn't bother me when he's quiet.

After I've had exactly six crackers, Roch finally hands over two pills. I swallow them down and push away his hand when he tries to shove more food at me. I've had enough I won't get sick off the pills, but any more and I'll throw everything up.

"Were you there? At the warehouse?" I ask. I'm still piecing together the puzzle in my mind. Working out the timeline and who all was there to rescue me. He lifts his chin. "Thank you for coming for me."

"S'okay."

"Did you kill people?" I ask and get another nod. "Does it bother you to kill people?"

"No."

"Why?" I ask and turn, as much as I can comfortably, toward him. "I'm trying to figure out how you guys do what you do and be okay with it. I was taught murder of any kind is wrong. Don't get me wrong, I'm glad you guys were there and I'm glad Dom and his men are dead. They were evil people and I think the world is better off without them, but I don't think I could ever do it."

"S'a bad world," he says, his navy eyes almost glowing with intensity.

"Loki wants me to stay," I say, snuggling back into the soft mattress. "But I'm afraid."

Roch swallows audibly and grasps onto my hand. Sometimes I think he might look at me as more than a friend, but other times I think he doesn't have words, so his body language and expressions have to do the talking for him. I try not to read into it and accept his friendship with an innocence I still see in him when he's with me or his dogs.

"Dom's gone, but there's always someone else, isn't there? Always a threat?"

He doesn't nod this time; he lowers his head. I think that's worse.

"So I'd never be safe?"

"Always safe." He lifts his gaze and his features harden.

"I wasn't safe when I was with Dom," I explain.

"Mistake," he says, leaning over and brushing stray hair from my forehead. I hear a tinkle of jewelry from under his shirt and reach for the chain of the necklace around his neck. I move slowly, giving him time to stop me, but he doesn't. He squeezes his eyes closed as I pull out the dog tags.

"William Pellman," I read aloud. The aluminum tags are weathered and damaged; they've seen some shit. "Army?"

His eyes open, and he nods.

"Is that why you don't talk much? Something happen to you out there?" I pry.

"Too much."

"I'm sorry, Roch. You're a good man. You deserve to be happy, but I think I understand about ghosts and nightmares."

He stands up and walks into the bathroom, slamming the door closed. The faucet turns on and runs for long minutes. I pull the sheet to my chin, feeling all kinds of guilty. I didn't mean to push him—no, that's a lie. I wanted to push him. I want to save him the way he helped to save me.

Some people are beyond saving.

Ten minutes later Roch appears. All the emotion clouding his features earlier is gone and back are his steely eyes and hardened expression. He really is beautiful. Not in the rugged way Loki is, but handsome just the same.

"Piss." Roch holds up Karen, I'm assuming telling me she needs to pee. Then he's gone.

I stare at the ceiling, contemplating my life. I wanted something more. I didn't want to shop and socialize my existence away. But is trading that in for a life with a criminal any better? And what would I do here? Cook, clean, take care of the overgrown boys who live under this roof? I don't want that any more than I want to sit around spending Daddy's money.

The only thing keeping me here are my feelings for Loki.

It's all-consuming.

It's overwhelming.

It's seeing my whole heart taking on the shape of a dangerous biker.

And that's the crux of my problem.

Chapter
THIRTY-THREE

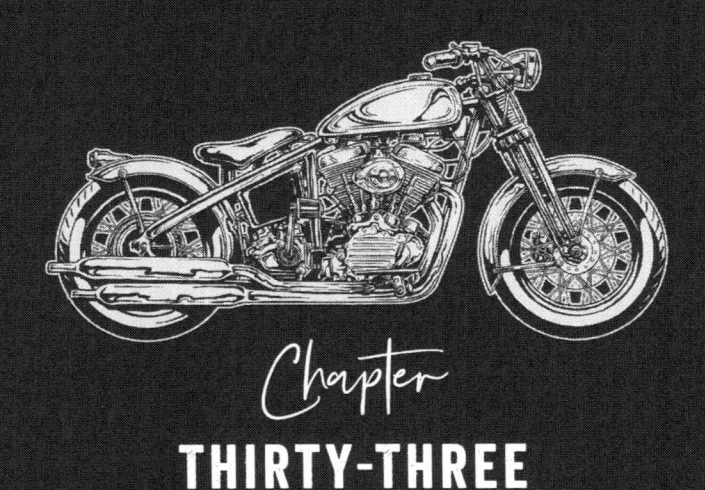

Loki

Trucker follows me into the basement and through the door to the kill room. Dom's being held up by the chains around his wrists. His head sags and his legs have long since given out. He's been stripped of his suit jacket and dress shirt. His shoulder and the side of his face took the brunt of the pellets from the shotgun at the warehouse, but the rest of him is unharmed.

I watch as Trucker steps closer, lifting Dom's head up by his hair. Dom's eyes flutter open and widen at the sight of his biggest enemy in front of him. Trucker slams his head into the wall and then spits on him before letting him go.

"You saved him for me?" Trucker peers over his shoulder at me.

"Yeah. Wasn't sure he was going to make it, but he's strong. Held on despite being shot by a sawed-off." I scratch my chin through my overgrown beard.

He looks like he wants to say more, but he purses his lips

and nods instead. That's enough for me. We're not a kumbaya, talk about your feelings around a campfire type of family. Actions speak louder than our words and me delivering Dom on a silver platter speaks fucking volumes.

This room is full of unique methods of torture. We all have our favorites, so we keep them handy. Trucker opts to pick up a baseball bat. He rears back and slams it into Dom's legs. His pained howl echoes in the closed off room. Trucker rears back again, this time aiming for his gut. The air in Dom's lungs leaves in a whoosh.

"I knew this day would come. The day I'd see your world getting taken from you the way you took mine from me." Trucker tosses the bat. "At first, I only dreamed of my wife. She was everything good in this world. She gave me a son to carry on my legacy. She spent days and nights alone while I was out doing everything she was against, but she didn't care. She knew me. She knew my brothers. She loved all of us. And with one bullet, you stole her from me. From us."

It hurts seeing this six-foot-seven, tough as fucking nails biker talk about his feelings. Especially when he's talking about Ma because he's right. She didn't like the things our club did. She didn't like the danger. But she loved every man who wore our patch. She knew we weren't built to work in an office or manual labor. We have wild blood that can't be tamed and instead of fighting it, she loved us enough to let us be who we were meant to be.

"Where's the key?" Trucker asks. I pull it from my pocket and hand it over. He unlocks the padlocks holding the chains taut and Dom falls into a crumbled pile on the ground. He wheezes loudly, so I know he's still alive. "Help me."

I grab Dom's arms while Trucker grabs his legs and we

maneuver him until he's on his belly with his hands and feet spread out wide. Trucker straddles him and reaches in his pocket for the knife he keeps there. He makes a long and deep incision down Dom's spine, causing him to scream unintelligibly. I think he offers money at one point, then turns to angered threats, which is fucking stupid considering the position he's in.

Trucker reaches into his cut and uses his knife to flay off sections of skin and fat until most of his spine and ribs are exposed. He's careful to avoid arteries or organs, which keeps the fucker alive. I don't get queasy easily, but this is pretty fucked up, even for me.

When he's satisfied with what he's done, he grasps onto one of Dom's ribs and twists it until it snaps. It must puncture or pierce something because a small spray of blood shoots up, painting Trucker's face. He doesn't stop taking rib after rib, twisting each one. Dom grows quiet after three, but even that doesn't stop Trucker. By the time each rib has been broken, both Dom and Trucker are a bloody fucking mess.

"When my nightmares about my wife turned into dreams about killing you, this is what I pictured." He dives into the open space he's created and grabs Dom's heart. His chest heaves with exertion as he yanks it from his body, and it doesn't look easy. The body's not meant to release its organs, but his body also wasn't meant to withstand Trucker's rage either. So eventually, he tears it free.

It would be fucking cool if it were still beating, but it's not. Dom's long since gone. Trucker doesn't seem to care, though. He squeezes the organ, sending blood spraying in all directions, I jump back to avoid having it hit me. I don't want to go back to the room covered in blood. Birdie's been too traumatized lately. That would no doubt not be good for her mental health and it wouldn't make a good argument for why she should stay with me.

"Take him, Hades. Keep him there for when my soul leaves my body. I'll come up with a new way to kill him by then." Trucker stands up, dripping red, heart in his fist. He chucks it at the dead body lying on the ground.

"Come on, I'll get you some clothes. You can shower upstairs." I open the door and start for the stairs.

"Wait," he says.

"Yeah?" I turn around.

"Thanks, kid." He rubs at the back of his neck, looking all kinds of uncomfortable and smearing red with each pass. "I'm, uh, sorry. You know, for disappearing."

"Does this mean you're back?" I ask, sounding hopeful.

"You kids don't need an old man cramping your style."

"You're not that old, and we need more of you old-timers around," I say.

"Well then, I think it does. I've missed it, you know? And your ma's probably not too happy with the way I've been going. She would've wanted me here with you, by your side. I never should've left."

"No, you shouldn't have. But I know we'll all be happy to have you back."

There's hang-arounds and patch pussy crawling around upstairs, so we sneak down the hall. People think they want to be close to the club until they see a man dripping blood, then their stories change, so it's best to hide that side from prying eyes.

Roch's standing outside Birdie's door when I reach my room. Even a brown-eyed, blond-haired, sassy Birdie isn't enough to make him want to socialize, so it doesn't surprise me he's no longer inside.

He sees Trucker and nods before walking down the hall. Birdie's asleep when I sneak into my room and grab some clothes. I hand them off and Trucker disappears into the bathroom. I shoot a text off to Sly and Moto so they can get things cleaned up downstairs.

I kick off my boots and climb into bed with my girl. I'm beyond exhausted and my mind has finally calmed enough to let sleep claim me. I brush her hair off her shoulder and rest my lips there for a long moment. I just need contact, need to feel her energy, but she's so broken, my options are limited.

She stirs and her brown eyes pop open. "What is it?"

"Shh," I hush her and lightly trail a finger down her arm. "Go back to sleep, darlin'. I just need to be close to you."

Her dry cracked lips tip up on the corners and she closes her eyes once more. God, I love being near her. She's better than any tequila I have stocked on my shelf. Better than any amount of weed I could smoke. I didn't know what I was missing before her.

I thought I needed the loneliness.

Needed a tormented soul to make it through this life.

I thought having someone would weaken me, make me soft.

That's not how it is, though. She makes me work harder, smarter, safer. She gives me a reason to live and to keep my club going; I need the fire she lights deep inside me.

Chapter
THIRTY-FOUR

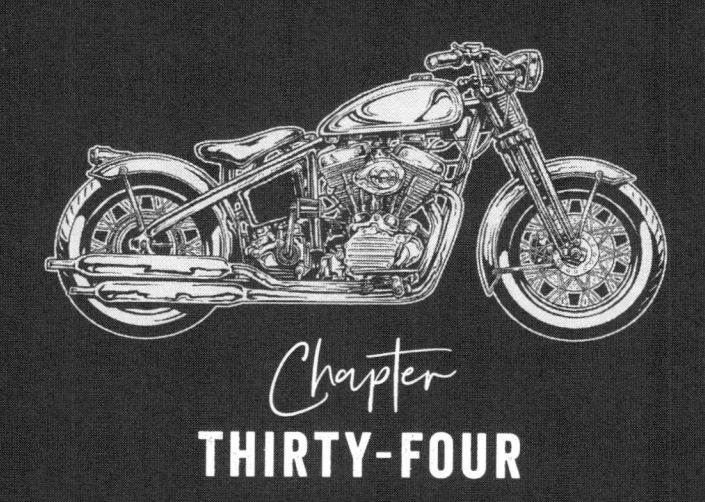

Bridgette

I wake up to Loki thrusting a phone at me. "It's your dad."

I sigh. I should've known he wouldn't be ignored for long. It's not that I don't want to talk to him or see him, it's just… I don't know. I'm embarrassed, as dumb as that sounds. I don't want to explain to him what happened to me. I don't want him to see his daughter and know I've been ruined.

I shake my head as my eyes weep even more sadness.

"I can't," I whisper. "Please."

Loki grunts and brings the phone to his ear. "Yeah, she's in the shower. I'll have her call you later on."

Loki pulls the phone away, cringing. I don't hear the words he says, but I hear the tone. He's pissed. It's been almost two weeks since I've even spoken to him, long before I was taken by Dom. I'm a terrible daughter. I'm all he has left. I snag the phone.

"Hi, Daddy," I say as cheerfully as I can muster.

"Bridgette. My God, I've missed you. When are you

coming home? I'll come get you right now." I hear keys jingling and it fills me with panic.

"No!" I say too gruffly. I take a breath and soften my tone. "You don't need to do that, Daddy. I'm fine. I promise."

"Bridgette. They took you. I don't even know what those people did to you, but it's over now. You can come home. I've kept the extra security, but things are silent. It's safe. Please, baby. Please come home."

"I will," I reassure him. "I promise. I just need a couple days to finish up some things I've got going. Roch has a sort of dog rescue and you know how much I love dogs. I've been helping and I… I just need to wrap things up. But I'm fine. It was scary, but like you said. It's over and I'm safe." *Lies.*

"I don't like this. You're hiding something from me."

"I'm not. Swear it. I'll call you every day and I'll come see you soon." *Bigger lies.*

"Come see me?" he spits out. "You mean come home."

"Right. Yes. I'll come home. Just trust me, okay?"

"It's not you I don't trust. Where's your phone?"

Crushed into a million pieces, probably in a landfill by now.

"Um, I'll get it back. Then you can call me whenever you want."

"You better. I don't want to show up at their door in order to see my daughter."

"You don't have to. I promise. I'll text you in a bit. As soon as I have my phone back." I give Loki a pointed look, telling him with a look he better figure out how to get me a phone and quick. He nods and leaves the room.

"I love you. I have a terrible feeling about all of us, but I trust you."

"Thanks, Daddy. I love you, too. We'll talk soon." I hit

end call before my voice betrays me. I'm surprised I made it through without it cracking.

I push myself to sitting. It's past time for my pain meds and I'm in utter agony. I scan the room until I see the orange bottles on the dresser. I stand up, using the bed to support my body weight. I make it to the nightstand and pop a pill from each bottle into my mouth.

It's then the door opens and my knight in shining leather appears. He's at my side in an instant.

"What the fuck are you doing?" he asks, a cigarette dangling from his lips.

"I needed my pills, but there's no water," I mumble around the bitter medicine.

"Come on."

He helps me into the bathroom and hands me a cup of water.

I swallow them and say, "I need to pee."

He helps me to the toilet and pulls my panties down before walking out of the room to give me privacy. What the heck? I'm perfectly capable of peeing on my own for days and he refuses to leave. Now that I could use the help, he ditches me?

His kindness pisses me off. I don't want a soft and squishy Loki. I don't want rainbows and butterflies. I want my badass biker.

I relieve myself and limp to the sink. Loki appears seconds after I dry my hands.

"Don't do that." I narrow my eyes on him in the mirror. I'm not sure if he can even tell because my face is so swollen, I might be expressionless.

"Do what?"

"Treat me like a delicate flower." My nose stings. I swallow back the emotion and push forward. "Everything that's happened to me? It doesn't change a damn thing. I'm not broken. Maybe I was once a happy little bluebird, naïve and fluttering through life, but I've shed those feathers. Now, I'm a blackbird. Smart and resilient. None of what Dom did to me defines who I am and when you treat me this way, it makes me second-guess myself. Like maybe I should crawl into the corners of my mind and never come back out."

"That's not how I'm trying to make you feel. You're the strongest fuckin' person I know. Most anyone would've come out of that warehouse destroyed. A normal person would've begged to go home, to get as far away from this life as possible. Not you, though. You're here and you're not running away. That tells me all I need to know about you."

"Then why are you being so goddamn sweet?" I yell.

He looks at me like I'm crazy for an entire minute before breaking out into laughter. I don't join. This isn't funny. He eventually calms down, but his smile doesn't leave his lips.

"You are a fuckin' psycho queen, you know that? Every other bitch would've eaten up all the nice." He scoops me up, not careful at all this time and even though it hurts, I'm glad. "Every other bitch would be pissed if I were anything other than sweet. Not my bitch. She's pissed I'm not being an asshole."

"I'm serious, Loki. When you're like this, it makes me feel damaged, like you see me differently. I never want you to see me as anything besides the thorn in your side you like to fuck."

"Language, Miss Davis," he chides, lying back in bed. "You better watch that smart mouth before I wash it out with soap, or maybe my cum. My dirty birdie would like that, wouldn't you?"

"I mean, maybe not right this second." I blush.

"Listen. Can we make a deal?" He sits next to me and holds my hand in his lap. "Can you give me a week to be a decent guy? I'm feeling like all this is my fault and I see your busted-up body and I feel bad. I may not be an honorable person, but I'm a fuckin' human and I have human fuckin' emotions. Let me do my guilty conscience thing for a week and I promise on all things holy I'll go back to bein' an asshole."

"Promise? It's not because you think I'm weak?"

"No, Birdie. It's not because I think you're weak. I'm the weak one. I see this swollen eye and busted up lip and I just want to baby you over it. Can you let me do that, please?"

"Fine," I agree.

"Thanks." He smirks in that sexy way he does. Just feeling the tingles low in my belly gives me hope I won't feel like this forever.

"Feed me?"

"My girl's hungry, huh? I'll go grab you something from the kitchen. I think you're ready to move on from crackers."

"Toast maybe? With raspberry preserves?"

"Now that you know this has an expiration, you're going to milk it for all it's worth, huh?"

"Sure am."

I spend a few days in bed. Sometimes alone, but most of the time with Loki plastered to my side. He waits on me hand and foot. He nurses me back to health little by little. He wakes me at night when my nightmares get to me and listens during the day when things come back to me.

Then I spend the next week puttering around the house because I'm bored. Loki has me on light duty and only lets me out of the room for a few hours at a time, and only when he's busy doing other things.

Roch lets me help him feed and play with the dogs. We take quiet walks together around the property. I learn the names of all the dogs and their unique personalities. They accept me into their pack, and I fall in love with each one. Karen will always be my favorite, though.

Goblin and I watch the news and talk about current events. He teaches me about politics and Sly teaches me how to hack cell phones and we laugh for hours reading through Lindsay's and Ruby's texts. Moto shows me how to tune up the bikes and soon, I'm doing it on my own.

Tabitha and Sissy let me help them in the kitchen. I learn how to cook for the first time in my life and discover I love it. It's rewarding to take a bunch of ingredients, put them together in measured amounts, and then have an entire meal. I'm good at it, too.

But nighttime is my favorite. It's when Loki and I tuck into bed and talk. We tell each other stories about our moms and our childhoods. We get to know each other and talk a lot about things we want in life. Well, he tells me what his hopes and dreams are, and I tell him I haven't figured mine out yet. He tells me I'm still young and there's time. He's right. It's easy to forget I'm just eighteen. He's twice my age and only now is he figuring out his future.

I call Daddy on my new phone every day and he begs me to come home. While I'm feeling better and healing, my face is still littered with bruises and my gunshot wound still aches. But by the next week, he can't be held off any longer.

"I don't care what excuse you have today, if you don't come home, I will show up there and drag you home," he threatens during our morning phone call.

"Two more days, then I'll come home and see you."

"No. You will come to stay by this afternoon, or I'll call the cops."

"No, Daddy. Don't do that. I'll come home."

He can't call the cops. Questions will be asked, and puzzle pieces will be put together. That won't be good for anyone.

"You have an hour." The line goes dead.

I'm in the room alone while Loki is handling "club business." While he'll be happy to take me home, he won't be happy if I *move* back home. I won't be either. I want to be here. I don't want to give this life up. I finally feel like I belong.

Not seeing any other choice, I pack my backpack up. The cage is still intact; I won't let Loki take it down. I explained how when I'm feeling the most scared, it helps me feel safe. He doesn't understand it, and he really doesn't like it, but since he's picking his battles with me right now, I win.

"What are you doing?"

I look up to see a red-faced Loki. "My dad threatened to call the cops if I don't show."

"He did what?"

"He said I have to go home today, or he'll call the cops."

"Like fuck he will." He tosses my backpack on the ground and helps me stand. I can walk okay, but it's changing positions that still hurts. "Come on."

"He won't like this."

"Don't care."

Chapter
THIRTY-FIVE

Loki

I stew from the driver's seat. Not only do I hate riding in a cage, but I hate that Birdie would rather leave me than tell her dad. I can't tell if she's embarrassed or just a pussy.

We pull up to the mansion I'll never be able to afford, nor would I want to, and I help my girl out of the car. A giant black and tan rottweiler bolts out the front door and rushes over to us. Birdie squats down, beaming at the mutt and loving all over her.

"Sophie! I missed you so much," she chokes out, laying kisses all over the dog's face. I tug her back to standing and pin her with a look.

Those lips are mine.

Those kisses are mine.

Birdie shakes her head in disapproval, but I see the grin she's holding back. She tries to act annoyed with my possessive tendencies, but her cunt doesn't lie and hers is always wet and ready when I assert my dominance.

Birdie reaches for my hand as we walk through the front door and come face-to-face with a furious man.

"What happened to you? You said you were fine."

"I am, just got a little banged up is all."

The swelling on Birdie's face is almost gone, and the bruises have faded to a pale yellow and green. She looks a million times better, but I don't think it'll help for me to point that out.

"This is more than banged up." He cups her face, inspecting every injury. Birdie gives him a minute before pulling from his hold.

"You should see the other guy," she jokes, and he scowls.

"And what is this?" Davis points to our joined hands.

"Daddy," Birdie whines.

"Don't 'Daddy' me." He turns his glare on me. "We need to talk."

"Anything you have to say, you can say in front of me," she says.

"Bridgette, not now. Run on up to your room."

"I'm not a child!" she shouts, sounding exactly like a child.

"Birdie, why don't you give us a minute?" I kiss the top of her head and give her ass a pat. She glares daggers at me but does as I say and carefully climbs up the stairs. I watch her until she reaches the top, just to be sure she makes it. When I turn my eyes back on Davis, his face is an ugly shade of red. "Mr. Davis—"

"If you think for one second I'll pay you that twenty grand for shacking up with my kid, you're wrong," he says through gritted teeth.

"I don't give a shit about your money, sir."

"I don't know what game you're playing, but Bridgette isn't a pawn."

"I'm not playin' no game."

"Then what the hell are you doing with her?"

"I care about her."

"You *care* about her? She's a kid and you're"—he gestures up and down my body—"in a biker gang."

"I know what I am and what I'm not. I'm sorry you're not thrilled with your daughter's boyfriend—"

"Not thrilled?" he roars. "That is the understatement of the fucking year."

"Listen, I'm trying to be respectful here, but you're making it hard."

"I don't care. You can leave now."

"If that's how you want it." I start up the steps.

"Where are you going?"

"To get Birdie."

"Who is Birdie?" he asks, confused as all hell.

"I am." My girl appears from her bedroom door holding a suitcase.

"Get back in your room," he orders.

I take the suitcase and hold out an arm for her to grab onto as she steps down.

"I won't, Daddy."

"I'm warning you, young lady."

My girl stands proud and wraps her arms around her dad's neck. She hugs him while he stews, completely taken aback at the direction things have gone.

"I'm sorry you don't understand, and I don't blame you. I never would've believed it if you'd told me a month ago I'd be living in a motorcycle club, but he makes me happy, Daddy. I want us to be close, I don't want to lose you, but it's time I lived my life. Plus, it's kind of your fault for sending me with them in the first place," she sasses.

"Should've stopped while you were ahead," I say under my breath. I pull Birdie toward the front door.

Davis follows us out, too stunned to say anything else. Can't blame the man. If my daughter showed up with a schmuck on a Harley, I'd beat his ass to the ground. Fortunately for me, Davis isn't capable of beating anyone up, let alone me.

I load her luggage into the car and then help her in the passenger seat. I've just opened my door when I turn back to the man standing on his porch with his hands on his hips.

"Did you take care of the vial?" I ask.

"Why do you care?"

"It made a lot of trouble for a lot of people. Just makin' sure it's no longer an issue."

"I destroyed it the day I got it back."

"Good. You know Dom's brother, Anthony, will come for you once he builds the syndicate back up, right?" I ask, and Davis pales. Guess he didn't know that. "Don't worry about it. We got your back. We're family now."

"No, we're not and I don't want you to have my back. I don't want you to have my daughter. This isn't how I thought things would go."

"It's true what they say about being careful what you ask for." I grin wolfishly because I'm a shithead.

I duck into in the driver's seat, place a hand on Birdie's thigh, and peel out of the driveway.

When we're back on the freeway, I sneak a peek at my girl. The window's down, blowing her blond hair in every direction. Her sunglasses are perched on her nose and she's smiling. It makes me feel like everything will be okay.

Her dad knows about us, Trucker's putting the bottle

down, Dom's dead. Now all that's left is getting my girl healthy, mentally and physically.

She says she's fine, that she doesn't need to talk about it with me or anyone else, but I don't think it's true. I see her slightly cringe when I wrap my arms around her. I still wake her from her nightmares where she's scrambling to get away from me before realizing I'm not fucking Dom. I hate that he made her this way. If I could, I'd resurrect the fucker and kill him all over again, only this time it'd be me squeezing the life from him.

Instead of taking the exit to the clubhouse, I stay on the freeway toward Tahoe. She doesn't notice at first, too caught up in singing along to the seventies rock channel I'm blaring through the speakers, but eventually, she pulls her sunglasses off and looks around at the scenery.

"Where are we going?" she asks.

"I've got a little surprise for you."

"What is it?"

"You'll see."

Twenty minutes later we're pulling up to my property. Only things look a little different now.

"Oh my God. Where did it go?" She jumps out of the car and spins around in the middle of what used to be a dwelling. All that's left is flat ground with capped off utilities.

"The second we got paid, I made a few calls and the construction company came out to demolish the place. We're ready to build."

"We?"

"I thought if you were going to live out here with me, you might want a say in how it looks."

"Wow. We're really doing this, huh?"

"What part of the last few weeks has given you doubts? When I bathed you and took care of you while your wound was healing?" I wrap my arms around her and tip her chin up to look me in the eyes. "Maybe when I held you in my arms every night? Or was it when I told you were it for me?"

"Isn't it kind of crazy to move so fast?"

"I've been known to be a little crazy." I chuckle.

"I don't want to sit around and do nothing. Or worse, take care of you guys full-time."

"What do you want from life?"

"I haven't figured that out yet, either."

"Darlin', I don't give a fuck what you do. The only thing I care about is havin' your sexy ass on the back of my bike and in my bed."

She bites her lip nervously, her pretty brown eyes leaving mine. "I don't know if I'm ready for that."

"We talked about this. My cock wants to be buried in you every chance it gets, but it's just fine waiting for you."

"What if it takes a year? Ten years? What if I never want to have sex ever again?"

Fuck, that's a painful thought. Could I really spend my life jacking off while sleeping next to the sexiest woman alive? If I'm honest, I don't think so. I don't say that, though. I'm not that big of a prick.

"I'd hope if it takes that long, you'd finally ask for some help. Not just for my wrist that'd end up with carpal tunnel, but for you too. It wouldn't be fair to shut that part off before you even had a chance to come into yourself." There. A non-answer she'll hopefully accept as a real answer.

She hangs her eyes, and I cup her cheeks, forcing her to face this. I'm not doing either of us any good by allowing her to keep avoiding the problem. My black heart breaks when I see her damp cheeks. Jesus fuck. This girl has made me feel more in a month than I have in a year.

"I'm scared," she whispers.

"Of me?"

"Of everything. I'm scared I'll fall in love with you and you'll figure out I'm not worth it. I'm scared Dom's brother will show up and want to take me as revenge. I'm scared my dad will never accept us and I'll lose him. I'm just scared."

"Do I make you feel safe?"

"That's not the point."

"Answer me. Do. I. Make. You. Feel. Safe?" I punctuate the words.

"Yes, and no."

"Well, then I haven't done my job very well, have I?" It hurts to think this is what's stopping her from moving on.

"It's not that. I don't know if you could. It was terrifying, Loki. I thought I was going to die before you could get to me. The only time I don't feel that way is—"

"In the cage," I finish, hanging my head.

I find her in there more often than not and each time she begs me to lock her in there. She flips when I threaten to take it out of our room. She's using it as a crutch.

"Yes."

"I don't think it's healthy."

"Healthy for who? Because I feel more like myself each time I go in there."

"This is so messed up."

"I've been thinking about it and if you just locked me in there sometimes and don't give me a hard time. Only when things are really bad."

Birdie's **BIKER**

I release her and walk over to the edge of the creek. I close my eyes and listen to the water rushing along the ground. It calms me and I can't wait to hear this sound every night when we go to sleep and have it be the first sound we hear in the morning.

My mind races with what Birdie's trying to convince me of because I don't know what the right answer is. Part of me wants to drop her off in inpatient therapy until she lets go of this dumb idea. But part of me thinks whatever makes her feel better. Whatever will bring her back to me. Mind, body, and soul.

Her arms snake around my middle, and she rests her cheek on my back. I went from being a bachelor, someone who swore they'd never get emotionally involved, to being in a relationship with a skittish, traumatized girl I don't know how to fix. Maybe she'd be better off with her dad. He could get her the help she needs.

"I know you don't like the idea. I know you think I'm messed up for even wanting it. Maybe I am, but when I think about you being the one trapping me. Having you be the one in control of my safety, you be my captor—"

I quickly spin around in her arms and put a hand over her mouth to stop her from spewing any more bullshit. "I'm not your captor. I never was. I know it felt like I was, but if you'd really put up a fight, I would've sent you back to your dad. I messed with your head and it was wrong for me to do. I don't want to be your jailer. I want you to be my partner. My ride or die."

She pushes my hand away so she can speak. "Most of the time, I can be that. But sometimes I just feel so out of control. When I'm in there, when I know no one can get to me unless they go through you, I feel safe. My chaotic mind calms. I know it sounds stupid and ridiculous, but it's what I need."

I study her for long minutes. She's starting to make sense, and it scares me. My brothers'll give me all kinds of shit for this. Admittedly, it was a huge fucking turn-on to lock her up before, when it was just for fun. I liked it. A hell of a lot. If I can convince myself we're the same people as back then, this could work.

"And you'll tell me if things change?"

"I will."

"And you're sure this will help?"

"I'm positive."

"Then I'll try. For you."

She beams up at me, looking more like her carefree self than she has since I pulled her from that warehouse. I press my lips to hers, not wanting to kill her smile, but needing to soak up her light. Her arms snake around my neck and I lift her off her feet, not breaking the kiss. Her tongue peeks out tentatively and I open for her. It's more than she's given me in weeks, and I soak it up.

Our tongues tangle and our lips move. She tastes like mint and sunshine. Like Sunday mornings and forever. Fuck, I love our connection. I'm addicted to her. I never want this to end. And maybe if I play my cards right, it doesn't have to.

Chapter
THIRTY-SIX

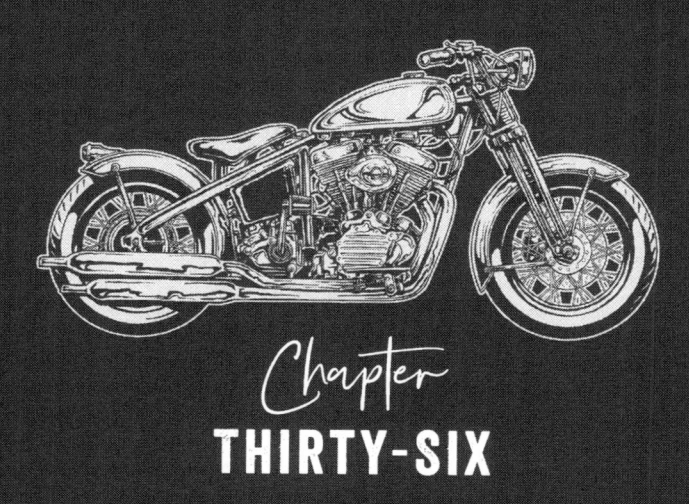

Bridgette

We drive back to the clubhouse with an electricity sparking between us. I've only felt trickles of happiness since Loki rescued me, but knowing he's on board with what I need, the dam has broken and I'm full-on excited. Like a child standing outside the gates of Disneyland for the first time. Not knowing exactly what's in store, but knowing it will be amazing.

I didn't tell Loki this, but I did some reading online. I wanted to know why I had this powerful urge. Turns out there's an entire community of women who like to be caged. Who like to turn over control to someone they trust. A lot of them are like me and suffered sexual and emotional trauma. I joined an online group under a fake account and connected with a few women, who gave me the words I couldn't find on my own.

By the time we park, I'm almost bouncing in my seat. I don't know if he expected me to want this the second we got home, but I do. Until now, he's refused to lock me in. When he finds me in there, he says nothing. He simply lifts me up and takes me back out. Now that we have an understanding, the only place I want to be is in his cage.

"Right now?" he asks as I tug him toward our room.

"Please?" I beg.

"Jesus Christ." He scrubs a hand down his scruffy face but allows me to direct us down the hallway.

I immediately take off my confining jeans, wanting to be comfortable. The second I step through the door to the hastily welded together metal, my heart slows and tranquility washes over me. I curl up on the foam pad and cover myself with the blanket.

Loki watches me intently. He doesn't want to do it. I see it in his eyes. I give him a reassuring nod and with a loud exhalation, he closes the door and turns the key on the padlock.

"So, I just leave you here? Go about my day?"

"If I need you, I have my cell. But otherwise, yeah. Do what you did before. Bring me meals, take me to the bathroom. Just give me a few hours, okay?"

"Sure, darlin'. Whatever you need," he says, but I know he's still unsure.

With a last glance, he leaves, closing the door behind him. I feel giddy. Amped up. Weirdly aroused. But most of all, I feel completely safe. It's not the same as having his powerful arms around me at night. I feel protected like that, but not completely out of harm's way. This place is my fortress. Impenetrable unless you want to take on my biker boyfriend and the one man who did is dead.

I reach under the pillow and pull out the latest dirty novel Tabitha has let me borrow. For the next few hours I get lost in the world of a bad boy hero and an innocent girl who falls into his clutches. It's naughty and filthy and only feeds the desire pooling low in my belly.

I read on as he pushes her up against a wall and runs his hand up her skirt. He toys with her and dominates her. God, how I want to feel this way again. I want Loki's hand smacking my ass. I want him to look at me like he did back then. Like I was a sin he couldn't wait to be guilty of.

The doorknob turns, pulling me from my fantasy.

"What are you doing?" Loki says, closing the door behind him, but his eyes narrowed at where my hand is.

It's then I realize I'm cupping myself, my fingers moving back and forth on the outside of my panties. I got so lost in the book, I wasn't even aware I was touching myself. My eyes widen and I jerk my hand away.

"Don't stop on my account." He smirks.

"It's this book," I say as I close it and tuck it away.

"What were you reading?" He sits down on the bed and rests back on his hands. He's wearing tight, faded and torn black jeans and the outline of his erection down his thigh is obvious.

"A love story."

"What kind of love story makes you want to touch yourself?"

"A good one?" I smile shyly, embarrassed to have been caught.

"Show me how good. Take off your panties," he demands.

His words send a thrill through my body that stops at my core. I may not be ready to have sex again, but this feels like something I can do from behind the bars. My side protests a little when I wiggle my panties down, but not enough to make me stop. Not even enough to take the over-the-counter meds I've switched to.

"Mmm," he moans. "You're so wet. Now take off your shirt and show me your tits."

I blush but comply. I still have a small bandage covering my wound, but other than that, I bare myself completely for him.

He sits upright and rubs his palm over his hardness. "Play with yourself. Rub your sweet clit, pinch your nipples, do whatever makes you feel good."

"What about you?"

"You want to see me stroke my hard cock while I watch you?"

I nod, too bashful to say the word aloud. He stands and removes his cut and T-shirt, then he pulls his jeans down his long, muscular legs. He's not wearing underwear, so when he stands, his stiff length stands straight and proud. The tip glints with a bead of pre-cum that has me licking my lips.

He lowers his head and spits a line of saliva down his erection. He walks to the cage and rests a hand on top, his other hand stroking himself slowly.

"Let me see those fingers move."

I realize I've been frozen watching him. I press two fingers inside myself and gather some moisture. I use it to lube my hard nub as I rub tantalizing circles. My other hand massages my breasts and pinches my nipple. I'm not a masochist, I don't think, but I like the bite of pain from being spanked or having my nipples pinched.

"That's my good girl. Imagine those are my fingers getting you off, my teeth biting your tits, my dick fuckin' your tight cunt. Can you feel it?"

"Mmhmm."

"Now stick a finger inside, tell me how you feel," he says as his hand strokes faster.

I insert a finger inside me while I muster the courage to talk dirty. If this is what I want, how I want it, I need to be able to be brave.

"Warm, wet, swollen," I say breathily. I clench down on my finger and it feels so good. I rub myself on the inside and find a spot that has my hips bucking off the pad. "Oh my God."

"You found your G-spot. Press down on it while using your palm to grind on your clit. Fuck, you're so hot. I want you to come with me."

"I'm so close," I moan and an orgasm washes over me. "I'm coming."

"Shit, yes." His mouth parts and his breaths come as fast as his hand works up and down.

Black spots fill my vision and my movements become erratic, uncontrollable. I chase the sensations until they're right there, blanketing me in endorphins. It's never ending as I watch ropes of ejaculate shoot from Loki's dick. He grunts through his release, our eyes locking as we share this moment.

We're both a panting mess by the time we've come down. Intensity rolls off both of us in waves, causing a torrent of emotion to pull us together. In a flash, Loki has the cage unlocked, and he's scooping my naked body up.

"Alone time is over, Birdie," he whispers in my ear.

"I'm okay with that." And I am. I feel so much better, especially knowing this is an option for me now. That I don't have to worry about the next time my mind gets away from me.

He tosses back the covers and lays me down before climbing in next to me. He wraps me up in his warmth. Our limbs tangle and our breaths mingle. This man is perfect for me. This life is perfect for me. For the first time, I'm excited about my future, even if I don't know what it looks like.

"I'm falling in love with you," I say.

"Of course you are, how could you not?" he asks smugly and I smack his chest.

"I'm being serious." I reach up and yank his beanie off his head so I can run my fingers through his black, coarse hair.

"I've never loved a girl before—"

"I don't need you to say it back. I just wanted you to know how I feel."

"You didn't let me finish." He leans in and bites my lower lip, giving it a tug. "I've never loved a girl before you."

A huge, dumb smile takes over my entire body. I feel it all the way to my toes.

"I got somethin' for you." He hops out of bed and I sit up, pulling the sheet up over my still naked body. He walks over to a black gift bag I didn't notice he'd brought in. He sets it next to me.

"What is it?" I ask, tearing the black tissue paper from the top.

"Proof that you're mine," he says cryptically.

I reach inside and feel stiff leather. I pull it out to find a black cut, a lot like his, only smaller. I look up at him questioningly. Girls can't join the club. Sissy and Tabitha told me that much when I asked why they don't just join since they haven't become "old ladies."

"Turn it around." He spins his finger in a circle.

I look at the back of the cut and see a huge RBMC logo

with the words "Property of" above the patch and "Loki" below it. "What does this mean?"

"It means you're my old lady. No one can fuck with you." He grins. "Except me."

"I love it." I put it on despite not having clothes on. "It fits."

"It was made for you." He crawls over to me, gently pushing me onto the mattress. He pulls the sheet down so the only thing covering my breasts is the cut. "Goddamn that's hot. I promise I won't take this too far, but I need to kiss you. Need to feel you under me. That okay?"

"Yes. I need it too."

His pillowy lips meet mine and I bask in the sensations. I relish in his cigarette and tequila taste and tobacco and motor oil scent. It's uniquely him and I wouldn't change it for anything. He kisses down my neck and suckles on my earlobe, gently nipping at it.

His mouth barely leaves my skin for him to say, "I'm happy to keep you in your cage for as long as you want. But I'll never clip your feathers, Birdie. When you're ready to spread your wings and fly, I'll be your safe place to land."

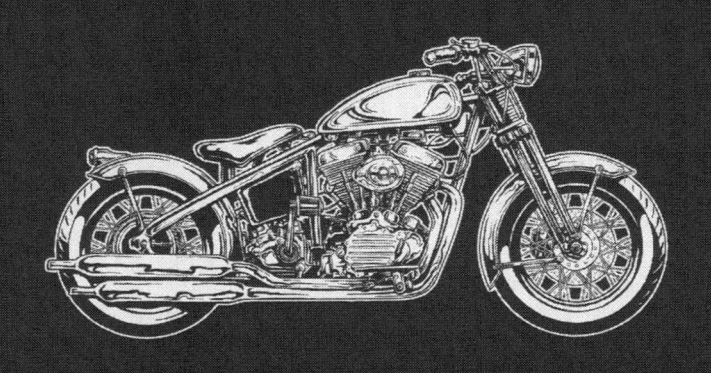

EPILOGUE

I kill the engine in front of mine and Birdie's tiny cabin in the woods. It's taken six long months and endless hours of planning, but it's finally finished. My brothers and I did most of the building ourselves, but inside is all Birdie. She painstakingly chose every piece of furniture and every decoration. Which is good, because if it were left up to me, there'd be a mattress on the ground and an oversized leather couch to match an equally oversized TV, and that's all.

It's a two-bedroom, one-bath log cabin made from trees we took down ourselves. The sides and back of the home are mostly windows. Since we don't have neighbors, except for the bears and other woodland creatures, there aren't curtains. Being able to watch the outside world from every room in the house is exactly what I wanted.

I walk up the steps to the custom front door that has an iron RBMC logo on it. Opening the door, I disable the alarm and am bombarded by two gray and white American Bullies and one giant rottweiler. The pits were a gift from Roch when we moved in. I think they were his way of keeping Birdie safe. I know it was hard for him to let go of two of his girls, and it choked me up when he stopped by to deliver them. Romy and Michelle are tanks and look mean as hell. I didn't understand, just by looking at them, that I was adopting two eighty-pound couch potatoes who like to cuddle. At least until they think there's a threat, then they crowd Birdie and won't even let me near her.

As for Sophie, Davis was all too happy to send her to live with us. He knew how protective that dog is and with his daughter living with a lawless biker, he wanted an extra layer of security. She gets along great with the other two bitches, and Birdie loves having her own pack of dogs living with us.

I open the door and let them all outside, off to protect the property from every squirrel who dares step foot near the house. I walk into the open concept living room, dining room, and kitchen. I don't see my girl. I know she's here because her periwinkle, pussy Prius is parked in the driveway. I hate that fucking thing. There's absolutely nothing badass about it. But she loves it, and since I only drive my Harley, I got her what she wanted.

The rich aroma of garlic and tomato sauce fills the air. Birdie's discovered her love of cooking back at the clubhouse and it's only grown in this gourmet kitchen she designed. She's even been talking about going to culinary school, maybe opening her own farm to kitchen restaurant all the rich fuckers she knows like to eat. I don't get involved in her dreams. My only job is to make sure they come true, so if she wants to slave in a kitchen all day, I'll make sure she gets it.

I turn to the table and coatrack by the door. I take off my cut and put my piece in the table's drawer. I kick off my boots and go looking for my girl. My first stop is the master bedroom. There are French doors back here that lead to a huge porch. More often than not, I find her back here reading her dirty books. It's always a good sign because she gets all worked up and I can expect some kinky fuckery to happen. But she's not in the room or on the porch.

I retrace my steps down the hallway and open the door to the only room I haven't searched. What I find sucks the breath from my lungs. There's a new piece of furniture in our guest bedroom. Front and center sits a birdcage. Not a normal one, a huge one. Big enough for a person. I know this because inside the cage is my birdie. She's perched on a small swing that hangs from the center and she's naked.

A blush creeps up her ivory skin as she rocks back and forth. Her tits sway with the movement and it's the fucking hottest thing I've ever seen. And I've seen some shit.

"This is new," I say dumbly. What else can I say?

"I had it specially made. I love our house. But it was missing something."

"I see that. Does this mean I'm going to have to start locking you up again? I thought you didn't need it anymore."

We moved into this house a month ago. Along with saying goodbye to living with a bunch of dirty bikers, we said goodbye to the cage. It served its purpose, but she was relying on it less and less. It transformed from something she used as a security blanket into something we used as a sex toy. I assumed with the move we'd find other methods of play, and we have.

We've explored all of Birdie's fantasies. She found her love of being tied up, of being spanked by not just my hand, but a paddle, a brush, basically whatever I can get my hands on. We've trussed her from the ceiling, clamped her nipples, plugged her tight asshole up, pretty much anything she reads in those damn books, we've tried. The only hang-up she still has is giving blowjobs. It's the one thing Dom did to her she can't forget.

It's fine by me. I don't need her mouth when I have her other two holes to take advantage of.

"I don't need it. But I missed it." She spreads her legs, showing me her dripping cunt.

Jesus fuck.

"So, what's the game tonight, Birdie?" I pull my shirt up over my head and unbutton my pants, letting them fall to the floor. I'm thankful I didn't put on boxers today. Less clothing to contend with. I grip the base of my cock and squeeze hard to push back my arousal. She's turning me right the fuck on and I want this to last.

Birdie hops off the swing and grips two of the bars in her hands. She presses her front against them, squishing her tits. I'm not walking away from this alive, I decide. My heart can't take all this fucking hot imagery.

"I want you to lock me up." She reaches outside of the cage and flicks a padlock fixed to the door.

"Where's the key?"

"It's a passcode. One-eight-four-three."

I punch in the numbers and hear the lock engage. "That's handy."

"Now I want you to fuck me through the bars." She turns around and presses her tiny little ass against the bars, showing me just how wet she is. Her cum is leaking down her thighs, making my mouth water.

I reach a hand between her legs, thankful the spacing on

the bars allows for it. The old dog crate had bars so close together, there's no way I could've done this before.

"Which hole do you want me in?" I spread her juices from her pussy up to her puckered back entrance.

"Master's choice," she breathes out.

Master is the other recent addition to our sex life. I think it came out accidentally one night, but she liked the way it sounded and how it made her feel like she was handing over control. So it stuck. Not gonna lie, it turns me on too. The trust she gives me is something I'll never take for fucking granted.

"As much as I want to feel your asshole around my dick, I prefer to do that when I can shove a dildo in your pussy at the same time." I line myself up with her cunt and shove in. She's so wet, the slide is easy.

"Oh my God," she gasps.

"Fuck, Birdie. You feel so good." I reach inside and grab onto her forearms. I use them as leverage to fuck the shit out of her. Hard and fast. Taking no prisoners.

Every time my hips meet her ass, she grunts in pleasure. From this position, I hit deep, her pussy sheathing me fully. My balls slap against her, adding to the erotic sounds coming from my girl. Goddamn, she's perfect.

"I'm going to come," she whines.

"Not until I'm ready for you."

Her ass shakes with the force, her tits bob rhythmically, and her hair swings to and fro. And it's all in front of a vast window looking out into the woods. There's no one to see us like this, but it still feels voyeuristic. My balls tighten and an orgasm builds from the base of my spine.

"Come now," I grit out, letting my own release spill free.

Birdie's **BIKER**

Birdie screams my name and her pussy clamps down almost painfully. She's a tiny girl and I'm a big guy; it's a tight fit already. But when she comes, fuck. It's like heaven and hell, all wrapped up into one.

I bring us down, slowing my thrusts. When I pull out, a river of cum spills from her pussy and onto the rubber-padded floor of the cage. If she hadn't just sucked every drop from me, the sight would be enough to have me wanting to fuck her all over again.

I rub my ejaculate all over her bare cunt, even pressing some of it back in. She's on birth control now, but I still like to test the odds and see if my super sperm can knock her up. She's still young, but I'm an old man. I want to start a family. She's not quite on board until she figures out what direction she wants to take her career, but accidents happen and I'm always hopeful. Yeah, it makes me an asshole, but everyone already knows that. I don't hide it.

I give her swollen bits a rough smack, and she cries out again. I grab onto the fleshy part of her ass, watching it turn bright red. Her skin is so fair and so sensitive, it doesn't take much for me to leave a mark. I fucking love that too.

She stands up on wobbly legs and I punch the combination into the lock and open the door. Just like always, I sweep her up and carry her to our bed. I don't know what I like more. When she gives it to me rough and nasty, or afterward when we take it slow and I'm able to explore every inch of her at my leisure. Both, I guess.

When I've got her body pressed to mine with the silky sheet covering us and the French doors open to let the fresh air and the sound of the creek fill the room, I kiss her temple and say, "I like your surprise."

"I didn't know if you'd be mad. I'm not reverting, I promise."

"I know. I can see it in your eyes. You're happy. Kinky as fuck, but happy."

She giggles, and it sounds as melodic as the birds singing outside.

"How was your day?" she asks.

"Good."

She never asks for specifics on what I do during the day. She doesn't want to know, and I don't want to tell her. She knows what it means every time I get my kit out and tattoo another tally mark on my pec, but still, she doesn't ask.

It's the life I've chosen, and just like I've given her the freedom to choose her own destiny, she gives me mine. I'm sure it's not what she'd choose, but she gets it. It's who I am.

"How're the guys?"

"Good. Roch's still on his vacation or whatever the fuck he's doing. Sly and Moto are probably fucking the brunette they were eyeing before I left, Goblin's organizing a rally this weekend, Khan has some tiny bitch he's been hiding away in his room for a week, and Bullet is on babysitting duty, keeping the prospects in line."

"It's still weird you guys named him Bullet. To me, he'll always be Clint."

"Don't say that in front of him. A road name is like a badge of honor. Once it's given, it can't be changed. If you use his proper name, it'll make him look like a pussy."

"Fine, I'll only use it when we're alone."

I pull her on top of me and narrow my eyes on her. "When are you and Bullet alone?"

"I guess we're not." She rests her cheek on my chest. "Bullet it is, then."

"Good girl."

Her head pops up. "Oh, I got accepted into UNR to their culinary program."

"Really? That's awesome. When does it start?"

"In a few weeks. I just made the cut-off."

"I can't wait for you to have homework. I love your cooking."

"I don't know if you get homework in cooking school."

"Well, you can always bring me home leftovers."

A buzzer dings from the kitchen. "Oh! I made lasagna."

She jumps out of bed, but I hold on to her wrist. "That's not how this works, Birdie. I get dirty with you, then you give it to me sweet."

Pink tinges her cheeks adorably. "How about we have lasagna, then I'll let you eat your dessert off my boobs?"

"Now that I can agree to." I release her. She pulls on a fluffy robe and disappears down the hall.

I don't know what good I did to deserve a life like this, but fuck if I won't enjoy every second of it. I reach into my nightstand and take out my tattoo gun. After this morning's visit to the mayor's son, I need another tally. I was the one to take his life after hearing what he's doing to some girls from the sorority at his college. He pissed off the wrong rich girl whose daddy has used us to take care of his own problems.

My bank account grew by five digits today, and my only repentance is this mark. The needle pierces my skin and although I should watch what I'm doing, I close my eyes and feel every puncture. Another soul gone by my hands. Another scumbag gone from this earth.

"You coming?" Birdie calls out and I quickly finish up.

It's difficult to balance a life of love and hate, but I'm made of tough stuff and someday, when I have a son of my own, he'll take my place. Just the way I did for Trucker. It's not a legacy most men would want to leave, but I'm not most men. I'm Loki, President of the Royal Bastards MC, Reno Chapter.

THE FUCKIN' END

Need more Royal Bastards? This series continues in *Truly's Biker*. Out now!

ROYAL BASTARDS MC SERIES SECOND RUN

E.C. Land: *Cyclone of Chaos*
Chelle C. Craze & Eli Abbot: *Ghoul*
Scarlett Black: *Ice*
Elizabeth Knox: *Rely On Me*
J.L. Leslie: *Worth the Risk*
Deja Voss: *Lean In*
Khloe Wren: *Blaze of Honor*
Misty Walker: *Birdie's Biker*
J. Lynn Lombard: *Capone's Chaos*
Ker Dukey: *Rage*
Crimson Syn: *Scarred By Pain*
M. Merin: *Declan*
Elle Boon: *Royally F**ked*
Rae B. Lake: *Death and Paradise*
K Webster: *Copper*
Glenna Maynard: *Tempting the Biker*
K.L. Ramsey: *Whiskey Tango*
Kristine Allen: *Angel*
Nikki Landis: *Devil's Ride*
KE Osborn: *Luring Light*
CM Genovese: *Pipe Dreams*
Nicole James: *Club Princess*
Shannon Youngblood: *Leather & Chrome*
Erin Trejo: *Unbreak Me*
Winter Travers: *Six Gun*
Izzy Sweet & Sean Moriarty: *Broken Ties*
Jax Hart: *Desert Rose*

Royal Bastards MC Facebook Group
www.facebook.com/groups/royalbastardsmc

Links can be found in our Website:
www.royalbastardsmc.com

ACKNOWLEDGMENTS

Tyrel, thank you for always supporting me, even when I overextend myself (which is all the time).

Kristi, just like Romy and Michelle, we laugh through all our ups and downs. I couldn't do this without you.

Lorelai and Mabel, I know this is the only part of my books you read, so I better put something in here for you. Thank you for being supportive, even when there's a naked man on the cover and it grosses you out.

Mom, thank you for being so proud of me.

Sultan, Sara, Sarah, & Elizabeth, you guys give me life with your feedback and your encouragement. Best BETA bitches ever.

Dily, you were MAGIC with the art you created. You are such a great friend and I'm so lucky to have you in my corner.

Ariadna, thank you for taking the mess that is my life, organizing me, and never judging me for it. You're the best.

Genevieve, my sister from another mister. Love you!

MY STREET TEAM, you girls are so insanely amazing. I don't deserve you, but I also won't ever let you go. #mineforever

Thirsties, thank you for giving me a place to post my TikTok addictions and always being such a motivating force.

Emily, I used the right gray this time. Did you notice? One issue at a time. Thank you for making me a better writer with every book.

Stacey, can't thank you enough for making my books so dang pretty. You're the best.

MISTY WALKER'S THIRSTY READERS

My private Facebook group of thirsty readers is the place where I go first to share news, give exclusive content, and post my covers before anywhere else. So, if you drink copious amounts of coffee, curse like a sailor, and enjoy talking about all the book boyfriends who are making you thirsty, this group might be the place for you.

Join here:

www.facebook.com/groups/mistywalkersthirstyreaders

ABOUT THE AUTHOR

Misty Walker is fueled by coffee and motivated by the forceful voices in her head, screaming to tell their story. If she's not reading or writing, she's spending time with her daughters, husband, and two dogs where they live, in Reno, Nevada.

But mostly, she's reading or writing.

AUTHOR LINKS

Sign up for my newsletter for updates on my books and alerts whenever I have something new for you!
authormistywalker.com/newsletter

Signed paperbacks are available from my website:
www.authormistywalker.com

Come stalk me in all the places, I like it:

Instagram: www.instagram.com/authormistywalker

Facebook: www.facebook.com/authormistywalker

Bookbub: www.bookbub.com/profile/misty-walker

Amazon: https://amzn.to/2NnrWhJ

Twitter: @mistywalkerbook

ALSO BY MISTY WALKER

Standalones:
Vindicated
Conversion (also available on audio)
Cop-Out
Crow's Scorn: Diamond Kings MC

Royal Bastards: Reno, NV:
Birdie's Biker
Truly's Biker
Bexley's Biker
Riley's Biker
Petra's Bikers

Brigs Ferry Bay Series:
Kian's Focus
Kian's Focus (also available on audio)
Adler's Hart
Leif's Serenity
Doctor Daddy
Brigs Ferry Bay Omnibus